Carnality

Carnality

LINA WOLFF

Translated from the Swedish by Frank Perry

OTHER PRESS
NEW YORK

First published in the Swedish language as *Köttets tid* in 2019
by Albert Bonniers Förlag, Stockholm, Sweden
Copyright © Lina Wolff 2019

Translation copyright © Frank Perry 2022
The cost of this translation was defrayed by a subsidy from the
Swedish Arts Council, gratefully acknowledged.

Production editor: Yvonne E. Cárdenas
Text designer: Jennifer Daddio / Bookmark Design & Media Inc.
This book was set in Bulmer by
Alpha Design & Composition of Pittsfield, NH

5 7 9 10 8 6 4

Library of Congress Cataloging-in-Publication Data
Names: Wolff, Lina, 1973- author. | Perry, Frank (Translator), translator.
Title: Carnality / Lina Wolff ; translated from the Swedish by Frank Perry.
Other titles: Köttets tid. English
Description: New York : Other Press, [2022] | "First published in the Swedish
language as Köttets tid in 2019 by Albert Bonniers Förlag, Stockholm, Sweden"
Identifiers: LCCN 2021058994 (print) | LCCN 2021058995 (ebook) |
ISBN 9781635420746 (paperback) | ISBN 9781635420753 (ebook)
Subjects: LCGFT: Novels.
Classification: LCC PT9877.33.O54 K6813 2022 (print) |
LCC PT9877.33.O54 (ebook) | DDC 839.73/8—dc23/eng/20211203
LC record available at https://lccn.loc.gov/2021058994
LC ebook record available at https://lccn.loc.gov/2021058995

Publisher's Note
This is a work of fiction. Names, characters, places, and incidents
either are the product of the author's imagination or are used
fictitiously, and any resemblance to actual persons, living or
dead, events, or locales is entirely coincidental.

If you bring forth what is within you,

what you bring forth will save you.

If you do not bring forth what is within you,

what you do not bring forth will destroy you.

—GNOSTIC GOSPEL OF THOMAS

Mercuro

As the plane dips toward the hinterland, she can look across at sand-colored high-rises and hills that are as dry and barren as the surface of the moon. This is not her first visit to the city. Some time ago she lived here long enough to learn something of its soul. The place is like a wild animal that has been tamed, or an ember still smoldering. You have to be on your guard, and if you sleep, you should do so with one eye permanently open. It occurs to her that the sum she was awarded as a travel grant could have been spent in Barcelona, San Sebastian, or Valencia, where closeness to the sea would have made the summer months more bearable. Then again you're not supposed to look a gift horse in the mouth. Besides, the thing about awards is that when you get one, the award also seems to get you.

Over the loudspeaker the steward is announcing they will soon be landing and the temperature in Madrid is currently twenty-nine degrees Celsius. She fastens her seat belt, leans back in her chair, and waits with her eyes closed for the plane to grip the runway.

The two-bedroom apartment she will be living in is on calle Goya. Its rooms are lined up in a row, and the first, which could be a guest room if she ever has any guests, is followed by the kitchen, the bathroom, the living room, and, at the far end, the bedroom that will be hers. She enters the apartment carrying her suitcase and then walks around on a tour of inspection while the owner remains at the door, drumming her fingers testily against the frame. The owner tells her that the neighbors can be touchy so she'd be grateful if things don't get too out of hand, because previous recipients of the award have held parties into the early hours. She tells her not to worry. She's forty-five and stopped partying like that a long time ago. Once all the practical matters have been sorted, she walks over to El Corte Inglés and buys a bottle of wine. That is the first thing she does when she arrives in Spain. A lot of people go down to the beach, or to a bar or a restaurant if you are in Madrid, to unwind and absorb the atmosphere of their new surroundings; they order a mojito and jot things down in a Moleskine notebook, but she drinks wine and watches television. Glass in hand, she arranges herself among the soft cushions on the sofa. She remains like that for the rest of the evening: bloated and reclining in the steady stream of overexcited voices pouring from the news, Venezuelan series, and rowdy talk shows.

A little after midnight she is woken by a cool current of air entering through the open window. She is still clutching the wineglass in her hand, and the hard tap water she drank earlier in the evening has left the taste of old plumbing in her mouth. The buzz from the square and the pubs has got louder. She gets up, moves over to the window, and looks out onto the square. It's down there, she thinks. Life. She decides to go out, and the nighttime pulse of Madrid starts pounding away at her once she's on the street. She remembers what it was like when she was a student here almost twenty years ago, immersed in a daily rhythm in which you never ate dinner before ten and always went out afterward. When did we sleep? She can't remember ever having slept in Madrid, or ever feeling tired for that matter.

She goes into a place with windows of tinted glass and furnishings in dark wood, sits at the bar, and orders a glass of cava. After a while she becomes aware of a man on the other side of the room. Several things make him stand out. He is sitting alone and keeps darting glances at the people around him; he appears to be sweating, even though the air-conditioning is going full blast and it isn't that hot inside. She must have been watching him for just a bit too long, because his eyes suddenly stop roving and look straight at her. She looks down at the counter. She isn't the sort of person who picks someone up in a bar, and even if she were, it wouldn't be anyone like him. But the ball has apparently been set rolling, because the man in question gets to his feet, grabs his glass, and starts moving toward her. She realizes she won't have time to get up and leave in a way that would seem natural before he reaches her. Once at her side, he asks her, in a voice that sounds muffled the way it can in people who don't talk much, if he can have a seat. When she fails to respond he pulls out a chair and sits. Then he turns to her and offers his hand.

"Mercuro Cano," he says.

She tells him her name. And that is where things stay. After a while she feels it's time for her to find another bar, as the man has failed to say anything more. She makes an attempt to get up.

"You leaving already?" he says in response. "We haven't even started talking."

There is something about the incomprehension in his tone, which sounds both genuinely confused and profoundly human, that makes her sit down again. Out of the corner of her eye, she watches him extract a handkerchief from his pocket and wipe his forehead.

"Are you all right?" she asks.

"No," he replies. "To tell you the truth, I'm not feeling well at all."

While he says this he runs a finger under his nose as if he were wiping away lather, or the traces of some powder he had sniffed.

"I could really do with a chat," he says. "Just to feel something in my life was normal. A little bit of normality, even if it's only for a moment."

Why not, she thinks. The point of this trip is to meet people as well, which isn't going to happen if you shy away the moment someone approaches you.

"Okay," she says.

The man nods, relieved.

"What do you do?" he asks.

"I write," she replies.

"Oh," he says. "You write. What do you write?"

"Articles and columns for a local paper," she tells him.

"Do you live here, in Madrid?"

"I've been awarded a travel grant," she replies. "Three months with everything covered, apart from pocket money and food."

"Congratulations," he says.

She tells him it's hardly worth congratulations. And if they had asked her, she would have told them she'd rather spend the grant somewhere else than in Madrid. She's lived here before and knows that arriving any time between May and August is madness. Someone told her that in some place in the interior, it might have been Granada, the mercury had reached forty-two degrees. Sheer hell. She talks quickly, as she used to when she lived here, and is delighted to discover she can still carry that off in Spanish.

"So where do you come from?" the man asks.

"Sweden."

He takes a swig of his drink.

"Sweden," he says. "The man-hating country."

"How do you mean?" she asks.

"The country you come from is supposed to be full of man-haters."

"I don't follow."

"I read—" he begins, but she cuts him off with a dismissive wave of her hand.

"Look, I came out for a glass of wine and to relax," she says. "So if you don't mind."

She empties her glass.

"Are you a feminist?"

"Didn't you hear me?"

"I want to know."

"Why?"

"To understand why you hate your men up there."

"Frankly..."

"All that hate and bitterness," he says. "Those outbursts of rage. Why?"

He looks her defiantly in the eye. She stares back. A peculiar contrast to the defiance in his eyes becomes evident when his hand starts to shake. He is still holding his glass, and she can see bits of ice jostling each other in the amber-colored liquid.

"What's the matter?" she asks. "Why are you shaking?"

He looks down at his hand and, to judge by the way the fingers are turning white, he must be squeezing the glass against his palm with all his strength. Once the ice cubes have stopped moving, he stares vacantly ahead for so long she starts to think he has forgotten her. But just as she is about to get up and go, he looks up from his glass, grabs her around her upper arm, and says, "Sorry."

"What for?" she asks.

"For what I just said."

She shrugs and pulls her arm away from him.

"Do you forgive me?" he asks.

"What do you mean?" she replies. "I don't care. You'll be going home any minute now and so will I and we'll never meet again. That's all there is to it."

"That's the problem right there," he says. "Because I wish it wasn't like that."

"Now you've lost me," she says. "Just a moment ago it seemed like you hated me. And now it almost sounds like you're going to say you're in love with me."

"In love with you?" he says with a laugh. "You've nothing to worry about there. I've only been in love with one woman my whole life and that's my wife. Soledad Ocampo, the one and only. What I wouldn't give to have her here beside me."

"Oh really. So why are you chatting to a stranger instead of being with her?"

"Long story. Nothing out of the ordinary to begin with. A bit of boredom, a bit of infidelity. Same old.

Only then her illness got worse and we started going to therapy."

"Illness?"

"She's got a congenital heart defect."

"Did it help?"

"What?"

"The therapy?"

"Did the therapy help?" he asks and looks at her in puzzlement. "No it didn't. It didn't help at all."

"I'm sorry. Sometimes it can be a solution."

"You don't understand," he says shaking his head. "This wasn't just ordinary couples therapy; this was marriage counseling straight from hell."

"Marriage counseling from hell?"

Her interest has been piqued. She likes listening to this sort of thing. Hearing what other people have done, how they've dealt with situations she has failed at, and, in a few rare instances, realizing she has dealt successfully with something others have failed at. She would like to know more, but the man is back to staring vacantly at his glass again. She senses that the conversation may have come to an end after all. She gets to her feet again.

"Goodbye," she says. "I really hope you sort things out with your wife. Good luck."

"Hang on," he says, and he grabs her arm once more. "Please don't go."

"What is it?" she says coolly.

"I need help."

"What kind of help?"

"A roof over my head for a few days."

"A roof over your head for a few days? In my apartment? You've got to be kidding?"

She can't help laughing. He wets his lips with his tongue and wipes his forehead again.

"How about this?" he says. "So what if... you let me stay at yours for a few days. And I'll tell you about the marriage counseling and the woman who ruined my life. We might as well call her the feminist. That could be interesting for someone like you."

She's got no idea what he means by that.

"Who is this woman," she asks, "the one you're calling the feminist?"

"Sor Lucia."

"Sor Lucia? That sounds like a nun."

"A nun!" he exclaims. "Dead right. Imagine a cross between the strength of a Belgian Blue bull and the evil of Hitler. Throw in a couple of armfuls of hatred for men and the concentrated essence of embittered womanhood, and that's her to a tee."

She is attempting to picture what he just said.

"Tiny and ever so slight," he continues. "Like a child. Only utterly *ancient* at the same time. Someone who's seen it all, done it all, and knows exactly how to . . . She's got a maimed hand as well. They say it was bitten off by a pig."

She is staring at him. The portrait he has been painting is too bizarre for her to visualize. Though it also occurs to her that anyone who writes knows the cliché "Truth is stranger than fiction" contains a great deal of wisdom. The image of the hate-filled nun with the maimed hand is intriguing.

"Hide me," the man implores her. "Just for a few days. You won't regret it."

Her spontaneous reaction is to dismiss the idea as absurd. On the other hand, an absurd idea is still an idea, and maybe she can write a column based on whatever he tells her. She says she is going to sleep on it and will let him know the following day. She gets his phone number from him. Then she goes home and falls asleep in front of the open windows in her bedroom. The night is out there. She dreams long incoherent dreams about strange men in bars and nuns in low-heeled shoes with rubber soles prowling the streets of Madrid in the hour before dawn, hunting something that never becomes clear in the dream.

She is woken by the light the following morning. She had forgotten to close the shutters, and the apartment does not have air-conditioning, so the sheets are damp from sweat. She gets up and has a cold shower. She realizes that spending time indoors during the day will be unbearable. She will have to find somewhere she can lie in the shade, maybe even beside a pool. Not that she would normally do anything of the sort. But everything is different in Spain. She finds a jar of coffee and a stove-top coffee maker in the kitchen, and when she has a cup in her hand a little while later she finds herself thinking about the previous evening. Daylight puts a different slant on everything, makes it seem unreal. Was she actually in a bar with a man who said he was being pursued by a nun? She shakes her head. Spain, she thinks, Spain. Things tend to get distorted; it's the heat. She packs her beach bag and sets off toward a *club social* in the Arturo Soria district. She has to pay twenty euros for a sun lounger in the shade and then lies there waiting for some kind of joy to appear. Any kind of joy at all: just to prove that her heart hadn't withered away during the long winter back home. The joy of the new. The joy of sunshine. Maybe even the joy of writing. The feeling you get in a new place, the sounds of a new language around you, the aromas from the restaurant kitchen or the sound of water in motion—anything at all. But she doesn't feel any sense of joy lying on the lounger; it's more as if her insides are a large wet ball of yarn that is refusing to dry out even in the sunshine.

After a while she can hear someone dragging loungers across the paving. Various people are re-arranging things alongside her to make room for a wheelchair. A woman, who looks to be just over sixty, keeps hovering, issuing instructions while two brawny men who look like bodybuilders carry out her orders. In the wheelchair is a man about the same age as the woman. He appears to be completely un-responsive and just sits there staring straight ahead with his mouth open. Drool is running out of one corner and dripping down toward his chest, and every so often the woman turns toward him and wipes it away. The gesture seems automatic, as if the woman had done it over and over again for many years. Set the table straight and lift his feet, turn around and wipe away the saliva, tell her helpers what to do, turn around and wipe away the saliva... Finally the bodybuilders lift the man out of the wheelchair and put him on the lounger. The woman asks them to place the wheelchair a little way off and then go and get a cup of coffee for her and Santiago. So Santiago is the man's name. When both the bodybuilders have gone the woman gets out a container of sunscreen and starts spreading it over herself and the man. The smell of coconut oil mixes with the inland breeze that is wafting across the pool area. The woman keeps chatting away to the man, and when the body-builders return with the coffee she helps him drink it by tilting the cup and holding a paper towel under his chin. That movement appears to be practiced as well, because not a single drop gets spilled, and the white napkin that has been draped across the man's upper body remains spotless. The woman continues to arrange matters for a while longer.

She must have fallen asleep soon afterward because she comes awake with a start when everything goes quiet. She lifts her head to see if the couple are still there. And they are: sleeping on their sun loungers.

A rolled-up towel has been wedged between the man's jaw and his shoulder. The woman is holding his hand, and the cool breeze is stirring their hair. It is a lovely sight, so lovely that her throat closes up. She may have been feeling some form of envy even then. She has begun to realize that the woman and her invalid husband are that very rare thing: two people who share both great suffering and great happiness. She knows something extraordinary is required for that to happen. This makes her think about some of her girlfriends back home. One of them absolutely loathes her ex-husband and cannot stop talking about him as if she were trapped in the viselike grip of a kind of Tourette's of hatred. Another refers to her husband as a "household pig," and although a third has got divorced, she continues to terrorize her ex with completely pointless texts and emails, just to disrupt the peace he has found with his new woman. A fourth girlfriend thinks that staying in shape amounts to the same thing as being enslaved by the male gaze and is allowing a lax but inexorable process of decay to spread around her waist. Not to mention herself: a veritable El Dorado of failures, incapable of making her way out of the labyrinth of a relationship no matter how she twists and turns. The woman in the neighboring lounger is completely different. Older, and with an invalid for a husband, but completely in harmony with her life. That might sound trite, but she knows it really isn't.

After a while a waiter comes over to ask the woman what time they would like lunch. She notices the respect, bordering on reverence, in his voice that Spaniards almost instinctively express when they encounter someone who is making sacrifices for a family member. Once he has left, the woman undoes the buttons on her tunic and rubs the sunscreen onto her belly as well. As she is watching her holding the tube of sun cream in one hand while massaging her flat stomach with the other, she finds herself in the painful predicament of a woman who realizes that someone a good bit older than her is also a lot more attractive. The other woman's skin is brown and slightly mottled, like the very finest parchment. She has short blond hair and freckles, or they might be tiny patches of pigment, all over her face. Suddenly the woman gets to her feet, runs toward the side of the pool, and dives into the water with the litheness of a twenty-year-old. She swims back and forth, snorting, laughing, and waving at Santiago.

"Santi!" she calls. "Santi, Santi, hi there! Can you see me, hi!"

A noise that sounds like a combination of pain-filled grunt and hilarious laughter comes out of Santi's throat. He smiles at his wife with drool spilling over his entire lower lip to soak his chest. The eyes of everyone around the pool are locked on the couple, lost in admiration. Even the waiters carrying trays come to a stop to gaze at them. The woman heaves herself out of the pool, runs over to the little table beside the lounger, picks up the handkerchief, and wipes the saliva away.

The hours go by. She is lying on her lounger, thinking about the man from the bar. The events of today and the presence of the couple beside her have made helping him no longer feel like such a strange idea. She does have a room to spare, as it happens. What would it cost her to take in someone in need for a few days? Besides, he has promised to tell her the story of the marriage counseling and the feminist as well. That could be interesting. But letting a complete stranger stay? Wouldn't that be more than a little gullible? It occurs to her that the best thing would be to trust her intuition. When she pictures the man from the bar clutching his glass while the ice cubes jostle each other, she immediately gets the sense he is harmless. And what if she's wrong? Then she'll have to live with the consequences. You have to take risks if you're ever going to experience anything in this life. She picks up her phone and texts him her address along with a message that he should come over that evening at eight. A few minutes later the man replies that he has no idea how to thank her and she won't regret her generosity.

She continues to doze in her lounger. It is coming up to two p.m. She listens to the sound of water in motion, the clatter of cups and spoons, and the hum of voices. And then the woman beside her starts talking on her phone while her husband is looking up at the tops of the palm trees above.

She's not the kind of person to eavesdrop on other people's conversations, but the loungers are so close together it's impossible not to overhear. The woman is talking to someone about a home helper. She gathers from the conversation that though the woman has placed an ad, she's not happy with any of the replies she received. "I can't see her with him," she says, shaking her head, "that's the problem, I just can't see any of the people I've interviewed with him, and I'd never forgive myself if he got neglected or hurt." The woman goes on to say you hear all kinds of things and Santi may not be able to talk at all soon and then how would she know if everything was being done properly? That's why she has decided to forget the whole thing; it's really just a lot simpler to look after him herself.

The idea, when it comes, is as rash as it is blindingly obvious. She doesn't even have to think about it. She sits up in her lounger when the woman has finished talking, offers her hand, and introduces herself. The woman shakes her hand after some hesitation and then introduces herself in return.

"Miranda," she says. "Miranda Reyes."

"I'm so sorry," she says, "but I couldn't help overhearing your conversation. The thing is, I'm actually looking for something to do like the job you advertised."

Why did she say that? She isn't sure, but as she was uttering the words she felt they were entirely true. She is looking for an occupation, and with it, a meaning in life. She is looking for the kind of work where you can both do some real good and not have to be on your own. What could be more meaningful than helping a person who is sick while also offering someone like this woman a break?

Miranda looks at her skeptically.

"You're not from Spain," she says.

"I'm not from these parts, but I'm here to write," she says. "I need to take a break from time to time, though, and do something else entirely. When I heard what you said, I thought it would be perfect. A few hours a day. Between one article and another, if you see what I mean?"

Miranda examines her carefully. She runs her eyes over her body, then gives her bag, her shoes, and the clothes she hung over one of the spokes of the parasol a long look.

"How old are you?" she asks.

"Forty-five."

"Have you ever looked after someone with Alzheimer's?"

She shakes her head. "No, but I'm sure I could learn how. The way I see it, where there's a will, there's a way."

"Not always," Miranda responds.

"Give me a chance in any case," she says. "It might just work out perfectly."

"Perfectly," Miranda says as though the word were a piece of bitter fruit. "I can't remember the last time anything worked out *perfectly*."

Then she turns around, adjusts the towel beneath Santiago's mouth, and wipes away the drool.

"All right then," she says, "why not? I can interview you right now before he wakes up."

So then Miranda Reyes interviews her. Where does she live, how many brothers and sisters does she have, where did she study, does she become impatient easily, how strong is she physically, what kind of food can she cook, and what does she know about various medicines? Is she squeamish, has she ever changed an adult's diaper, and is she punctual? Miranda Reyes also wants to see what is inside her bag and to inspect the inside of her shoes. It is just as they are finishing all of this that Santiago wakes up.

"Chat to him," Miranda says. "Put him in a good mood."

She does the best she can, even though chatting to someone you don't know is far from easy, sitting next to a woman like Miranda when her eyes are boring holes in you. She isn't convinced Santiago understands that much of what she says, but he never stops smiling at her for the duration of the test. In the end she has no idea what to say and just smiles silently back at him. Then Santiago does something unexpected and takes her hand and squeezes it.

"How much were you expecting to be paid?" Miranda Reyes asks when she sees that.

What she realizes there and then is that she does not want to be paid, even though her funds for this trip are by no means unlimited. She wants *to help*. She has already planned out this trip and is not counting on any more income during the coming weeks; her grant covers most of the outlay, and she doesn't have any expensive habits. Someone said no one can ever be happy if all they do is receive. She needs to be able to give something of herself too, which is what she tells Miranda and feels a soft, almost pathetic, rush of goodness course through her veins when she notices Miranda's eyes slowly fill with tears.

"Thank you," she says softly. "I gave up my secretarial job with the city council to take care of him. Not that I'm complaining, I manage okay. We get by. But you're a godsend."

A godsend. No one has ever called her that before. She has no idea what to say in reply and can feel herself beginning to choke up, so she gets to her feet and goes to the toilet. When she returns, Miranda has recovered from all the emotion as well and announces briskly that she is welcome to come around at ten a.m. the next day. She writes down the address Miranda spells out to her. Then Miranda asks about her writing and says that being a writer must be the most romantic career of all. Though she nods in reply, all she feels inside is a profound exhaustion.

She goes home after that. Several hours later the man from the bar turns up. Mercuro Cano. He looks pale, dogged, and is not very talkative when he comes into the flat. Although he is barely recognizable as the same person, she shows him the guest room and hands him some sheets and towels. She asks if he wants anything to eat, but he doesn't. He just smiles politely and closes the door to his room. She goes into the kitchen and makes dinner for herself. She spends the rest of the evening sitting in front of the television in the living room, watching soap operas while feeling that something inside her is starting to thaw and that everything might actually be different from now on.

The next morning when she enters Miranda and Santiago's spotlessly clean apartment on the sixteenth floor of a building on the outskirts of Madrid, she finds it almost impossible to imagine that this is a home afflicted by serious and chronic illness. The scent of mildly perfumed cleaning liquids and fresh air is wafting throughout the flat, and Miranda, whose short curly hair is damp as though it had just been washed, looks indecently youthful. Santiago, freshly showered and shaved and his hair neatly combed, is seated on the sofa with the television on in front of him. The curtains are moving in the lukewarm current of air entering through the balcony door behind him. The balcony itself is covered in colorful Castilian tiles; the patterns are taken from the themes of old folk songs. There is a table outside and two chairs. She pictures Miranda making a huge effort to help Santiago out through the door so he can sit there with her and drink cold beer and eat pistachio nuts before dinner, as though they were still newlyweds and his illness did not exist.

When she is told what her duties will be, she realizes Miranda has made no concessions at all when it comes to the routines that have to be carried out each day. Every morning Santiago is to be showered, shaved, combed, and dressed in a freshly ironed shirt and clean trousers. He is to have aftershave applied to his cheeks and moisturizer rubbed into his hands. He is then to be seated at the dining table to drink coffee and eat slices of toast with oil, tomatoes, and salt—just as he has done all his life, with a spotless napkin tucked into the collar of his clean shirt. Afterward he will sit on the sofa while Miranda cleans the apartment, gets herself ready, and prepares lunch. During this time she is to help Miranda with the cleaning and laundry and also read the paper aloud to Santiago. Every afternoon Santiago has to be taken to a day center for Alzheimer's patients for a couple of hours of social stimulus in a group setting. The day center sends a car to fetch him and once he has left, she too can go. Miranda shows her around the apartment. The bedroom is a pale blue confection of satin pillows and lace with spotlessly white wall-to-wall carpeting. Beside the bed is a pair of small slippers with heels and powder-white puffs. The bed has, of course, been made in the Spanish manner and not a single crease is visible on the tightly fitted cover.

After lunch Miranda tells her over coffee that she has just booked a hotel for their summer holiday in Catalonia.

"Are you really going to take him on holiday with you?" she asks.

"To Salou," Miranda replies proudly. "A room with a view of the sea, the same one we had on our honeymoon forty years ago and that we've stayed in every summer since. You can leave the balcony doors open at night and fall asleep to the sound of the waves breaking."

"What about all the travel arrangements for Santiago?" she persists.

Miranda Reyes tells her about the vast amounts of preparation that have been required to complete the journey in the last few years. First there is the train between Madrid and Barcelona, where her son-in-law picks them up and drives them to Salou. At the resort both daughters and their families take turns at caring for Santiago together with Miranda. He has to swim in the sea every day, and to get him down to the beach, she hires three men from the local gym who carry him from the hotel and out into the water in a chair. He has a specially adapted swimming ring that keeps him afloat. Once that is done everyone gets together on the beach: daughters, stepsons, grandchildren, and the bodybuilders. They all go swimming, laugh, and play games.

"They really are moments of total happiness," Miranda says. "The illness is forgotten, and with the help of the bodybuilders, Santi can lie floating in the water and look up at the sky. He has always loved the sea and he is going to swim in it every summer as long as there's still breath in my body."

Miranda says that with just a hint of defiance, and she is about to praise her for her strength when they are interrupted by Santiago, who raps the table with his hand and says, "I'm going to kill you all one of these days."

"No you're not, darling," Miranda immediately exclaims with a little laugh. "You don't mean that, now do you?"

Miranda Reyes appears to be trying to gloss over his words as best she can, only then Santiago swipes a saltcellar onto the floor. When Miranda bends over to pick it up, his hand lands on her delicate back with an audible thwack. Dumbstruck, she can only look on. She feels awkward and has no idea how to intervene in an appropriate way. It is as if the previous Santiago had ceased to exist all of a sudden. There's a muscular monster on the wooden chair in the kitchen instead. His face is grim, and his lips look almost black.

"Nothing to worry about," Miranda says when she has got to her feet. "Nothing at all."

"Are you okay?" she asks.

"You can't take it personally," Miranda says. "It's the illness acting through him. It's not him doing it."

Miranda tears a sheet off the roll of kitchen paper and wipes away the string of drool. Then she turns to her and says in a steady voice, her back straight, that she can go now.

A while later she enters the flat on calle Goya feeling exhausted. It smells of fried sausages, and there's the clatter of dishes from the kitchen. All she wants is just to sink into a chair and tell the man from the bar about what happened, but any such notion vanishes completely the moment she sees him. When he comes out of the kitchen into the dim hallway to say hello, he is so pale it looks like the outline of his body is dissolving and he is turning into a shadow. If anyone needs to talk, it is very clearly him. They eat dinner in silence. Then they take the wine bottle with them into the living room and sit on separate sofas. What happened at Miranda and Santiago's feels increasingly remote. With the window half-open and all the sounds of the city down there in the background, she listens to his story.

We knew what kind of show it was, my wife and I, so we've got no grounds to play the innocent. It's just you'd think with a nun behind it there'd be limits, some kind of safety net. Not because I'm a believer. I don't believe in any religious communion or system. But an institution has always got something to lose, if only its self-image, which is why there are things you never believe it capable of doing. What we'd both heard about Lucia was that she could work miracles. I don't believe in miracles, but Soledad insisted that a miracle was exactly what we needed at that point: some vast, unbelievable miracle that would transform everything. Even though we were already separated, we continued to attend marriage counseling and to work on our relationship. I was the scapegoat whose unbridled lust had got us into this situation in any case, so all I could do was be grateful. When Soledad said she would consider one more attempt but that it would be the last, of course I said yes and even felt I'd been blessed. I knew how tired she was and that her sick heart was getting worse and worse. She needed a new one, but you can't just get a new heart like that. There was a long waiting list, and all we could do was hope. We were going to do our utmost to find our way back to each other in the interim. Soledad might have a new heart one day, and we could have a new relationship. That was the paradise that beckoned, and it was worth all our efforts, every attempt we made, no matter how melodramatic and desperate they may have been.

Once we had applied to be on the show, it felt like making a huge bet on the lottery, a game of poker or Russian roulette. The risk involved had a surprisingly stimulating effect on me, and my senses immediately felt sharper. Real life seemed to me to be a bit less hazy, that bit clearer and more interesting even— as if an inner window through which you looked out onto the world had been properly cleaned. When I was walking through a park, say, I might look up and actually *see* the tops of the trees. It made me think: All those leaves, all these details. How long have I been blind to them? How long have my surroundings and the natural world been lavishing on me a generosity I have been completely incapable of receiving? What a waste of beauty on a dead soul. One morning on my way to work, I noticed there was a pond full of black water, and swimming around in that water was an orange carp whose scales appeared to fluoresce in the early morning sunlight. I stopped and watched the carp for a long time and thought the carp was watching me as well. I remained standing there for so long I got to work late. No one saw me arrive. No one noticed I wasn't there. The slow fading away of the man without love. Sometimes I thought I had faded so far away I had become invisible.

Although, to begin with at least, I didn't think we had wagered that much on the show, not compared with Russian roulette and other high-stakes games. The way I saw it, how could my life get any worse? I had all but lost the woman I loved, and with her any sense of meaning. If this was a success, on the other hand, everything would turn out right and I would be a whole human being once more. I had a taste of those words and thought they tasted wonderful. I am tasting them again right now, and they taste just as good. *A whole human being. A whole human being.* Do whole human beings still exist? I had done things I shouldn't have done, and when you've done things you shouldn't, you can't afford to be picky. You have to grab whatever bits of rope come your way and allow the hand that reaches out to you to haul you up.

We filled out the forms on our own and I was meticulous when completing mine. I took my time and read through everything I had written several times before I pressed *Send*. I went out to shop at Mendez Alvaro immediately afterward and felt light on my feet as if a weight had been lifted off them. It took me twenty minutes there and back, and I was untroubled by the feeling that would come to haunt me after I took part—that people were pretending not to see me while actually looking at me out of the corner of their eye. Our separate applications were dealt with quickly, and I got an answer after only a week or so. We had been accepted. That sense of having been galvanized got stronger. I've been having a difficult time because being a person is difficult and the choices you make are often the wrong ones, but then again incredible things sometimes happen, like the chance to make a fresh start. In their reply it was stated that both Soledad and I should each turn up at the studio on our own, and that it would be almost a month before my session would be recorded. I was urged not to watch the program in the interim. In their experience the people who applied and were booked for a particular installment would sometimes watch an episode closer to their time and get cold feet and decide to turn down the chance to appear at the last moment. That created huge gaps in the scheduling of the shows, they went on to say, and the hope was that they could prevent gaps of that kind by encouraging future participants not to watch several episodes. I could see what they meant. I've worked in planning myself and am familiar with the importance of rules of conduct. But I also knew how hard it would be for me not to watch the show. I had no problem admitting I was totally hooked and if I didn't get to see an episode every day it felt like that day had been erased or become entirely pointless at any event. While I still had a job, I would feel a pleasurable tingle as the end of the working day arrived and I set off for home because the next item on the conveyor belt of the day's events would be to sink into the sofa and watch Miss Pink and Mister Blue on the living room screen. You rarely got to see Lucia in person, and when she had something to say, it would usually be communicated by the ravishing

Miss Pink. For me the show was a blissful hour of life distilled to its essence. An hour when I was spared the boredom of existence. That feeling became even more pronounced when I lost my job. The fact is that on some days I would wake at seven, as I always did, only to feel that my sights were already set on the beginning of the show that evening. That made the day seem like an ocean I would have to steer across—or rather a plain I would have to traverse while suffering from a raging thirst. Everything I did, or failed to do, was in relation to the time of the episode—a whole afternoon left, half the afternoon left. Anticipation created new ways of measuring out those intervals.

So naturally I failed to obey the instruction not to see more episodes. I fell ill on one of the last days before the recording. I lay in bed drinking water with the computer on my stomach and rewatched episodes I remembered as being particularly involving. There was one I liked especially in which a couple were happily reunited following an infidelity. A seasoned Miss Pink guided them through what she referred to a bit dramatically as "every instance of betrayal." At the end of the program the couple came together in an embrace that developed into a passionate kiss. Mister Blue and Miss Pink looked at one another, and I thought I could see tears in their eyes. In my feverish state, a new aspect of the show would be revealed, however. Everything seemed—how should I put it—ever so slightly *distorted*. One of those tiny shifts that can change the whole way you see things. Now and then I thought Miss Pink's and Mister Blue's faces were transformed for a moment in a way I had never noticed before and that I can only describe as *horrific*. This was just for an instant and barely noticeable, a bit like an optical illusion. I also managed to glimpse a silhouette in the background in one episode and when I paused and enlarged the image—that had to be the nun standing there. Lucia herself. I felt an anxious stirring in the pit of my stomach at the sight of her. An inexplicable anxiety, I should say, because I knew nothing about her at that point, apart from what people had said about her ability to work miracles. Even though it was also said she had helped a number of people end their lives. I took a pill to bring my fever down, closed my eyes for a moment, and after a while I could feel myself being swept away by the show again, just as usual. As I was lying there in bed, I was also trying to work out the principles that determined how the catalogue of episodes and the information about the participants had been put together. Understanding the principles that underpin a system is to understand the mental skills—or the intelligence, if you prefer—of the people behind it. I like people who can perceive the beauty of a well-structured system. I like people who can see things from the perspective of administrative systems. Because we always talk about the system from the perspective of the individual and never about the individual from the perspective of the system. From the perspective of the system the individual is always organic and desperately in need. From the perspective of the system the individual has always just bashed his thumb with a big hammer and requires assistance. The truth is, though, that the individual is an ant, and no one is going to bring an entire system to a halt just to relieve the completely insignificant pain of one ant. I know that now.

My own words make me shiver. That is the person I have become. Cynical, hardened, contemptuous, spiteful, and scared to death—all at the same time. I'm not well at all, as you will have realized. I've really got to get my life in order, find my way back to Soledad and get everything put back to the way it used to be. Where was I?

The day of my appearance on the show had come and all I could think about from the moment I woke up was that I had to stay calm. Calm, calm, calm, I said to myself, but whenever I said it my heart rate seemed to accelerate even more: a muscle running amok. I can feign calm, and even simulated calm is something I consider to be calm in a sense, but calm isn't something you can fake with people as intuitive as the program hosts in question. It has to come from inside and it has to be genuine, otherwise they will sniff you out. And the moment they catch your scent, the smell of blood sets them off. They love to bring down people who cannot keep their anxiety under control. Figuratively speaking, I mean. Participants who fail to keep their nerves in check will bite the dust, and it feels like you can hear this very particular sound when their heads hit the ground with a smack.

The day had arrived in any case, and my time had come. I chose my clothes with care and opted for a white shirt and a pair of beige linen trousers. Then with only a few centimeters between me and the bathroom mirror I examined my face, hunting for any unsightly stray hairs. I know young girls can be touchy about them. I also knew that if I turned Miss Pink off, or if she found me repugnant in some other way, I would be out of the running. "Failure is not an option," my boss used to say, and that phrase seemed to me perfectly suited to the moment. There are times when failure is not an option and this was one of them. I really don't feel well. I'm really not feeling well as I'm telling you this and I'm convinced there's someone standing outside the entrance to the building at this very moment. If I went to see a psychologist, I'd probably be told I am paranoid. The day of my appearance had arrived at any event and as I stood there in the bathroom, I tapped the tweezers against the sink and watched the long black hairs fall onto the white enamel. Hair. This stuff made of dead cells. This quintessential matter of dead cells that is an adornment and a scourge for both sexes. My hair is as thick as a horse's, or that is what Soledad told me a long time ago. And she added with a glint in her eye that men with thick black hair exude virility. That was then. That was then, and it must have been said on a whim, a kindly one, because some time later it was my hairy body in particular she expressed revulsion at. Your body hair is like a wall-to-wall carpet, she said, and not a particularly clean one at that. You need vacuuming or cleaning with the high-pressure hose from top to toe. That's the sort of thing a woman cay say, but not a man. Imagine if I'd said to her that her crotch was like wall-to-wall carpet, and not a particularly clean one at that, and that I'd like to give her a good going over with the high-pressure cleaner—I'd have had to put up with her sneering or, even worse, tirades about my corrupt, dirty, and male chauvinist ego, for days on end. Anyway. I'm not complaining. Though I am, of course, but not about that. I like all women. I like the female as a phenomenon, its cyclical character, and that includes the smell of your genitals. I do apologize. Only when you are telling a story, you have to tell it properly and, even though I'm a reserved person, I cannot help the odd intimacy while doing so. I never wanted to get separated. Separations are ghastly. That's what I wanted to talk about, and what I wanted help with: how to get Soledad back and undo the separation, how to wake up from this nightmare, how to support Soledad in her illness and how to be her husband. *Help me get my wife back and I will be grateful to you forever*, was what I was going to say, *help me remove the thorn from her heart, no, help me remove an entire thicket of thorns from her heart. Do that and I will pay whatever you want, provided I've got enough to live on afterward.* I don't care about money in any case. I've never had that much, but I've managed fine all the same. Soledad hated me. I, on the other hand, loved her in every way imaginable. I loved her groin that she used to wax every three weeks like clockwork while she was still in love with me and which she then allowed to grow as hairy as an all but impenetrable jungle when she hated me. Not that I was allowed to touch her there any longer. I knew all the same. The jungle was there, an impenetrable no-man's-land of unruly hairs. When I asked why she didn't get waxed any more, she said: "Try it yourself. You do that, Mercuro, go and get waxed. All those hairs, your whole crotch while you're at it. I think we'd have better sex if you were making an effort along those lines as well." Better sex was what she said, and who could resist that especially when you're not having any sex at all? And while there may be many things I can be accused of, being unwilling to accommodate Soledad is not one of them. I called the woman who waxed Soledad and asked her for an appointment, only then she said she preferred not to wax men. "Why not?" I asked. "Your skin is looser and more sensitive. When I'm waxing a man I have to pull the skin tight with one hand and pull off the wax with the other, or else it feels like I'm going to rip the whole show away." The whole show? I shivered. I'm sorry to have to bring this up now. I'm an intuitive person. Paranoia and intuition go hand in hand, a psychologist once told me, and I thought that sounded worrying because how would you know in that case what was paranoia and what intuition? Where the dividing line goes, I mean.

I had nothing against Soledad aging. I would gladly have made love to her as she was in her slightly overripe form. I would also have considered—and it is here I think I am unlike many of the men I know—doing some work on myself if she would only give me the chance. Just a chance. What would that have cost her? What does it cost womanhood to give manhood a chance? Women can be so hard. You dictate the terms of the present. On the surface at least. Though the surface is important; sometimes it is all there is, so kudos to you for that. Nietzsche said man is evil but woman is mean. By the way, that is something Lucia would say later on. "Nietzsche says man is evil but woman is mean." What kind of nun would quote something like that?

There was this pressure on my sphincter the morning I was due to go on the program. All of my innards were concentrated around that one point. I ignored the pressure and looked at my reflection in the mirror. That was me standing there. Me, and I've always been a battler. Me, and I was loved by my mother and my father. Me, and I had loved and had fallen and was now trying to pick myself up again. I wondered how I would remember this morning in the future. I thought I would remember it as if I were at the bottom of a well just before being hauled up. But I had no idea how deep the well was. I know now that you can think you are way down in the dark even though you're actually splashing around in the shallows, still bathed in blessed light.

You're looking at me like I'm an idiot, I know. But at least I'm an idiot who knows he's an idiot, and that's more than you can say about a lot of people.

I took a taxi to the recording studio, even though it left a dent in my wallet. I've never been really rich, but well enough off for long enough to have forgotten what being poor is like. As I was being driven, I could watch the character of the city changing through the taxi window. You never think the neighborhood you live in amounts to that much, but the well, as they say, is always deeper than you imagine. Wide avenues lined with horse chestnut trees gave way to concrete blocks with peeling facades and narrow sidewalks. Overweight people eating chips and drinking beer, even though the sun had not yet passed the zenith, sprawled on cheap plastic furniture outside the bars. I thought I must have given the driver the wrong address when the car stopped outside the entrance. The door looked as though it led down to an unlicensed subterranean nightclub, and obscenities had been tagged across its iron surface, obscenities it seemed no one had bothered to clean off. *SUCK MY COCK* was written in bold white text across the darkened rust. A diversionary tactic maybe because no one—including me, who had the actual address noted down—could ever have imagined the kind of thing that went on behind a door like that. And why not, when I think about it, suck my cock. You can do that, all of you out there. I cannot remember when someone last did, with commitment and devotion, as though there were pleasure sensors in the oral cavity capable of relishing the penetration. On the other hand I remember something Soledad always used to say before she started hating me, and that was that if a man was going to exude masculine self-possession, he needed to feel that a woman wanted to have his member in her mouth. Whores don't count, she added with her finger raised, as if she could read my thoughts. It only counts if you are doing it of your own free will. She looked at me as if she had played her trump card, set me a mathematical problem I would never be able to solve, as if she had just deprived me, once and for all, of any real possibility of believing in myself. I don't really understand why I always attached so much importance to the contemptuous digs she would direct at masculinity, and thus at me, at every opportunity, and that she kept stabbing me in the back with out of sheer irritation. And, hand on your heart, is there really any woman out there who likes practicing fellatio? Honestly? Cross your heart. There are things we do to give a lover pleasure, we all do, we're made to work that way.

I can still feel the pressure of it all on my sphincter even now as I am telling you this. I said that to Soledad once: "I could feel the pressure of it all on my sphincter," and she laughed and asked why I couldn't just say it, that I simply had to shit. Say that three times, she said, virtually jumping up and down with excitement, say it: "*I've got to shit, I've got to shit, I've got to shit.* Get down and dirty, Mercuro!" I didn't like it when she was vulgar like that. I'm not feeling at all well. I have to get my life in order.

I got out of the taxi and paid the driver. Then I stood in front of that graffiti-tagged door and wondered for a moment how long it would be before I was forced to move to an area like this. I looked at the facades of the buildings around me and noted their dirty green awnings, the withered flowers on the balconies and the faded, forgotten washing hanging on lines in front of the kitchen windows. I said before that I'd never had that much money, but I'd felt I was doing okay. The truth is that poverty has always scared the pants off me. I raised my hand and knocked firmly three times in the middle of the word SUCK.

I knocked once, twice, a third time, but no one opened the door. *Miss Pink, hello, I'm here,* was what I wanted to yell and I felt this sudden impulse to laugh at myself, although I became serious again almost immediately. After a while I decided to try the handle to see if the door was unlocked. Maybe you were just supposed to go straight in. That was it. The door slid open. I could see a staircase leading down into darkness. As Dante descended into

Hell, he was met by the reek of sulfur. I made my way down those stairs and was met by the stench of a distant sewer. That's the underworld for you. The air has been treated with metals and fossilized plants. It was impossible not to think about death. As I went inside I felt very tall. The ceiling was low, and I had to stoop a little as I walked down the narrow staircase from the front door to the entrance to the basement. I felt clean and neat as well, but most of all I felt tall, as though I were fully occupying the space that was my due. You should be proud. You should pull your shoulders back a touch just to make sure your posture is perfect. It was a good feeling, a feeling that probably had something to do with the sensation of the ironed shirt against my skin and the scent of my new aftershave. I ought to do this more often, I thought. Dress well and wear cologne, because I was aware of what an uplifting effect it was having on me. A *caballero* like myself ought not to be dressed like a beggar. I had let myself go for such a long time. I had been neglecting myself. You really shouldn't neglect yourself, because then you lose respect for your own person. That is how depression works. It opens the door to a lack of self-respect and to self-loathing. After a while you can't even remember why you are depressed, because all the discomforts, the unease, have congealed into this sludge of unpleasantness. An untidy home, an unwashed body, and general intellectual lethargy. A sticky, monotonous, and tepid limbo it is impossible to see any way out of. Life makes demands on you. You can complain and find reasons for why things turned out the way they did, but the fact remains: you have not moved, you have fallen behind. But I hadn't reached the age of fifty-five for nothing. I know something about life and about you women. Your whims and your internal contradictions in particular.

"Please come in."

I peered into the darkness in front of me.

As both figures began to take shape, the first thing to occur to me was that they looked completely different in real life from how they did onscreen. Mister Blue was fine-boned and could have been taken for a woman in that moment, while Miss Pink was chunkier than I had expected. They weren't at all how I had imagined them. They were standing side by side, what's more, with their eyes locked on mine, which made me think of the twin sisters in Stanley Kubrick's *The Shining* just before the blood erupts from the wall behind them. I wanted to turn around and walk back out that rusting door, which is what I should have done, of course. And just forget the whole thing. What a stupid idea to imagine this would solve anything. Like I said, the show isn't freely available. There are all these codes you need to log in, the cryptocurrency and the amounts debited from your account every month, until I filled in the form and got accepted, which meant a free pass. So Soledad had already been here and told them her side of the story. What was her version like? You couldn't watch that episode from my computer. All I had been told was where and when I should turn up. I wanted to laugh. An abrupt edgy laugh that would help channel some of the nervous tension I was feeling, but I was all too aware of what kind of situation I was entering, and so I stifled the laugh, or rather I didn't have to stifle it, all I had to do was meet their eyes for any desire to laugh to vanish abruptly.

"Welcome to *Carnality*," Miss Pink said.

"Thank you," I replied.

"My name is Miss Pink, and beside me is Mister Blue."

I had imagined Mister Blue's skin would shimmer with a celestial blue color, and that Miss Pink's face would be of a rosy hue and there would be tiny light-brown freckles scattered across her nose. That would make her the kind of person who can seem a bit porcine and still be lovely. I wished I could say something. How beautiful you both are, for instance. But I couldn't get a word out.

"Come with us," said Mister Blue.

They turned and I followed them. My eyes were becoming accustomed to the half-light. We entered a large room that was dark as well—apart from a corner at the far end that was brightly lit.

"Have a seat," Miss Pink said, while pointing to the illuminated area.

I sat on one of the chairs, the one I knew the guest was supposed to sit in, and they seated themselves across from me. While they were setting up the camera and arranging the lighting, I had a chance to watch them undisturbed. The sudden brightness cast everything in a whole new light. I'm skeptical about perfection as a phenomenon and old enough to know that there are always flaws, but even so I'd been expecting something very different. It was not for nothing they were referred to in some of the comments as "the God" and "the Goddess," although I had always considered this to be a combination of exaggeration and groveling. And now I could see I was right, because both of them had pimples and, in addition to her freckles, Miss Pink had little patches of pigment and black dots on her nose—dark spots that could very well be blackheads. Youth may be desirable, but it lacks the kind of mature glamour I had become used to in Soledad. Like the lovely warm autumn sun on a still afternoon in October, that is Soledad. Miss Pink was more like a sunny but stormy spring day in May. I no longer had the vigor you need to fully appreciate that. I thought her breasts looked hard, as if they had balls surgically inserted, and I longed for Soledad's soft maternal bosom where my hands had found peace for so many years. I had a look around. I wondered if Lucia might be sitting somewhere in the room, but I couldn't see her. The notion that a nun might be keeping silent in the darkness made me feel that pressure against my sphincter again. And I had imagined the studio to be very different as well. The warm red pattern of the tapestry that hung behind Mister Blue and Miss Pink onscreen was only big enough to cover the background as the camera zoomed in, and where it ended there was just the rough, untreated surface of the exposed wall. Onscreen the tapestry looked as if it was covering the entire wall of a magnificent castle, an impression that was reinforced by the Latin inscription running across it, which I did not understand. I'm not a learned man. When I mentioned Dante I was repeating something I'd heard. I haven't actually read him. I've always wanted to be well-read because I've realized that appearing to be cultivated can make things easier. Though I have to wonder, where would I start? But right then my lack of literary refinement was only one among my many problems and far from the most important of them.

"Are you ready?" asked Mister Blue. "Sixty seconds now."

During the minute that remained I kept wetting my lips with my tongue. I was also thinking about the fact that when she arrived Soledad must have come through the door with SUCK MY COCK written across it. I was picturing her getting out of a taxi, coming over to the door, seeing those words, then opening the door and going in. Though I wasn't feeling well at all, the feeling that I needed to relieve myself had suddenly disappeared. I felt comfy inside and empty, as if all I was made of was warm fluff like a cloud. The cement walls were bare, and there were water stains on the floor, the ceiling, and the walls. Like huge roses, they appeared to have agreed among themselves to bloom at the same time, a subterranean cement garden of mold and damp. The air was slightly sour. Both the cameras had been rigged, one in front of me and one behind, and Mister Blue appeared to be controlling them from the computer he had in front of him on the table. I was aware that everything that happened from the moment we began would go out live. They had never edited an episode and they refused to cut away even when the situation got out of hand. I had seen that happen several times from the safety of my sofa, not without some malicious satisfaction, I'll admit. Besides, that was what I really liked about the program. The God and the Goddess never wavered, not about anything. Though it all seems very different, of course, when it's about you. When you're the one in the hot seat, I mean. I was picturing the section of the screen for comments as a field beneath a gentle breeze. The ears of corn were nodding slowly, silent and expectant. But there were dark clouds on the horizon. And as soon as the program began, the wind would pick up and the ears of corn would start to thrash around, whipping against each other in anticipation of the coming storm. I felt as though my tongue had swollen inside my mouth and that if I tried to say anything, all I would be able to produce would be a choked wheeze from the back of my throat. And your voice—as they told you in the introductory email—was crucially important. That was why you were supposed to breathe deeply and avoid tensing your vocal cords, because if those cords did become tight your voice would be altered, and a particular vocal pitch could make the Comments section fill with a rage that was as illogical as it was relentless.

"Right then," Miss Pink said. "Five seconds."

I nodded. I cleared my throat without making a sound, and it felt like a clot of hot phlegm had come loose, which made me think that my voice would carry after all. Then Mister Blue looked up and into the camera next to me. He came out with the usual opening lines and then turned to me.

"Welcome to *Carnality*."

"Thank you," I say. "I'm happy to be here."

Immediately I wish I hadn't said those words. There's nothing to be happy about. They know that, which is why I can already detect a hint of scorn in their eyes. There's nothing to thank them for, not yet. There's no guarantee they will save me. On the contrary my fall will be all the greater if I make an effort to be polite and all the more satisfying for their followers.

"You know the rules," says Mister Blue. "You have exactly one hour. You tell us about your problem, and then together with Lucia we decide if we can help you and, if so, how. While you are taking part in the program you have to allow us free rein and trust that we will do what is best for you. You are giving us a kind of authorization. You are agreeing that we are allowed to do whatever we please."

"Yes," I say. "I know the rules."

"And you agree to them?"

"Yes, I do."

"Right then," Mister Blue says. "I'm going to read aloud a few facts about you after which it will be your turn."

Miss Pink angles the computer so that Mister Blue can see the screen and then he reads aloud: "You are fifty-five and male. You are married but separated from your wife, Soledad Ocampo. When you were working, you earned forty-five thousand euros a year. You are now unemployed. Your home address is in the Cuatro Caminos neighborhood. Your job was in requisitions as part of EU-funding."

"Yes," I say to confirm.

Mister Blue goes on: "Since *Carnality* chooses on occasion not to reveal the real names of participants, you will be given one by us that you will use in all your dealings with the show and that we will also use when we address you and when we talk about you to the viewers in your absence. Because we will be talking about you in your absence, and in ways that could be perceived as insulting. Do you understand this and do you consent to it?"

I don't understand the point of this formality. It's not like it would be possible to sue the show in the courts if something went wrong. So it's playing to the gallery. A way of demonstrating who has the power in this setup, and of dodging any kind of comeback later on into the bargain. Though, in retrospect, I do feel grateful for the pseudonym. I wouldn't have wanted to appear under my real name.

"Our name for you is Lee Peng," Mister Blue says.

I don't get it. First off I don't understand why Soledad wasn't given a different name as well. Second I don't get the particular name they've chosen. Lee Peng. It's not as though I'm Chinese. So I say this and receive two supercilious smiles in response.

"Let's make one thing clear to you. The fact that you respond to the name the way you do reveals a set of values. Conscious or unconscious? That's something we'd like you to think about."

Silence falls as if they were actually expecting me to think about it. I want to ask them how I'm supposed to think about something they just said I was not conscious of, but I realize that would undermine any sympathy I might get from the followers so I say nothing and try to look as though I really was thinking.

"The name we have given you doesn't necessarily have anything to do with the person you are in real life. Maybe there's some other name you'd like to suggest?"

It occurs to me that Maddox, Osbourne, or even Bruce would sound better, but I shake my head.

"Lee Peng is fine," I say.

"You're welcome," says Mister Blue. "In that case you may begin. Tell us and our followers what you want help with. Start at the beginning and take your time."

I take a deep breath but just as I am about to speak there's the sound of knocking on the iron door. Even though the knocks are hard they're barely audible, as if they're being made by a very small but very powerful hand. Mister Blue gets up from his chair.

"Excuse me," he says with a smile.

I remain in my seat along with Miss Pink and don't know where to look because I don't dare look at her. Mister Blue soon returns, a very small person walking at his side. It is Lucia. I get to my feet immediately. The old woman is clutching Mister Blue's arm even though she is walking—or rather striding—swiftly ahead, and not moving like an old person at all. Mister Blue is still smiling and has even put his hand over her thin bony one.

"So this is Lucia," Miss Pink says when they have sat down.

"I didn't know that—," I start to say.

"She's decided to grace you with her presence," Mister Blue cuts me off.

I thought I was going to be alone with Miss Pink and Mister Blue. It is completely impossible to ignore the nun's presence, and I no longer feel taller, but small and shriveled instead, as if I'd been stripped of any personal authority. The nun refuses to look me in the eye; she sits down and just stares at the table. She looks ancient. Ancient and expressionless. Not that her wrinkled stone face seems to inhibit Miss Pink or Mister Blue; their spirits have very obviously been raised by her being there. They look at her and smile, and then smile at each other, as if the three of them were one happy family.

"Right then," Mister Blue says once more. "Now we're all here. Mr. Peng, the floor is yours."

All three of them look up and at me in silence. I clear my throat and all of a sudden I've no idea how to begin. Even though I've thought it through so many times. So I do what I'd decided to do, which is to tell the truth: that I've been unfaithful and I've been a liar. My urges, my desires, kept hounding me and led me to make mistakes. It feels good to be able to say that. It feels good to get it said straight off, to get it out of the way.

"Not another adulterer," Mister Blue says, the smile vanishing from his face. "It feels like we get infidelity served to us for breakfast, lunch, and dinner on *Carnality*. What is it about all of you men that makes life so difficult? You should be lined up in a row and mowed down, the lot of you. What's your view on that, Lucia?"

What I think is that the exaggeration is exaggerated, so to speak. He knew all that already; I told them about it on my application, and Soledad must have told them too. Besides, he's a man himself and ought to know it isn't always that easy to resist. The nun says nothing. My eyes are glazed as I stare straight ahead, because I know this is the sort of thing you're meant to put up with. This is only the first test. Humiliation is part of the entertainment value, and the people who do best are the ones who manage to ignore it, let it roll off them like water off a duck's back. Miss Pink will step in soon enough. That's how they operate. Mister Blue wades in with the sledgehammer, testing your mental strength in the hope you'll break and the tears will flow, or you'll flip out. Both strategies come at you like wads of spit in a headwind.

And I'm proved right because then Miss Pink says in a gentle voice: "Infidelity is, as I am sure you know, Mr. Peng, run-of-the-mill stuff for us. It's the carnal. You can find no peace, because the carnal is in your blood."

"That's right," I say. "That's exactly what it's felt like to me. It's as though there has always been something gnawing away at me, something that can only be appeased with sex."

Miss Pink nods sympathetically and then goes on: "Most people, however, don't actually want their infidelity and their lies undone. It's the consequences they are appalled by. Does that apply to you too, Mr. Peng?"

The question is left hanging. Does that apply to me? I haven't thought about it. I haven't considered whether what I feel is genuine remorse or if I am, in fact, just appalled by the consequences. And what is genuine remorse, in any case? It dawns on me that I am, in all honesty, mostly appalled by the consequences, and if I could still have committed the adultery but escaped the consequences, I wouldn't say no. Deep down I'm glad I don't feel any real regret because I don't think regret serves any purpose.

Fear, what I am feeling now, clearly does serve a purpose: fear of the consequences makes you want to be a better person. That is about the best you can hope for from a human being. I look Miss Pink in the face and realize from the gleam in her eye she has seen that realization dawn on me. Which is why I say in as firm a voice as I can muster: "To be perfectly honest, I am mostly appalled by the consequences."

The nun starts drumming her fingertips against the surface of the table. I can make out that it is the rhythm to a well-known piece of music but not which one. Suddenly she stops drumming and places her entire hand on the table. I can see she is missing a thumb and only has a bluish one-centimeter-long stump instead. I hear a gasp coming out of my chest and before I have time to think I am looking up and at her face. She is looking right back at me. I gulp. I'm thinking, you've got to breathe, whatever happens, because those breaths calm the brain as well as the body. But breathing doesn't help the way I hoped it would, because there's a ringing in my ears and I feel dizzy. I'm expecting Miss Pink to tell me that I have to leave, in which case I will have to go back to my festering home and my stagnant life. If you can't do better than this, there's no hope; they can't work with a pile of shit, because piles of shit fall apart however hard you try to shape them. I heard them say that in one of the other episodes. You can't build towers out of shit because they simply fall apart. Some people you can work with, while others are just hopeless. Only I realize at the same time I did the right thing, because if I had lied they would have sniffed that out. They possess that ability; I've seen it for myself and more than once. I swallow, and take stock in the silence. I've staked everything on a single card, and that card is *Carnality*. If they refuse to help me—I might as well throw myself in front of a train or jump off a bridge. I just wish it wasn't so bloody unpredictable. I can see that that is part of their attraction, only when you're the one in the hot seat it feels like being on a roller coaster in the dark. Deep pits can suddenly yawn right in front of you even though you've been slowly moving uphill for hours. I remember one woman, shortly after I started following the channel, who turned to *Carnality* for help with her addiction to social media. In tears she told them how her life had been wrecked by her inability to tear herself away from her mobile phone. Though she really wanted to, she just couldn't. She'd be sitting there clutching it and staring at the screen, which was covered in dirty marks from the grease on her fingers, as though she'd been hypnotized and forced to tap at apps that promised some kind of instant kick. Facebook, Instagram, Twitter, the paper, the bank, the weather. Though she felt an instinctive distaste for almost everything she was shown, she just couldn't break free, and she realized the same was true of the rest of her family. Her domestic life was falling apart. She was doing less and less with her kids, and meals were consumed in haste so everyone could go back to their computers, tablets, and mobiles. On *Carnality* the woman displayed genuine despair, and her story had a powerful effect on me. A person who wanted to do better but was just too weak. All she needed was a bit of resolve, and I was totally convinced Miss Pink and Mister Blue would help her, take her under their wings and steer her toward freedom, toward the calmness of a strong and healthy mind—but they opened up the pit instead. A stern Mister Blue gave her a long lecture that even had me quaking on the sofa in my home. He said the woman had allowed "sewage to swamp the shores of her inner life" for far too long and that it was impossible to "cleanse some kinds of filth from the human soul." He also said the woman's brain was bound to resemble Swiss cheese by now, filled with the kind of holes that are created when you choose distraction over concentration. Miss Pink, who was nodding beside him, referred to some philosopher who said you should only open your mail once a week and take a long bath afterward. The nun must have been there too—I realize that now—without being visible onscreen, and she may well have been drumming her maimed hand against the surface of the table just as she's doing now. In the end the woman got up, sobbing, and rushed toward the door while only the faces of Mister Blue and Miss Pink remained onscreen. They were both wearing exactly the same expression of amused indifference. Throughout the afternoon the Comments section was inundated with the kind of excitement that presumably follows a public execution. A few days later I read a brief article in the paper about a woman who had taken her own life. There was no picture but something made me associate what I had read with the woman who had been on *Carnality*. That might have been the result of all the different emotions the episode had stirred in me, an attempt by my brain to connect the bits of information it was privy to. There's no denying, though, that it could have been her.

And now I'm the one sitting here. Hope is the last thing to die. I'm trying to banish any thought of the woman and her mobile. You're not supposed to think about anything while you're here. That was in the introductory mail as well: when you're facing them, you're supposed to let go of any thoughts and simply focus on Miss Pink and Mister Blue, as if they, and you, are all there is.

"As you realize, Mr. Peng," Miss Pink says, "we do not like adulterers. But we've always done our best to help them."

She is growing larger as she speaks. It's like the space is being filled up with her—both her spirit and whatever judgment she is about to pronounce.

"We've already had Soledad Ocampo in here," she continues. "Lucia was moved by her story, and that's why we've decided to give you a chance. We want to help your wife, and by helping you, we'll be helping her."

I ought to respond but can't think of anything to say.

"Doesn't that make you happy?" Mister Blue asks.

"I'm just wondering," I say with an ironic little laugh before I can stop myself, "if what you really mean is that, if it weren't for Soledad, I might just as well have been thrown to the dogs."

I meant it as a joke, like a little barb, but all three of them are now looking icily at me.

"You're the one who messed it all up, though," Mister Blue says. "If you'd only been able to keep your cock in your pants, you wouldn't be here now, would you?

No, I wouldn't. You couldn't put it any more clearly than that. Suddenly I feel exhausted. No pressure on my sphincter, no bodily sensations at all, just a sense of crippling fatigue. I've been struggling for so long. There has to be an end at some point, a light at the end of the tunnel. It has to be possible to atone for a crime, doesn't it?

"Mr. Peng?" Miss Pink says then, and the sudden kindness in her voice makes me want to cry.

"I'm so tired," I whisper. "I've been struggling so hard and for so long to keep it all together, to stop it cracking, and now...the shards of my life have been hurled into the cosmos like a slow-motion explosion..."

Mister Blue picks up a pack of chewing gum and starts to fiddle with it ostentatiously.

"Stop, stop, just stop," he says. "No shards being hurled into the cosmos, thank you very much. And very definitely no pseudo-poetry."

"What do you mean?" I say. "Pseudo-poetry?"

"We loathe pretentiousness."

"What about when you want to say something lovely?"

"You just have to find another way of doing it."

I open my arms wide. "I've no idea how to respond...I realize I may have tried to deceive you
with words. It's just, I'm a verbal person, and verbal
people will try to do that."

"What a good liar you must be," Miss Pink says,
sounding genuinely interested. "You'd have to be a
really extraordinary liar to have pulled the wool over
the eyes of someone like Soledad Ocampo for so
long. Tell us about that."

"About what?"

"Your lies."

"What do you want me to say about them?"

"How you come up with them, and how you go
about putting them to work?"

I don't know what to say. My instinctive answer
would be that my lies occur to me quite naturally
and that I've never even had to think about them.

"I've constructed my whole life to make it un-
sinkable like the *Titanic*," I say. "I built different
rooms inside that were isolated from each other so
they could fill with water without the whole thing
capsizing. In theory it was impossible for the *Titanic*
to sink, as you no doubt know, because any damage could only have led to a limited number of areas
flooding. In much the same way it was impossible for

a catastrophe in one part of my life to spread to another. Unless the utterly improbable were to occur, that is, and one entire side of the ship was ripped open by an iceberg because the ship was moving at high speed and..."

I lose the thread when I catch sight of their expressions. You can see the contempt and revulsion glittering in their eyes.

"You don't really mean," Mister Blue finally says, "that you came all the way here, and dragged Lucia out of the convent into the bargain, just to tell us how the *Titanic* was built."

"What...? No, I..."

Then the nun says, "Are you extremely intelligent, very rude, or just stupid?"

She looks at me as if she were actually expecting a reply. Mister Blue and Miss Pink are doing the same. There is silence all around us, the kind of silence that only exists in the underworld.

"I apologize," I say.

"Let's move on," Miss Pink says and takes a sip of water from her glass. "We've arranged a little surprise for you."

The nun puts her hand on the table, and once again I can see the stump where her thumb should be.

"Surprise?" I repeat, my voice thick.

"There's someone here to see you," Miss Pink says cheerfully, as though the nun's hand were not where it was.

"Which someone?" I ask. "Who?"

"Penelope."

Oh shit. Penelope. I have to resist the impulse to get up and run out of this place. My cheeks are burning. I can feel sweat running down the inside of my thighs. Although I'm trying to control my facial expressions, I can clearly sense how one eye has started to twitch. I can feel the nun's eyes on me and I look back at her. That is the moment I know she hates me, and there's no defense against that kind of hatred. Such an ancient and powerful hatred.

"Come on out, Penelope," Miss Pink says, and Penelope emerges from the darkness.

My eyes fill with tears when I see her. I can't hold them back.

"Penelope," I say, and I get up to go over to her. "At last, it's been so long, how are you..."

"Sit down, Mr. Peng," Miss Pink says sternly.

I do so. I am aware that Penelope has been studiously avoiding my gaze and also that it feels like winter has invaded the space we are in, as if the temperature had just plummeted below zero. I rub my upper arms and shiver. The nun gets up to offer Penelope her chair. Then she disappears from my field of vision.

"It's good to see you, Penelope," Miss Pink says.

I wonder what is happening in the Comments section. Is it still displaying the calm before the storm with the ears of corn moving slowly in the breeze, or have they been whipped into a frenzy of insults, jeers, and calls for violence?

"Maybe you'd like to say something first?" Mister Blue asks.

"Of course," I say. "I'd be happy to."

Only I have no idea what to say. The chill from my wet shirt has made one side of my body go into a kind of spasm from the shoulder blade all the way to the kidney. I pull my shoulders back. And then I say, "Penelope, I am so sorry. So sorry. Can you forgive me?"

"I loved you, Mercuro," she says through her tears.

That sounds to me like a line from a soap opera when she says it, but I am hoping it comes across differently to someone watching at home.

"Though you had Soledad at home, you still came to me. For two years. Two years of filthy lies and adultery. And that's leaving out..."

There is nothing I can say. She's right. That's how it was, and now it has come out there's no defense in hindsight. I know I have to get through this. All I have to do is let myself be humiliated. If I can only swallow my pride and let myself be humiliated, and if I can just find a way to demonstrate genuine remorse, then maybe they will help me. They've got every resource at their disposal. Lucia is supposed to be one of Madrid's richest women, because when people die without issue they often choose to leave their assets to the convent and on occasion to someone specific within it, someone who has been particularly supportive. *Carnality* can send people to tropical resorts. They can mediate, bring psychologists in, makeup artists and influencers. They can do anything at all, because *Carnality* has access to money, resources, muscle. If I manage to get through this, they might send Soledad and me on a trip to Mauritius or the Dominican Republic. They could even help us with the hospital waiting lists. Soledad could have her operation and then we could go. Get away from it all for a bit, make a new start and *do it all right* this time. *Do it all right, do it all right, do it all right.* Only nothing is for free. A new start is going to cost me, and the currency I have to pay in is humiliation. That is how I see it.

"Just focus on Penelope," Miss Pink says. "What do you have to say, Mr. Peng? Do you believe you can be forgiven for what you've done?"

"If someone shows genuine remorse, forgiveness ought to be possible," I say.

"Let's see what our followers think," Mister Blue says and pulls the computer toward him.

He presses some of the keys.

"Right then," he says. "Here's the current situation: twenty percent think that Penelope should forgive Mr. Peng because he so obviously regrets what he did. But a good *eighty* percent think he's a swine who deserves to die."

"Is that what it says?" I say.

"That is exactly what it says."

I clear my throat. This is how it can go for some people. There's no telling exactly why but there are some people it just feels so incredibly rewarding to hate. And while they're hated for what they have done, they also get hated for something else, for things other people have done, as well as things you might even have done yourself, and it feels like these people are a magnet drawing all the hatred out of you, only it doesn't make you feel any better because while that is happening it feels as if the same hatred keeps on being created inside you, even faster than the magnet can draw it out. I want to say that to the followers. To plead with them. Don't hate. Come to your senses. Stop, nothing good can come of this, you're being sucked in. Only that won't work when you are the person being hated. You'd have to do it when it's someone else being hated, and that is of course not something I've ever done. Though, to be perfectly honest, I did my hating as well when other people were being hated and it felt so good, so satisfying, to lie on the sofa and feel hate, to hate with all you've got, like tickling the very back of your throat with a feather and taking pleasure in both repressing the urge and keenly anticipating the awful vomit about to erupt, relishing it intensely beforehand, the sweetness of delicious hatred.

And now I'm the object. I'm the herbivore fleeing the carnivores. I'm the one whose flesh you can't help sinking your teeth into. Soft, white, quivering, and utterly chewable flesh. I take a deep breath and turn toward Penelope.

"I am so sorry," I say. "I am so terribly sorry, Penelope, can you forgive me?" I keep going even though I can hear how trite it sounds: "I accept that I'm responsible and I admit *everything*. I had you and Soledad at the same time. For two years I hopped between you and between your beds. I was in love with both of you and couldn't choose. I was too weak. Weak but devious as well, because I managed to keep both of you in the dark. Two clever, not to say brilliant, women. Now it's all been exposed and here I am. Spat upon and hated. The only chance I've got is to try and clean up the mess. Starting with admitting everything and then doing my utmost to make it up to you and get Soledad back."

"Get Soledad back?" she whispers and her eyes narrow. "So *she's* the only one you're thinking of?"

"She *is* my wife."

"You bastard..."

All of a sudden it's like she's possessed as she hurls herself across the table, digs her nails into my cheeks, and yanks them down very hard. It is incredibly painful because Penelope's nails are treated with a kind of varnish that makes them as tough as metal and allows her to grow them as long as she likes. Though it is not the pain that strikes me first but the force of the rage in her eyes, which are bloodshot from weeping.

"Tell them about the abuse," she whispers.

"What?" I say.

"The abuse. Tell them, so they know what kind of person you *really* are."

I realize I'm bleeding. Blood is dripping onto my white shirt. Penelope is still sprawled across the table and staring at me with those hateful bloodshot eyes. I keep my hand on my cheek to stop the bleeding, though that's of secondary importance now. Her bringing up what she calls "the abuse" is absurd. Abuse is when four men hold you down on the street and keep kicking and punching you until you can't walk. That's being abused. Getting into a fight at home, over a lover's spat, isn't abuse; it's a temporary loss of control, a *mistake*. A contemptible mistake, a mistake that deserves to be punished, of course, but no one's been killed or ended up in the hospital. Not, of course, that I can say any of this to these people. Oh Penelope, why bring it up at all? Don't you know the expression "don't wash your dirty linen in public"? Bring a couple of thugs around to my place one night and have your revenge. This though? Airing our dirty laundry for everyone to see?

Though I feel so tired of all the lies. I don't have the energy to keep lying. This is the first time in my life I've ever told the truth about something as intimate as my own lies, and it feels like I am speaking a new language all of a sudden, one I realize I can speak fluently and without effort. I want to speak this new language. Loud and fast, and test its boundaries. There is something so uninhibited and intoxicating about the truth. Being able to expose yourself, reveal all your flaws while declaring *here I am, this is me.*

"Mercuro?" Mister Blue asks. "Do you want to reply? What kind of abuse is Penelope talking about?"

I tell them. One night at her place I woke up and needed to go to the loo. I took my mobile to light the way and so as not to wake her by putting the lights on in the bedroom and because I wanted to see if I'd got any messages during the hours I'd been asleep. Is that a crime? Could you really call that a crime? Countless people do it. Check their phones, I mean, at night. I was convinced she was asleep on her side of the bed, which meant that when I heard her distorted but completely alert voice say in the dark, "Are you off to chat with your whores?" I was so terrified the blood almost stopped flowing through my veins. I think my rage was born from fear. I've been told it can work that way and there's always another feeling behind the rage, which is usually grief or fear. Fear that I had been caught out so unexpectedly and the shock because I was so convinced she was asleep. And then there was her voice, because, trust me, she sounded like a demon. An offended evil witch who'd been lying awake beside a man, working out how she was going to punish him for some flaw in his character, something at his very core, which he is not responsible for and can do nothing about. "Are you off to chat with your whores?" And just who were those whores supposed to be? Soledad, my wife, who was at home with a damaged heart and who I already had pangs of guilt about, did she really have to be called a whore *by my mistress* on top of everything else? I wouldn't have been able to hold back if I'd tried and instead I threw myself at the bed in a blind rage.

"You came flying at me out of the dark," Penelope says, "like this huge, furious bat."

"I admit it. I came flying at her out of the dark. She screamed from terror. I hit her with a clenched fist on her arms and legs, and all I can say in my defense is that I didn't hit her on the parts of the body that can sustain internal damage. And I didn't hit her in the face. And I did it because of all the things she had done to me, all the suspicions she had vented in tiny puffs of marsh gas, because of all the lies she had forced me to come up with in order to justify the old ones and because of the way she had forced me to spin a web of new lies around myself, which meant I could no longer move without the web swaying and vibrating and winding me even tighter in its sticky threads. And I hit her because of the wonderful woman she had deprived me of when she deprived me of herself, the person she was before she allowed suspiciousness to sour her mind. She kept screaming like someone possessed. She was screaming 'Stop, stop, you're killing me,' which made me even more furious because I was doing my utmost to hit her on the very places that *couldn't* kill her. I did think in the heat of the moment she deserved to die for screaming what she had screamed, and because of all the moronic things she was also screaming, like 'Sorry, sorry, sorry, I take back everything I ever said, you're right I'm too suspicious,' when it was obvious she hadn't taken anything back but was only screaming those words because she was so bloody scared of dying. I held her head up. 'I'm going to crack your skull, you fucking witch,' I said, and I headbutted her.'"

I can see Mister Blue and Miss Pink freeze. It's like they have suddenly turned to ice. They look away as if they cannot bear the sight of me. Only I'm in the middle of my story now and cannot stop.

"I remember how all my rage just disappeared the moment that Penelope collapsed in a heap on the bed. I was watching myself from outside as if on film. A furious savage in an ocean of tangled, wrinkled sheets. The woman I loved in a lifeless heap in front of me. The night wrapped around us. Penelope, I whispered. Penelope, for God's sake, say something. My darling. Please, please forgive me. I don't know what happened, I've no idea what got into me. I touched her and to my tremendous relief I could feel her moving. Her hand fumbled its way into mine, and her terrified face turned toward me. Sorry, she whispered. And I felt a sense of relief soft as cotton and the warmth of the sun bloom inside me, because not only was she not dead she was also showing me she understood even though I didn't deserve it in the slightest. My wonderful, beloved Penelope! My refuge among women. To show understanding to a man, to all his base and violent impulses, the unfortunate leftovers from our primeval condition, somehow she was able to show me she understood all that despite the harm I had just done her. I don't deserve you, I wept. I don't deserve you. I took her in my arms and no embrace has ever been as lovely, not in my entire life. Penelope cried as well, and that felt like she was sharing the guilt with me, like she was taking her share of the responsibility for what had happened. Don't get me wrong. I was the one who hit her and even though that was unforgivable, of course, she had driven me to it. She had pressed every button a woman's finger can press and she had done that as if what she really wanted was for the bomb to go off. Some people do things like that. They seek out destructive situations because of what they went through as young children. They feel driven by this desire inside them to solve those childhood problems and they can only do that once they are adults."

I paused for a moment and then continued.

"Of course I didn't realize at the time that she was still so terrified she wouldn't have dared put the blame on me for what I had done; that came later. She was crying from fear, fear and the grief that affects a woman when she realizes the man she is closest to is prepared to kill her. Something gets broken. I realize that now. A groundwater that ceases to flow, an artery that dries out, an elixir in the soul that disappears. *You are not loved* is the realization that dawns, *but hated.* When you wake up in your bed, you are hated. When you struggle with all of the reverses we suffer in this life, with illness, aging, and bitterness, you are hated. I couldn't see that then. But I can now, and believe me, seeing it is punishment enough."

"Go on, Mr. Peng," Mister Blue says.

"I don't know if I can."

"Give it a try."

"It took a while before we could find our way back to each other. There was something oppressive about the air in the flat. Penelope got out of bed, went into the bathroom and showered. She put on a lovely, thin summer dress in a bright color. The bruises were not visible yet. We became acquainted with the life cycle of the bruises over the days to come. A red patch appears first. Then a violet blue mark that turns black and ends up green. The constantly shifting reproach of the flesh. But that night when she came out of the bathroom her arms were still smooth and clear, covered in a gentle transparent down that would occasionally glisten in the sun and could evoke surges of tenderness inside me, just as it did on Soledad's skin. She had made herself up with a pearlescent powder and mascara. The impression she made when she came out of the bathroom was softer than usual. I went over and held her in my arms and in that moment I couldn't understand how I could have hurt her only a little while before. That I could have *headbutted* her. I mean who in God's name does that? That's the kind of thing you'd do to a thug who was attacking you on the street while you were being restrained by two other thugs, and you had no other option. That's when you headbutt someone. I could have broken her skull. Or my own. I felt deeply ashamed, of course, because if there is one thing everyone agrees on, even my most male chauvinist friends, it is that you don't hit a woman. Everyone hates a man who hits a woman. Only does anyone ever wonder why a man, as man, hits a woman? Of course not, that question can't be asked. That question is too politically incorrect to even merit a response. That question is too scandalous, too male chauvinist, too white (although I doubt that white men beat their women more than other men), too hegemonic, too reductive. It meets the criteria for every category of the taboo. Still, if I were to put it to you who are listening to me at this moment, who are listening to me very patiently, a patience I am grateful for even though I'm not sure I deserve it, if I were to put the question to you, rhetorically, and then have myself answer it, what would you say to that?"

"We are all ears, Mr. Peng."

"Right, you see the thing is that a woman appears to have something inside her that has been genetically engineered to annoy a man. I apologize for saying this. As you know, Nietzsche says that man is evil but woman is mean. A truth I've also experienced for myself on many occasions. Women have learned how to fight from a subordinate position and how to turn the strength and energy of the man against him. After all their provocations, their childish attacks and endless nagging, you reach a point when you can no longer control yourself. Don't tell me women are unaware of this; they know exactly what they are doing. They know exactly what they are doing when they turn themselves into demonic victims. Though you can only be a victim when you are dead is how I would put it. And if you're not dead, then what you are is a *survivor*."

I stop speaking and look over at them. It is only now I notice that Penelope is smiling. At some point during my story she must have squared her shoulders and sat back in her chair, put her arms over her breasts and started *smiling*. I have never seen her smile like that. She is smiling so much there are tears in her eyes, though no longer from rage but a profound sense of joy. She moves her lips at me shaping words I cannot quite make out, but that for a moment seem to say *They're going to murder you*. I am also aware that the silence in the room is deafening. There are no longer any sounds at all. No distant whir of fans, no hum from the computer, no sound of breathing. Miss Pink and Mister Blue are looking at me as if I were something *monstrous*. And they keep doing it for a long time, a long time during which the awareness returns that I am speaking on camera and that a great many other people can also hear what I say. What does the Comments section look like now? I can picture it—not the stirring of a breeze, not the force of the wind, but *blazing coals*. I have talked my head off. I have opened myself up. I've allowed myself to be split open like a dead animal, and all my innards have been exposed to the light of day.

"Mr. Peng."

"Yes?"

"How are you feeling?"

"Good. Very good."

"Are you sure about that?"

"No."

"We can see that. You're not feeling well at all. You're aware you've said too much, and that it is going to come back on you."

"Yes."

"It is the first time you've spoken to anyone about this."

"Yes."

"It is very painful for you because you feel deeply ashamed."

"Deeply, yes. I feel deeply ashamed."

"It is that shame which will save you."

"Will you help me?"

They do not reply.

"You're not going to help me," I say. "You're going to throw me to the wolves and you're going to enjoy doing it because that is all part and parcel of your declaration of war against the patriarchy."

I can hear Lucia clearing her throat in the darkness.

"Did you say patriarchy?" she asks.

"Yes."

"You're flattering yourself, Mr. Peng, in that case. What you just told us has got nothing to do with patriarchy."

"Yes it does," I say. "It does because it is about the exercise of power."

"Is that something you've read, that that is its nature?"

"Yes," I reply.

I look at Miss Pink and Mister Blue, asking for confirmation, but they refuse to meet my eye and simply stare into the darkness without any expression.

"All this unfounded talk about the patriarchy," Lucia says. "All these casual simplifications." She clears her throat again. "Now, listen to me. Patriarchy is a tree with deep roots; those roots are at least three millennia old. We all grow from that tree and we are all tied to it. To try and take it out of us would be to behave like the merchant in the Shakespeare play. Take thy pound of flesh but not a jot of blood. Take thy pound of flesh, but no nerves and no sinews. Not only would that be futile and self-destructive, it would obviously be impossible as well. We all come from that tree, and it would be to disrespect ourselves as human beings not to consider it in all its breadth and depth or to fail to understand that it is a formidable tree whose primary task is to *strengthen* and protect."

"I never thought I'd hear anything like that from someone like you," I say.

"The problem is," she goes on, "that the tree has become sick. It has continued to grow unconcerned that other plants are being deprived of light. There are diseased branches on that noble trunk. And you, Mr. Peng, are one of those diseased branches."

I wipe my brow with the palm of my hand.

"Only what about forgiveness," I say. "In the biblical sense. So how does that really work then, Sor Lucia?"

She says, as though she had not heard me, "So what do you think, Mister Blue?"

"I think you've done a marvelous job, Lucia."

Forgiveness, I want to yell again, what about that then? What about that, you hypocritical bloodhounds?

"Are you going to help me or not?" I ask.

"We're going to consult with our followers," Mister Blue responds. "They don't always react the way you'd expect. They may want to know what should happen next. After all, this show is not about social work but providing entertainment."

Entertainment? I can't help laughing.

"Even though they may have been in therapy for many years, some people," Miss Pink says, "never manage to be entirely honest. You've only been here for a very short while and you've already succeeded. That is good, Mr. Peng. Very good. Whatever happens, both Mister Blue and I, and no doubt Lucia as well, think you've grown a great deal in what is a very short period of time."

She smiles at me.

"Yes," I say.

"So kudos to you for that."

Kudos. Since when do they hand out kudos on *Carnality*? I dig around in my jacket pocket and come up with a handkerchief. I run it over the blood on my face and tidy my hair with the other hand.

Lucia appears out of the darkness and puts her hand on Penelope's shoulder.

"Come, dear," she says. "I've ordered a taxi for you, and it's waiting outside."

Penelope gets up and goes off with the nun. I watch her walk away. She is moving freely in the shaft of light, her gait is free, and just before she steps outside it and enters the darkness, she turns back to me and smiles. I can hear the iron door open and shut, and then the steps of the nun as she comes back. No one speaks until she has taken her seat at the table.

"Well then," says Miss Pink. "Our followers have now heard Soledad Ocampo's story as well as meeting Mr. Peng and his mistress Penelope. That means we've reached the next section of the program."

Miss Pink looks at Mister Blue.

"We're going to propose several ways to solve all this now, Mr. Peng."

The red light on the camera is blinking at me, as steadily as a heart with a regular pulse. I am assuming the humiliation phase is over and we will now be moving on to the next one. The *constructive* phase. The phase when you may actually get help. I clasp my hands on the table and look at them. One by one. Miss Pink, Mister Blue, and Lucia.

"We think struggling to get Soledad back would be futile," Miss Pink says.

"What?" I say. "How do you mean?"

"There's no point beating about the bush," Mister Blue says. "Soledad Ocampo hates you. She couldn't stop talking about that when she was here. She told us how much she hates you for a whole hour. She had so much hatred stored up, after accumulating it for years, that it had become compressed, concentrated."

"But that's exactly what I'm asking you to help me with," I say. "To rid her heart of the hate. I'd do anything for that. If you can help me get rid of the hate, the resentment, and remove that forest of thorns from her heart, I could have another chance again."

"Are you certain that that is what you want, Mr. Peng?" the nun asks.

"Absolutely," I say. "I'm certain that is what I want. Get rid of the resentment in my wife's heart and replace it with tenderness toward me."

"In that case there's only one option."

She has clasped her hands on the table so that you cannot see the stump of her thumb.

"I would be so grateful," I whisper. "So tremendously grateful."

She nods and looks up at Mister Blue and Miss Pink with a slow shrug of her shoulders, as though they had all suddenly understood something they were unwilling to say out loud.

"Well?" I say. "What's happening?"

"Do you have any idea what a heart is?" Lucia asks.

"A heart?" I say. "A heart is a muscle whose sole purpose is to continue beating no matter what."

Lucia nods. "That's right, that's exactly what it is."

I haven't got a clue. What do they mean? What's going to happen now? How much time is left?

"There's a shortage of hearts at present," Lucia says.

"I don't understand."

Miss Pink and Mister Blue look as if they are struggling not to laugh.

"No, really," I say, "I don't understand..."

"She means donors," Mister Blue says. "What Lucia means is that there aren't as many donors as are needed. If there were then your wife would have been given a new heart long ago."

I take a deep breath and swallow and then do it again. I am completely at a loss and as I've only got the one thing to say, I say it: "I love Soledad Ocampo with all my heart, and I'd do anything for her. Anything at all."

"Fine words," says Miss Pink.

"I'm starting to get tired of all this fencing," I say. "Are you going to help me? Yes or no."

"I think Lucia really does want us to help you, don't you, Lucia?"

"Yes," the nun says. "It's just I've spent almost my entire life trying to help people and I'm not sure it's that simple. I want to help Soledad, and in order to help Soledad, we have to help Mr. Peng. Mr. Peng, Soledad. Soledad, Mr. Peng. So that is what we are going to do. Somehow."

What follows are those last dreadful minutes. And though I could obviously tell you about them— maybe another evening, another night, just not now. Once they're over, Mister Blue finally says to the camera that that is it for today.

The blinking red light on the camera went out. Silence fell. I tried to catch their eye, one of their eyes. Then Mister Blue and Miss Pink began to collect up cables and headphones, and no one paid any attention to me. I moved toward the door and just before I reached it I was considering whether to turn around and yell something in farewell. Such as: *What's going to happen now,* or *Fuck off, the lot of you.* But I didn't say anything. I walked slowly up the stairs from the underworld and out into the fresh air. Despite the light up there I thought I could see a few stars looking down at me from the sky like eyes shining out of a swarm of insects.

What did I do after my appearance on the show? I went home and lay down on the bed. I stubbornly pushed the image of myself out of my head. The man who had confessed to everything on *Carnality*. What a terrible mistake. Digesting something like that takes time. The only thing I could see in my mind was Soledad. Soledad in a different flat. Soledad with another man. Soledad sitting next to another man, who is putting his hand between her thighs as they are watching a film and letting it stay there, enjoying the warmth. Another man she is making dinner for, who then falls asleep beside her and can reach out for her in his sleep. Soledad making meticulous plans for her old age with another man. Where are they going to live, where will they travel, where will they spend the Christmases and the summers? Soledad discovering she has a soul mate she will be with for the rest of her life. That all felt horrendous, unnatural, and unreal. At the same time there was a kind of bizarre pleasure in tormenting myself, as though I were sinking into a quagmire of self-pity. A sweet quicksand I could swallow in huge, deep gulps, and even though I knew it would make me sick I was gulping it greedily down with appalling eagerness.

The evening ended with my masturbating while visualizing Soledad. My orgasm was long, protracted, painful. Afterward I lay on my bed, out cold as though my body was a building whose main fuse had blown, and everything had faded to a dumb, nocturnal blank.

The next day came and went. Two more days passed, maybe three. I didn't take a look at *Carnality*, and my mobile stayed silent on my bed. No one rang, no comments appeared. As though the episode in that basement had never occurred. But the scratch marks on my face were still there, and I could see them every morning in the mirror. The scabs were getting darker, and the bruises around them changed color from blue to black and finally green. I wanted to ring Penelope and persuade her to forgive me. My body ached with longing for Soledad. I thought about going into town to look for temporary sexual release, but didn't have the energy to get out of bed. I dreamed that I had experienced my last orgasm. It was unnaturally drawn out and painful, like a kind of final goodbye to everything still alive inside me.

Then one morning I was woken by someone knocking on my door. I had had a deep and dreamless sleep and actually felt rested when I opened my eyes. I got out of bed, went to the front door, and opened it. There were two men standing there who appeared to be Chinese. They were both wearing suits, white shirts, and ties.

"Lee Peng?" they inquired.

"Yes?" I replied.

"We're here to inform you about the practical aspects."

"The practical aspects?" I said. "Of what?"

They looked at me blankly.

"The organ transplant," they said.

"The organ transplant?"

"Aren't you Soledad Ocampo's husband?" they asked.

"Yes, I am."

"Then you're the person to speak to. About Soledad Ocampo's organ transplant."

All of a sudden I thought I understood. Lucia's magic wand had been waved over our heads, Soledad's and mine. She had waved it over us, and the first part of her help was on the way: the new heart. Lucia, I thought, you are a beacon of light after all. Now the humiliation was over, all that trouble would prove to have been worth it. Because who would they be contacting if not me? I was her husband, I was the one who would have to sign all the papers and I was the one who would be present when the operation was carried out. Of course I would have to be involved at an early stage.

"Please come in," I said and held the door open. "I'll put the coffee on."

Both men entered, straight-backed and dignified. They sat at the dining table I showed them to. One of them looked down at the crumbs on the top, so I fetched a cloth from the kitchen and wiped them away. When I put the cloth back in the kitchen I noticed there was a sour smell coming off it that I hoped they hadn't been aware of. An elegantly expensive scent of cedarwood and eucalyptus had pervaded the flat since they entered. While I was making the coffee in the kitchen, I could hear them talking to each other in Chinese. I hummed to myself for a bit before I returned, carrying a tray with three cups.

"There we are, then," I said and took a seat on the other side of the table. "I'm all ears."

"My name is Liu Huei," one of them said, "and this is my assistant."

He gestured with his hand to the other man and said a name I can't remember. The assistant nodded amiably. I nodded back.

"The name of our company is Metamorphosis S.A., and we deal with almost a thousand transplants a year. You are in good hands, in other words. I don't think it would be boasting on my part to say you won't find a company with a better reputation in the entire market."

"Market?" I say. "What do you mean, what market?"

They glance at each other.

"What sort of world do you think we live in?" Liu Huei asked. "The black market, of course. Surely you didn't think we were here from the public health service?"

"I didn't think anything," I said. "I had no idea you were going to turn up at all."

"People who rely on the health service die before they even get a diagnosis," Mr. Huei stated.

"I understand," I said.

"Our focus, in contrast, is on more 'creative solutions.'"

"I understand," I repeated, despite not understanding anything.

Liu Huei and his assistant were both smiling at me. In front of them on the table was a perfectly squared-off pile of papers.

"Let me say first that you should know how much we admire people like you," Liu Huei said.

"Is that right?"

"People who have worked out how to leave the stage with their heads held high. So that once you are gone, other people can say though you may have lived like a dog, you had become a man by the time you died."

I didn't understand. Or rather, at first I didn't understand and kept looking at them with my hands folded over my stomach. I could hear the neighbor's wife in the flat upstairs, opening the balcony doors while singing to herself as she moved around what must have been pots. Then, it slowly dawned on me, very slowly, and I did understand. My first impulse was to laugh. Loud and long as if it were a joke, an over-the-top joke. Only then did I realize it wasn't the slightest bit funny. There was nothing to laugh about. It was a very bad joke, an outrageous and pathetic joke.

"May I use your toilet?" Mr. Huei said.

I pointed toward it. Mr. Huei went off, and I was left with the assistant. He pushed a page torn from a newspaper toward me across the table, and I started reading. The article was about a village in Pakistan in which nearly all the inhabitants only had one kidney, because they had sold the other one to wealthy individuals who had traveled to the village with the sole purpose of obtaining a new organ. They received $1,700 a kidney, which represented great wealth to these people who were living in dire poverty. Someone was making a huge profit, however, because the price the foreign clients were paying was $15,000 a kidney. *An entire industry exists,* the writer of the article wrote. *Few things generate as much related activity as this meat we live in. The resourceful buyer will always find what he wants on the market in human flesh, because we live in an age when anything to do with the carnal aspects of human life is possible.*

"So you want me to sell my organs?" I asked when I had finished reading.

The assistant cleared his throat softly and shook his head.

"*We* don't want anything," he said. "*We* don't have any particular desires. But there are others who do."

I nodded. "Of course, I should have realized. *Carnality* is behind all this."

"Help can come in a variety of ways," the assistant said, "and *Carnality* provides it in a form that is all its own."

Mr. Huei returned from the bathroom.

"Right, then," he said as he sat down. "Let me tell you a bit about the market."

"I really don't know if I have time for this," I said.

"The black market is a wonderful place," he began. "There are no needs it cannot meet. You can find people there who need everything and anything, hair, nails, livers, kidneys, and of course hearts. Someone is supposed to have said, 'In the kingdom of the blind the one-eyed man is king.' People can go from not amounting to anything to having it all."

"This is absurd," I said.

"You have everything," he said and patted me on the hand, as if I had won a race or married a particularly beautiful woman.

"Yes," I said. "Apart from Soledad."

"Because you are healthy, aren't you?"

"Completely healthy," I said, nodding,

"A veritable *feast* of life and health," Mr. Huei exclaimed, and he offered me his hand.

We stayed like that for a while. I looked at them and they looked at me. I could hear a tap dripping in the kitchen. I immediately realized that all my efforts on the program had been in vain, and I would have to give it all up now. I would end all contact with them. Withdraw. Lick my wounds. Not see any more episodes but simply log out forever and try and forget the whole thing.

The sun popped out at that point and I could see how filthy the table was, even though I had just wiped it. The surface was greasy, and there were crumbs in the grooves between the glass and the wood. I was debating whether to go and get the cloth again, but then I remembered it smelled bad; I felt it was better to end the discussion and deal with any other stuff afterward.

"No," I said. "Something's gone wrong. They're playing a bit of a joke on me."

"A joke? I find that hard to imagine."

"You work with them often, do you?"

"Our work is almost entirely on behalf of Lucia. She is like a little empire all of her own."

"A little empire of her own? How do you mean?"

"Lucia has always done her utmost to help other people. And she has helped so many of them. She has helped people on the run go into hiding and she has helped people suffering greatly from terrible illnesses to cross to the other side."

"What you mean is she has killed people," I said. "Why not just say that?"

"She's never done anything to people who were unwilling," Mr. Huei responded.

"Only now you're telling me she wants my heart. That's what you are saying, isn't it? But I am unwilling. So how does that make sense?"

Mr. Huei looked at me blankly. "Soledad Ocampo is the one she is helping," he said.

"But what about me? Let's just pretend this isn't a joke. What about me?"

"You can't always help everyone equally and at the same time. And presumably, she is counting on you being generous enough to assist her. You will be getting a wonderful transition in return, after all. Do you have any idea what that costs? Do you know how many people wish they could have had that? If we could hear the people on the other side speak, you would realize how privileged you are. You will be passing over without any pain. You have no children. No partner. No job and no motivation. As you are now, you're just withering away. What have you got to lose?"

"I think you should go now," I said.

"The way we see it, life is cyclical. The human being is an array of exceptional components, each of which possesses the ability to continue into new dimensions. Seen from that perspective, death seems like a terrible waste. You will be living on in four different individuals, instead, and one of them is your wife."

"No, no . . . no. Like I said, you should go now."

"Not yet, Mr. Cano."

He raised his hand and looked at his nails. He was very well groomed. The way a man is when he has a woman who loves him and who looks him over every time he leaves the house, who brushes a piece of dry or flaking skin off his shoulders, plucks an eyebrow that has grown too long, and says his shoes need polishing when he comes home. Which means he is loved, I thought, and felt that familiar twitch of envy in my heart.

"Does Soledad know?" I asked. "Is Soledad in on this tasteless joke, does she know you're here now?"

"Soledad? No, she doesn't know anything. We can't let her know because then she would be against the operation out of sympathy for you. And once the operation has been carried out, any guilt she might feel could interfere with her body's acceptance of the new organ. The heart could be rejected. In China we are very aware of the impact of mental states on the way the body functions."

Despite how crazy everything the two men had said was, I heaved a sigh of relief that they had not been messing around with my wife's head to persuade her to join in this madness of her own free will.

The assistant clasped his hands on top of the table and asked if I was ready for the details of "the final step." It was going to be wonderful, he assured me, not to say exhilarating.

I shook my head. "Leave now."

"Allow me to put a proposal to you," Mr. Huei said. "One you are, of course, entirely free to accept or reject. We have many options available. But events of this kind require a good deal of preparation. We need doctors, surgeons, and nurses, and we need the individuals who will receive organs to be on-site so that the transplants can take place immediately. In one part of the building a group of people will be gaining a new life while in another part a number of individuals—we call them 'the life sources'—will be moving on to the next dimension. As I said, this all requires planning. Everything has to take place in an efficient, competent, hygienic, and dignified manner. Furthermore, the people whose lives are going to end usually have quite a few last wishes, with regard to food and to *company* in particular."

At this point Mr. Huei winked at me suggestively.

"And that means?" I asked.

"Mr. Cano," Mr. Huei said, "I would like to congratulate you because you are going to be ending your days happier than you have ever been in your life. You will have a gorgeous woman to die with. And both of you will be served a dinner the like of which you have never seen. Afterward you will enjoy several hours alone together in a suite and, when all your needs have been met, you will be served a drink we call 'Mozart,' which will make you feel intoxicated and exhilarated and will also make your memory start to fade. You will, in other words, no longer remember why you are where you are. You will just slip into the mists as if riding a *wind organ.*"

"A wind organ?"

"Being given the chance to die," the assistant filled in, "without having to worry about the transition from life to death. That is a gift, a luxury, true mercy."

"My God," I whispered. "You're both completely mad."

I got to my feet and said I had no more time available and, more importantly, that I did not want to die. Though I loved Soledad Ocampo very much, I was not willing to give her my heart. And that was that. In all honesty I wasn't sure I was willing to donate any of my organs, not even if I were to die now, not even if I were to drop dead in front of them this very moment. I was much more the kind of person who would take it all with him to the other side, in the event.

"In the event that?" the assistant asked.

"Leave now," I said.

"That last bit you said was among the most selfish things I have ever heard," the assistant said.

"They're *my organs*," I said, "and I'll do with them as I please. Leave."

I started moving toward the hall, but they remained in their seats.

"Perhaps you didn't hear me," I said, and I moved a step or two back. "But I really did ask you—"

Mr. Huei shook his head and looked down at the table. "It's really not that simple," he said.

"What do you mean?" I stared at him. Was I going to have to grab hold of him and *chuck* him out?

"We've already been promised," he said.

"Get out!" I yelled.

"And we've already lined up the recipients for all of it. While your wife will get the heart, other people will be receiving your kidneys, your liver, and your spleen as well. They are looking forward to that. Some of them are looking forward to it so much they cannot sleep at night but just lie awake thinking about those body parts."

"Those body parts? My body parts, you mean!"

"Your body parts," Mr. Huei said with a nod. "Exactly. Your body parts."

"Get out, or I'll throw you out," I said with clenched teeth.

They got up, gathered up their papers from the table, and moved toward the door. They turned and smiled at me as if they were keen to maintain some form of civility or appear to be gentlemen at least.

"So we'll call you then," the assistant said, "when everything has been arranged."

"That's right, we'll call you," Mr. Huei echoed. "We'll call you when everything has been arranged and let you know the date."

"Fuck off!" I yelled and slammed the door behind them. "You, *Carnality*, and Sor Lucia can all fuck off, the lot of you."

I stayed in bed. Now and then I got up to have a bit of bread or a few cookies and drink water from the tap. In an attempt to find out who she really was, I did some half-hearted searches on the net into Sor Lucia, but the only thing I came across was her name on a list of the nuns living in the convent. Nothing else. Nothing about miracles or obscure shows on the Internet. Nothing about her and the black market, nothing about her and Mr. Huei. She was effectively invisible, and I realized what a feat that must be for someone like her to achieve. If only I had got up and done something different. Packed my bags, abandoned everything, left the country or, at least, Madrid. While I was dozing in my dirty sheets, events in the outside world were spinning a fateful web.

Then one morning Mr. Huei rang.

"Good morning, Mr. Cano," he said, sounding happy. "How are you doing?"

"What do you want?" I asked.

"I've got it all arranged now," he said, "and the day it can be carried out will be in two weeks' time."

"I'm not up to this," I said.

Without appearing to have heard me, he said it would be a combined event. The involvement of many parties needed to be coordinated, as he had mentioned. Several "life sources" would be participating and many more recipients. There would be five donors in total and sixteen recipients. In addition there would be four luxury prostitutes, five chefs, and all the other staff that formed part of their teams.

"You donors will be the kings of the event," he said with considerable satisfaction. "You will enter on a red carpet, and everyone there will owe you a debt of gratitude."

"Didn't you hear what I said?" I asked. "I said I don't have the energy for this."

"I have also been having a look at the numbers," Mr. Huei continued. "And once our fees have been deducted, there will be twenty thousand euros left over. I presume you want them to go to Soledad? Or for some of it, perhaps, to go to your mistress as compensation for pain and suffering?"

"You're lunatics," I said tiredly and hung up.

After a few more hours spent in bed I got up and had a shower. Then I went out.

Madrid. My city, my beast. This is where I was born and where I have spent the best hours of my life. Where I lost my joie de vivre and experienced loneliness, where I broke hearts and had my heart broken. Madrid, so diverse it lacks an identity of its own. And even so—the streets of Madrid, the traffic, the whores on parade, the beer barrel deliveries at night, the bullfighting arenas—I loved it all. I remembered the time when Soledad and I had just got married. And the way we would go to work, come home, and take care of each other. All those utterly genuine efforts on our part to create a life that would give us an opportunity to grow and to feel secure. When I looked back, I realized that time was the loveliest part of my life. A tremor runs through the cosmos when love is broken. I was carrying that quiver inside me, a wave front that, though it would vibrate every now and then, could sometimes be as powerful as an earthquake. I had been carrying it inside me for a long time, and now

I understood it would not stop until Soledad could forgive me . . .

With all the stress the events of the last few days had involved and even though I didn't take any aspect of the organ transplant business seriously, it felt like my senses had become even more acute. All of a sudden I was able to see how beautiful everything was, just as men condemned to death or people who are extremely ill are known to do. I could see the woman who sat on the street, begging with an infant in her arms. It wasn't her poverty, her dirty clothes, or her emaciated face I could see, but the love with which she embraced her child. I saw the bright, open gaze of the child and the mother's smile when she looked at it. And I saw a man who had lost his legs to a land mine and was now forced to drag his body along on a skateboard while wearing a placard on his back. I watched the extraordinary pattern of his movement, the suppleness with which he shifted his body along the street. I gave them both money, not to help them but because they seemed so pure to me, so much themselves, so superior to everything else. I listened to people who were ill talking on the metro. Someone who had got cancer, someone else who knew someone who had got cancer, someone who butted into the conversation to declare that everyone gets cancer nowadays, everyone!...

I walked to Plaza Manuel Becerra and ate a burrito. It may have been while I was sitting there that I realized that I loved my life more than I had for a very long time despite Soledad's absence. The spark of life had flared up more strongly than ever inside me and I was able to feel the joy of the moment. The beast, the demon that had taken up residence inside me, had departed, it had fled. Here I am, I thought, sitting on a step in the evening sunlight eating a burrito, with all my body parts intact and enough money in my account with good prospects at least of lasting the month. I was visualizing how I would go about finding a new job, and how to work harder at it. In a more focused, complete, and wholehearted way. I could see myself cleaning the flat, chucking away lots of stuff that was simply lying around, and getting the place back into shape in an inexpensive but comfortable way, and how Soledad would come around to say hello. We would sit at the table with the doors open onto the little interior courtyard and, as time passed, we might move back in together again, acquire a circle of shared friends, and... But at that point the very idea of happiness seemed too vast to be contained in my chest, and I was forced to stop imagining all these wonderful things just so I could breathe.

My heart, I was thinking, and the way it has always beaten for me. My body and all the heroic battles, the conflicts it has fought to keep me alive. I read somewhere that the mind usually dies before the body. Just imagining all those living bodies without minds is a dismal notion... I had a living body, on the other hand, and a living mind...

The next morning I called Liu Huei to tell him about my newly reawakened lust for life. I was going to make clear once and for all that he and Lucia had to stop this ridiculous harassment. I thought it might make him happy to hear about my conversion as well. We're often told that Asians think we Europeans have lost our inner core, that we have been ruined by the desire to consume, sexual liberation, and a general wimpiness—and no one can deny they have a point. Besides, if there really was going to be an organ transplant event in the underworld, Mr. Huei would need ample time to find another "life source" for his four recipients.

So I told Liu Huei about what I had realized, about how blind I had been to all the possible sources of joy in my life. I was at pains to ensure there was genuine warmth and joy in my voice. But the silence at the other end was so deafening I ended up wondering whether he was still listening.

"Mr. Huei," I said. "Are you there?"

"Yes," he replied.

All I could hear after that was his calm and imperturbable breathing.

"Hello? Mr. Huei?"

"This is not a joke, Mr. Cano," he said then.

"How do you mean?"

"You're behaving as though this were a joke. But it isn't."

"Mr. Huei, I realize you and Lucia have been playing a little game with me. Maybe Mister Blue and Miss Pink have been in on it too. You may even have been filming me for the last few days as well, what do I know? But that doesn't bother me. I just feel I've finished with this whole business now. Finished, once and for all."

Then he said in a quiet voice, all sober and controlled, that I could not withdraw at this stage.

Everything had been arranged down to the last detail, and the paper I had signed when I applied to go on *Carnality* was legally binding. The text stated very clearly that it served as a form of authorization and that Miss Pink and Mister Blue had the right to avail themselves of whatever help they thought appropriate. I objected that the piece of paper in question was meaningless, what possible value could it have? He could hardly go to the courts with it, as the very existence of the program was a gray area, wasn't it?

"Not in this world," he said. "Not in the world of Spain, or in the world of Madrid. But another world exists as well, and that world is ours. And in that world the paper you signed carries great weight and applies in full."

Although I laughed, it felt right then like I was slowly starting to sweat ice cubes from my armpits.

"We grew out of the cement, Mr. Cano. No one has ever helped us to achieve anything. We had to learn to help ourselves and now we have created a whole world of our own."

"Why don't you take your fucking world and shove it up your ass!" I yelled.

"Do you really have any reason to resort to disrespect, Mr. Cano?"

"You're terrorizing me. You're persecuting me."

"You have nothing to fear. I promise. You should be feeling happy and not tormented."

In a subdued but kindly tone he told me that he had signed contracts with a man who would get one of my kidneys and a woman who would get the other one. A reformed heroin addict would be getting my liver.

I think that it was then I felt panic stir inside me for the first time. I remember I was standing in the middle of my apartment and I could hear Mr. Huei breathing over the phone. I was thinking I ought to have a shower, and then, completely out of the blue, I remembered a scene from García Márquez's *One Hundred Years of Solitude* when a rain of tiny yellow flowers starts to fall outside the window of the main character, who is dying. But the only thing that occurred to me to say was I didn't want a heroin addict to have my liver.

"Why not?" Liu Huei said, as indignantly as if he were the one I was refusing to give my organ to.

"I want someone else to have it," I said. "A child for instance."

"Your liver is too large for a young child. The ex-heroin addict deserves it just as much as anyone else. He was a child too once, and a child, besides, who was not given what he needed when he needed it most."

I hung up. I went into my study and stood facing the bookshelves. It took a while for Mr. Huei's words to fade. I found the book and the episode with the little flowers and I read it over and over again, and while I was reading, it felt like the words were a small animal, a rodent, scampering around on tiny cold paws across a froth of dirty scum, just as I was trying to consume the episode, to make it my own, to take it into my mouth and swallow it. But the door to the elation that comes from reading had closed, and I could not find my way into the story.

Another five days went by before Mr. Huei rang again.

"This is Mr. Huei," he said, but this time there was none of the usual amiability in his voice. It sounded harsh and metallic, instead, and his Chinese accent was stronger than ever, as though he couldn't be bothered to make the effort to try to communicate in my language, but had chosen to pollute as much of it as possible with his own.

"The time has come, Mr. Cano," he said. "I ask you to be like water. Yielding and advancing."

"Water!" I exclaimed.

"Yielding, Mr. Cano, yielding."

"I can get away from you," I said. "Go underground."

"You should have thought of that before," Mr. Huei said in response. "It's too late now."

"Too late?"

"We've got a man outside your building."

I moved over to the window and parted the slats of the blinds. On the other side of the street I could see a man of Chinese appearance leaning against a building with his arms crossed over his chest, waiting. Sweat broke out across my back.

"This is completely out of proportion," I mumbled.

"Sorry?" Mr. Huei said.

"The punishment," I said. "It's disproportionate. The punishment is not in proportion to the crime."

"What do you mean?"

"I deceived them, it's true, I pulled the wool over their eyes and lied and I may have banged one of them about a bit at one time or other. But that doesn't mean anyone has the right to yank the heart out of my rib cage. No one has that right just because I made a few mistakes."

I yelled the last bit so loudly I could hear my own voice echoing between the walls. It sounded like a cry of despair to me, but Mr. Huei cannot have thought the same because I heard laughter as loud as an avalanche from the other end of the line, a sound that seemed impossible to imagine coming from a man like him.

"Proportionate!" he shouted. "Proportionate! Since when, Mr. Cano, has anything ever been proportionate? Since when has anything ever been in proportion to anything else? I'm dying here. You're making me laugh so hard you're killing me, Mr. Cano. Explain the word 'proportionate' to me."

I remained silent until the laughter had ebbed away. When it had, I said I had to go out.

"Goodbye, Mr. Huei."

Then I went for a walk. I walked through the city and every now and then I would turn around just to check that the man was still following me. When I went into a bar for a cup of coffee, he took a seat at the table opposite me, making no attempt at concealment. He was staring at me and nodding slowly as though he were already visualizing that terrible operation and all the money.

———

In the course of the next few days I did my utmost to convince myself that the whole thing was a joke. It was a gag they were doing on *Carnality*—the followers might be in on it too—as a form of punishment for the harm I had done to Soledad and Penelope. I tried to convince myself that the punishment (which had to consist of my fear and discomfort) was justified and that I simply had to put up with it, allow them to keep at it until they finally invited me back to that basement, and when I entered the underworld Miss Pink and Mister Blue would laugh out loud, and Penelope and Soledad would say they forgave me. Heaven after purgatory, life after forgiveness. I tried logging in to the program but discovered I had been blocked and could not access any of the program's functions. I tried ringing Soledad but all I heard was the kind of sound you get when someone has changed their number but not left any notification. I even tried to get in touch with Lucia, without success of course. I considered ringing the police but what kind of claim could I make? The program was invisible to anyone who had not been invited. I had no evidence, no visual material, just emails sent from an encrypted address.

Wherever I went, the Chinaman followed. I could be in the park, watching children playing in the sun or the elderly in outdoor cafés. If I turned around I would always see him sitting a little way off.

I focused on keeping myself occupied for the duration of the punishment. I tidied up my little apartment. I cleaned out all the cupboards and the other spaces where junk had accumulated. I saved anything that was important but donated the rest to the needy or sent it for recycling. And then I continued the process for several days, dusting and window cleaning. Every so often I would look out through the blinds to see if Huei's man was still on the other side of the street, which he always was. But I thought I could make out something more casual in his posture, as though he wasn't on guard quite as much. Maybe they were relaxing their grip on me? Maybe the joke had begun to wear off? One day I took a cup of coffee out to the man. A way of breaking the ice, I thought. He looked up at me in surprise but there was something so utterly cold about his eyes that I took a step back out of sheer terror. I went back inside the apartment and poured the coffee into the sink. Then I sat at the table, my arms shaking and a leaden feeling in my knees. The sun broke through the cloud cover and shone in through the window. Strongly, generously, effusively, as it does for the chosen few. Though chosen for what?

I made one last attempt to escape my fate about a week or so ago now. In the early dawn I left the apartment on the ground floor wearing a hoody and a cloth backpack, mostly to escape my insomnia but also as a way of proving to myself I really could leave my home unobserved. I crept into the stairwell and then out the back door into the courtyard and climbed over the six-foot-high wall at the rear and into the neighboring courtyard, which exits onto a different street. It was completely quiet and the only thing I could hear was the sound of my own steps, my breathing, and the beating of my heart, which was pounding all the way to my temples. The morning air was so lovely, and I felt spurred on by the idea of escaping from my own home in the half-light of dawn, of setting off for the new and the unknown, toward somewhere that might be completely different, although the choice would be mine and only mine. This was who I was; this was the nomad who had been living locked away inside me and had allowed the spark of his life to be stifled by confinement. I had reached the bullfighting arena by the time Huei's man appeared. He was standing by the entrance to the metro station, leaning against a litter bin with his arms crossed as always.

"We're going home now," he said calmly and put a hand on my shoulder. We went back.

The day arrived when I was due to be picked up for the bizarre culmination of the punishment. There was a knock on the door late that afternoon. It was Liu Huei, his assistant, and the sentry.

"It's time," said Liu Huei.

It all happened very quickly after that. In the space of a few seconds I was escorted into a black car parked on the street. I was sitting between Huei and the guard in the back. We'll be arriving at the basement studio and *Carnality* any minute, I was thinking. Lucia, Miss Pink, and Mister Blue will be standing there, and they will all be laughing and talking about methods for combating urges and the Chinamen will be laughing too.

But *Carnality* was not where we were headed. The car stopped outside the Hotel Europa instead, and we were dropped off at the entrance. One of the porters opened the door and because I am not used to people doing things for me, I caught his eye and thanked him as I got out. He failed to reply. He just looked through me as if he were staring at something on the other side of my body, as though my physical self no longer existed and he were holding the door open for a phantom. We walked through the lobby and took the lift to the top floor. I had been feeling relatively calm until this point. The lift ran up the outside of the building, and at our feet was a view of the sprawling city. The ugly city in the interior, home to so many flaws, the city of Franco, the nest of the fascists, the city of burnt facades, but my city nonetheless. The sun was about to set on all those disparate buildings. I was struck by the realization that I might not be alive when it rose again. "I don't want to," was the only thing I could get out. But we had reached the top of the building, and the lift doors were opening in front of us.

There was a small crowd assembled in the foyer. We stepped out of the lift and I stood there for a while watching the gathering. All the invited guests were well dressed and making small talk. Soft vacuous music was playing in the background. Young women dressed in bikinis moved around carrying tall glasses on trays. The event seemed rather somber and subdued like a private view or a ceremony to thank some high-up executive who was retiring. A woman carrying a tray came over to us straightaway and I took one of the glasses. Mr. Huei took one as well and then raised it toward me as though we should make a toast.

"Cheers," he said. "To this world and all the other worlds."

I avoided drinking from the glass and asked if I could go to the toilet. Mr. Huei gestured toward his assistant who put down his glass and offered to accompany me. As we were passing the lifts I could see out of the corner of my eye that a set of doors was just about to close and managed to hurl myself inside before they shut. I pressed the button for the ground floor like a man possessed, and the lift started descending. I reached the ground floor with the blood pounding in my ears, and before Mr. Huei's assistant could do the same I slipped (as swift as running water!) past all the soberly dressed people who were also staying at the hotel, and out onto the street and headed straight for a viaduct beside the building that carried the elevated motorway. I ran like a condemned man. I made my way up onto the motorway, gesticulating wildly at traffic, and a truck driver, who must have thought I was suicidal, stopped to pick me up.

I've been living among the rough sleepers in the Retiro park ever since. I've done my best to remain hidden while staying as clean and decent as possible. I haven't touched my accounts and I've had a wash every day in a fountain to spare my clothes. I haven't dared return to my apartment. I'm begging you to let me stay. I'll do anything. The only thing I can't offer you is sex because I suspect the events of the recent past have left me impotent.

That is how Mercuro Cano ends his tale. Dawn has come and a blue light is spreading across the sky. Air is coming into the room through the open window, and it feels dry, crisp, and cool the way it does in the interior in the morning. The cleaning machines that have begun washing the asphalt before the traffic gets going can be heard from the street below, and on the coffee table in front of them are the empty wine bottle and their equally empty glasses. Later on, when she looks back on the course of events in an attempt to determine the point at which she committed the act of subversion that set the ball rolling, it is this moment she will think of. Though she will also be aware that nothing had been disturbed as yet. She had not done anything she wouldn't do again. She had simply offered to help Miranda and Santiago and listened to Mercuro Cano all night long.

"Impotent?" she asks.

"Bound to be temporary," he says, making a dismissive gesture. "I had to say it all the same, just so you don't get your hopes up."

She shakes her head. She hasn't been getting any hopes up. That happens to be true. Having listened to his tale, she feels neither tenderness, compassion, or attraction, but just mild repugnance and some curiosity about what is actually going on in his head. He really does appear to be the victim of a joke of some kind. He doesn't seem to be entirely well either. She says this to him, and he replies it's a good thing that's the way she sees it because the last thing he wants is for anyone to feel pity for him. He is looking back at her as if waiting for her to pronounce judgment.

"Weren't you going to say something?" he finally asks.

"What might that be?" she responds.

He shrugs. "I thought what I told you would make you loathe me. The violence, the infidelity."

She shakes her head and says, "The way I see it, you are someone who has got some things wrong and who wants to do better. And you are in the fortunate position of sitting opposite someone who would also rather be different from the person she is today. Who is struggling to become that. So there are two of us.

It makes a kind of obvious sense for us to join up on this trip."

She smiles at him. That all sounds so easy when you say it. He gives her a weak smile back.

"I do think though that you're suffering from paranoia," she says.

"Paranoia?" he replies.

"You think people are pretending not to see you while actually watching you out of the corner of their eyes. It can suddenly strike you that people look different, that they seem grotesque, twisted. And then you believe you are being persecuted by a program that no one apart from you appears to have seen. I really do think you've got all the symptoms."

"Well, I'll be damned," he says. "A hopeless case, that's what it sounds like."

She looks at the clock. "I have to go soon," she says. "I've got my job to go to."

Mercuro Cano gets off the sofa and heads for his room. She stays where she is and looks at the paintings hanging on the walls. They tell her nothing. A little while later she gets up as well, makes herself ready in the bathroom, and then has a cup of coffee in the kitchen before heading for Miranda and Santiago's flat.

———

She is still a bit dizzy from the wine, but entering the apartment on the sixteenth floor feels just as good as it did the day before. Last night's conversations seem infinitely remote once she has slipped her handbag onto a clothes hanger and taken a look around. The airy apartment is spick-and-span, the door to the balcony is ajar, and there is a smell of freshly brewed coffee and dishwashing liquid. The sound of the television has been replaced by calm classical music from an old gramophone on one of the bookshelves. A freshly showered and neatly dressed Santiago is sitting on the sofa; he gives her a radiant and demented smile as she comes into the room. The incidents of yesterday afternoon appear to have been entirely forgotten, and there is no longer even a suggestion of the muscular monster about him. Sitting up straight and listening to the music, he is as neat as he is absent.

"Hello," she says and sits next to him.

"Have you come to read the paper to me again?" he asks.

"Yes, I have," she replies, surprised and delighted at how lucid he is. "Shall we get started?"

"Yes, please."

She opens the newspaper and asks him what she should read.

From the kitchen Miranda shouts that he'll want to listen to an article about the liberation of Catalonia, another about poisoned mussels at a restaurant in Galicia, and a column by Javier Marías in the arts pages.

While she is reading, she can't help stealing glances at Miranda, who has come out of the kitchen and is tidying and arranging things in the living room. She is wearing a thin pale blue dress and an array of bracelets that jangle when she moves. After a while Santiago falls asleep against the back of the sofa. He is snoring with his mouth open, and the angle seems to keep the saliva inside his mouth. She asks Miranda what she should do next and is given the task of ironing the pile of Santiago's shirts Miranda has put on one of the chairs. She is also given a spray of scented liquid Miranda wants her to dampen the shirts with before pressing them. While she is ironing, Miranda continues to arrange things in the living room, chatting good-naturedly the whole time. She notices she has put on the powder-puff slippers that were in the bedroom the day before. Miranda tells her the holiday to Salou has been arranged. She is already looking forward to it. She goes on to tell her about when Santiago and she were young and had just met. What a catch he was at the time, and how many women were after him.

"And then he chose me," says Miranda. "Of all the women he could have picked, I was the one he chose."

"Most members of the male sex would probably have done the same," she responds.

"Oh," Miranda responds coquettishly, "now you're flattering me."

She goes on to tell her about their daughters and the grandchildren and then returns to the subject of Salou and the summer. The sea at Salou, the dawns at Salou, the evening walk along the edge of the water and the dinners at restaurants along the promenade. About Santi's annual custom of going down to the beach in the morning, leaving his bathing slippers at a certain spot, and then running along the shore-line. Meanwhile she would be drinking her coffee on the hotel balcony and could watch him vanish into a point on the horizon, only to pop up again thirty minutes later and wave at her before he hurled himself into the waves.

She can feel admiration for Miranda growing inside her. Where do you find the strength? she wants to ask, but doesn't feel she knows her well enough to put the question. She makes do with listening. She realizes these stories are the family legend—an enhanced version of the past that can always be invoked to bring everyone rallying round and to account for the present and the loyalty they owe one another. By listening she is lending Miranda the strength she needs to keep going. That's how she sees it. She is trying to find something inauthentic about Miranda's manner, something to prove that her goodness is a facade and that there are *flaws*. But she cannot find any cracks. Miranda is the genuine article. She continues to iron the pile of shirts. Miranda keeps talking while Santiago is asleep on the sofa. In the kitchen lunch has been in the oven for a while now, and the aroma is spreading through the apartment.

Her days pass like that. It becomes a routine, a positive routine, maybe the best one she has ever had. She can feel something inside her slowly thawing. It is the closeness to other people; no long, lonely hours spent on columns that never really seem to touch her readers, and then there is the appreciation she gets from Miranda when she helps her. Mercuro appears to have been given a boost by confiding in her, and he has begun what he refers to as a self-cleansing, which is basically about him not only saying he is going to get a grip and put his life in order but actually doing it.

"Enough is enough," he says. "It's now or never."

He seems to be feeling a lot better and no longer talks about Mr. Huei or Lucia. She gets a sense he may even be considering the possibility that the whole thing was a joke after all, and, if it wasn't a joke, that he has actually escaped his pursuers. Although she is curious about the show and about Lucia, she is reluctant to ask him anything more. Let sleeping dogs lie. The "self-cleansing" process also brings with it several advantages as far as she is concerned, because she wakes up nowadays to the smell of coffee and when she enters the kitchen she is met with the breakfast he has prepared and the coffee in the pot on the stove. After breakfast she makes the journey to Miranda and Santiago and stays there until the late afternoon. By the time she gets home, Mercuro will have worked out what they are having for dinner. Sometimes they eat together; sometimes he will dine alone in his room while she eats in front of the television. It is getting hotter and hotter, and she buys fans he positions at various points around the apartment. He makes lemonade with mint, which is kept in the fridge and topped up whenever she drinks it. There is a cheerful feeling about the apartment. It occurs to her that everything gets easier when she makes no attempt to write. Her shoulder no longer aches and she no longer has to come up with topics for her columns. Somewhere deep inside her she knows she has never been a good columnist. The travel grant is a charade, perhaps even a means for the newspaper to get rid of her for a while. She would make a huge effort every time a piece was due, but always felt uncomfortable when she saw what she had written in print. As if she had done her best for king and country, but all she had achieved was a ridiculous little squeak. No one ever commented on them, and she was convinced they never said anything because they didn't want to hurt her feelings. In any case, she thinks, when you are writing you have to create the situations and the links between them yourself, but when you are living you get them for free. She says this to Mercuro, which is when he says that writing is the kind of occupation that consumes you. You pay for it with your soul, and one fine day your soul has been used up.

One night she dreams she is peeing on Miranda Reyes's sofa. She is leaning comfortably back against the sofa in the apartment on the sixteenth floor in one of the outer suburbs of Madrid. Everything is perfect apart from the fact that she needs to go to the toilet but does not have the energy to get up. In the dream she gives in and can feel the liquid pleasantly warming the inside of her thighs. In the dream she is smiling to herself. But then the liquid gets absorbed by the cushions, and it all goes cold. So there she is on a sofa she has peed on just as Miranda is telling her from the kitchen door that the food is ready, and she should join Santiago and her. She gets to her feet and looks Miranda in the eye. Miranda appears just as appalled as she had feared. She looks from her to the sofa and then back to her again. "What have you done?" she says. The shame that reddens her face blazes so fiercely that she wakes up. She is still feeling embarrassed when she tells Mercuro about it over coffee. But then he puts his hand on top of hers on the table and says that there is nothing to be ashamed about. The peeing in the dream wasn't about bodily fluids or dirt, but about *territory*.

"This is a lovely thing," he says. "You're simply becoming like Miranda. She possesses a femininity that is becoming part of you."

She looks at herself differently afterward. She even thinks she has begun to walk differently—more slowly and a little more ladylike, just like Miranda

Reyes. She has been watching her from the balcony when she goes off to do some shopping for lunch. Miranda Reyes never seems to be in a hurry and yet she gets everything done in time. She also thinks she is beginning to speak differently, quickly and yet softly, with short bursts of rippling laughter inserted here and there. On reflection she realizes she has acquired an entire collection of Miranda accessories without thinking about it. Long white linen blouses and necklaces made of natural materials. Eye shadow in a warm shade of apricot that does not suit her own colder coloring at all, but which she bought without a second thought.

Much later she will fantasize about how it would all have turned out if things had continued in the same vein. If she had completed her transformation, and Mercuro Cano his. Though it would have been utterly bizarre if anything in this life were ever that easy. That easy and that clean. Djuna Barnes writes that there is no pure sorrow, because it is bedfellow to the flesh, to the gall and the guts and the innards as a whole. You always have to take the many layers of the carnal into account. Ben Okri writes that the route destiny has planned for us is always different from the fate we imagined, and though our dreams may be fulfilled, this occurs in ways we couldn't have expected.

She knows that Miranda is devout because she goes to mass every afternoon and takes Santiago with her in his wheelchair. Other members of the congregation help her get the chair up the stairs to the church because there is no ramp. Miranda also has a cross above her bed with a tormented Jesus on it and she has inserted a dried olive branch behind his back. She may just be devout in an everyday Spanish way, based more on custom and social affiliation than on actually making up your own mind that a supreme being exists. In any case Miranda shows no sign of wanting to talk about it whenever she tries to steer the conversation toward the church in Spain and convent culture. Mercuro's story has made her curious about Lucia, and she's doing some nosing around. And it could just be that pent-up need to talk about the nun that makes it all fall apart.

Everything is the same as usual to begin with. Santiago is dozing on the sofa, and Miranda says they need to help him into the bedroom so he can lie down more comfortably.

"I'll do it, Miranda," she says.

She moves over to the sofa, gets hold of Santiago's arm, and wraps it around her neck. Then she pulls him up with all the strength she can muster. He is a lot heavier than he looks, but she has learned how to compensate for his weight. She grips him around the waist and starts slowly guiding him forward. Only now he has just been woken up, he gets confused and struggles against her while yelling for Miranda.

"Miranda!" he shouts. "Miranda, help me!"

"No, I won't," Miranda calls from the kitchen. "It'll be fine, you'll see. I'm here, my darling. I'll wake you when it's time for lunch."

"I want you to do it!" he yells again.

"This time we're going to do what I say," Miranda replies.

She pushes the bedroom door open behind them with one foot and continues to steer him toward the bed. Their progress is very slow and she can hear from his breathing that he is upset. She draws back the cover on the perfectly made bed and lowers him carefully onto it. But then he grabs her by the hair, yanks on it, and screams at her, "I don't like you! I want Miranda!"

The rage takes hold of her so abruptly she has no time to think. She grasps his chin hard, raising his face toward her and stares into his eyes.

"So this is how it's going to be, is it?" she says.

She squeezes so hard his mouth opens and his tongue is forced out. His face looks so distorted and grotesque she feels scared. She suddenly remembers this is a person with dementia and releases him immediately.

"Lie down, and I'll pull the cover over you," she says.

"You hurt me," he says.

"Just lie down," she repeats.

"I hate you and I'm going to kill you," he says.

She sits down on the edge of the bed and squeezes his hands, so hard she can see the pain in his eyes.

Then she says in a soft voice: "So here's the thing. I know someone who takes care of people like you. An evil monster, a tiny female one, who rips the hearts out of people who do not behave. So watch it. If you keep behaving like this, I may have to introduce you to her."

While she is saying this, she can feel all her good intentions collapsing around her—like a rain of glass splinters. What am I doing? she thinks. Santiago is watching her calmly though, and asks without any anger in his voice: "Do you think she could help me...?"

"Help you with what?" she says and lets go of his hands.

"The female monster...If she could..."

He falls silent and looks over at the door. They are being observed. She turns around and sees Miranda standing there, looking shell-shocked.

"What are you doing?" she says softly.

"Let me explain," she says.

"I've been watching and listening. Have you gone mad?"

"Sorry," she says.

"Do you realize how much I had to trust you to leave him in your hands? Have you got any idea?"

Miranda comes over to her. She is wearing the shoes with the puffs on, the kindly shoes with the puffs, though that is deceptive, because there's nothing kindly about Miranda now. She raises her index finger and her eyes are shining with rage.

"Sorry, Miranda," she says again.

Miranda lowers her index finger and looks at Santiago, who is sitting on the bed with a smile plastered across his face. She leans over him and wipes away the drool, straightens the sheet, and caresses his head.

"Is everything okay?" Miranda asks.

"Yes," he says. "I'm fine."

"Sorry, Santiago," she says. "Sorry, Miranda."

"Never mind," he says.

"I did tell you it was the illness," Miranda says.

"I'm so ashamed. Please forgive me. It won't happen again."

"No, it won't, because you're leaving." Her voice is trembling with fury.

"What...," she says, and shakes her head. "No, no, no. I want to help you."

"Get out," Miranda hisses.

"I got impatient," she says. "You must be able to forgive me for that."

"Out," she says, pointing toward the door. "You're leaving now, even if I have to go and fetch the cleaver from the kitchen."

She cannot hold back tears. "You don't understand," she says. "I need this."

"*You* need this? Why?"

"I don't know, I just do. I feel better when I'm here. There's a meaning to things and I don't want to be without that meaning."

Miranda clears her throat and her voice shakes with the effort of controlling herself as she says: "I'm the one to decide who'll be here. And like I said, I no longer trust you at all. Get out."

She looks at Santiago on the bed.

"She wants me to go," she says to him in the hope he will oppose Miranda and say he needs her, she helps him, and he wants her to stay.

But he says nothing just smiles his demented smile and waves at her.

"Goodbye," he says. "See you again maybe."

She is still crying on the metro. People are staring but she doesn't care. When she gets back to the apartment, even though Mercuro does his very best to console her, she feels she might just as well go home now. What did she imagine she was going to accomplish? Someone told her there is a saying in some language or other that if you are born square, you won't die round. She might just as well forget the whole thing, and go on being the person she always has been until she eventually dies, and that will be that.

Mercuro lets her finish her story and cry herself out while plying her with alcohol. In some strange way her breaking down seems to have given him another boost, and he says maybe they should go somewhere, to one of the islands, one of the Balearics? It has been getting hotter and by noon the temperature in the apartment is unbearable. The idea of the sea is irresistible, and she is picturing it the way someone in the desert glimpses an oasis in the distance. Mercuro keeps on about the idea. There's no point being in Madrid in the summer. It is almost forty degrees Celsius outside, and if they were older or weaker they could die. The situation is harmful to humans; it's dangerous.

"Let's just go," he says. "Let's just leave this hellhole behind us, come on."

"But you're so scared of going out. How are you going to cope with going on *holiday*?"

"All we've got to do is get to the airport, and then we'll have left Lucia and Huei behind us along with this city and its infernal heat. We can manage that. Imagine being gone, let's just get away from this place!"

She shrugs. "Fine by me."

A few hours later he comes out of his room to tell her he has booked the flights. They leave the next morning.

———

Leaving Madrid and arriving on the island feels wonderful. She can see it from the plane as they come in for a landing, and though it looks small and bleak, it is surrounded by dark blue water. There are azure patches she thinks are swimming pools, but which the pilot tells them are salt marshes. She can see beaches, bays, islands, large rocks, and sailboats. She has been drinking steadily for the hour the journey lasts, and so has Mercuro. He is fast asleep with his head on her shoulder. A man traveling on his own is in the seat closest to the aisle. He ordered two small bottles of spirits that he has been cheerfully swigging. When the man becomes aware she is watching him, he turns toward her and introduces himself.

"Hello," he says in English. "My name is Johnny. I'm from Sweden. What's your name?"

Brusquely she tells him her name and says she's from Sweden as well. She prefers not to meet other Swedes on her travels. This man is overweight, besides, and has a regional accent. He looks like he comes from some little village in the country. She decides to keep her distance.

She pretends to read the paper but keeps glancing furtively at Johnny out of the corner of her eye. She is wondering what it would be like to make love to a man like him. He seems like the sort of man you could fantasize about, even though you haven't got the faintest idea how you would deal with him in real life. Like a large green piece of furniture you buy because you liked it in the shop but which looks out of place in the living room when you get it home. When it comes to comparing men to pieces of furniture, she has only had a single solid one her entire life. Martin, her ex-husband from Bjuv, was like one of those spindle-back chairs from IKEA. There were no refinements, and you couldn't expect romantic indulgences like the luxurious dinners or underwear some of her friends were sometimes given by their husbands. On the other hand you were never in any doubt about what you had. Every evening when you came back from work, the wooden chair was there to receive you, and you could just let go and stop pretending because that was something the chair would never do. Her divorced friends, in contrast, are endlessly preoccupied with coordinating their lovely designer furniture, while competing with a horde of gorgeous twenty-five-year-olds at the same time. She would never have the energy for that. *Better safe than sorry,* they say in English, and there's no denying there's something to that.

She glances at Johnny again. If he was up for it, would she be as well? The idea is absurd. But a lot of ideas are absurd, and that doesn't stop you thinking them.

A little while later they are taking the transfer bus to the hotel. Johnny is sitting a few seats away. His face is already red from the sun, and he has a ridiculous-looking cap on his head. She doesn't tell Mercuro she has spoken to him and looks away the moment he glances in their direction, because she doesn't want them saddled with some nutcase on this trip. There don't appear to be any mufflers on the island's mopeds. The architecture is gaudy and ugly. The houses have aluminum windows, and the inhabitants' underwear has been hung out to dry on lines that have been strung up in makeshift fashion, with skin-colored panties and bras with large compressed cups fluttering in the wind. There are patches of grease and oil on the sidewalks.

Though the hotel apartment lacks charm, it is practical and comes with a balcony that overlooks the swimming pool. Mercuro and she each have a room of their own. This is the first time she has been on holiday with a man she is not in a relationship with, or who is not Martin. Although she tries to act naturally, she is aware the new place is making Mercuro tense. He tells her he saw a man at the airport who could easily have been Mr. Huei. She says he has to let go of Mr. Huei. He has to let go of Miss Pink and Lucia. The whole *Carnality* circus. He has blown it all out of proportion. He nods and says that's bound to be the case. And though he may have blown it up to a quite extraordinary degree, he just can't let it go. He asks if he can borrow her tablet to see if he can access *Carnality* from it. She tells him under no circumstances whatsoever. They haven't come all the way here to get stuck rehashing old battles. If he logs on to *Carnality*, then she will ring Miranda. And if she rings Miranda and can hear that Miranda is still angry with her and still despises her while she can also hear the sounds of the apartment in the background, which will make her remember the smell of Miranda's fabric conditioner and the purple bougainvillea on the balcony, then she will break down. So she won't be doing that; she's going to resist temptation. And in that case it's not asking too much for him to have to do the same.

Just as she has said this she catches sight of Johnny walking past beneath the balcony. He sees her, stops, and then starts to wave and shout. She pretends not to notice, but Mercuro has seen him and tells her there's someone down there calling to you; he looks like someone from your country, maybe you should find out what he wants?

Johnny asks in English if he can come up. He doesn't know anyone here, and it's not like you go on holiday to be on your own. Mercuro looks a question at her. She shakes her head but Johnny persists.

"Come on up," Mercuro shouts back in English with a strong Spanish accent. "Come up and have a glass of wine with us."

Johnny arrives and they get a couple of bottles out of the minibar. The whole thing feels stiff. She and Mercuro move rather awkwardly around an apartment which is not their own, opening cupboards on the hunt for knives and chopping boards, because Johnny has brought a melon with him. What are they going to talk about? They raise their glasses in a toast. The wine is sweet and sticks slightly to the corners of your mouth while laying down a film over your teeth, but it tastes good anyway and she keeps drinking it. They're on holiday after all, and the more she drinks the more remote it makes Miranda and Santiago seem. They introduce themselves, and Mercuro tells him he is on sick leave for mental health problems. Johnny does not ask what kind of psychological issues; he just keeps looking at her instead. She says she works on a local newspaper. Johnny nods.

"So what do you do?" Mercuro asks.

He tells them he is due to start training in a few weeks to be a chaos pilot.

"A chaos pilot?" she asks.

"The people who get called in following an accident to find out what went wrong in the sort of setup where everything should have gone right."

He provides a few examples of lifeboats after shipwrecks failing to right themselves and remaining upside down, even though the people in the water had struggled to turn them over.

"Some people have got it," he says. "They know exactly what to do in a catastrophe situation. They're the ones who can immediately take command, get to the heart of the matter and say you go here and you go there; they get it sorted, keep a cool head, and make sure things get done the best possible way."

She gives a little laugh and says, "So are you someone like that?"

"I don't know. Not the kind of thing you can know before you've been in a catastrophe situation for real. That's when your *real* self comes to the fore."

She nods slowly and lets the muscat wine go to her head while she looks out over the tops of the pine trees. The air is hot and carries the smell of resin. Mercuro goes into the kitchen to look for something in one of the drawers.

"Though there are other kinds of catastrophe as well," Johnny says. "The catastrophes we carry inside us."

"I see," she says. "So what kind of catastrophe have you got inside you then?"

Johnny shrugs. "None, except I sometimes lose self-control. And do things I regret later."

"Like what?"

"It's come on as I've got older. When I was young I was completely different. Everyone respected me. I could beat *anyone* up. Anyone at all. Get it? It was like I had this power inside me. Only now . . ."

He gestures at his body. She wonders how old he is. Forty? Forty-two? You just wait, she wants to say.

"It's like there's a sense of disappointment inside me," he says. "At myself. You feel you're not up to it. You can't get it together. The loser shows through. And then the dam just bursts . . ."

"Nothing fucks you harder than time," she says. "Ser Davos. *Game of Thrones.*"

He nods.

"Ser Davos," he says, "comes out with some fucking brilliant lines. *Nothing fucks you harder than time.* That's it exactly. Fuck's sake, 'nuff said..."

"Right," she says. "The thing is, though, it can get so much worse. Mercuro, for instance..."

Mercuro comes back onto the balcony and she stops herself.

"What?" Johnny asks.

"Nothing," she says and looks down at the floor.

"Here's the thing," Johnny says, leaning forward toward her. "Catastrophes are like latent illnesses that get activated by a particular signal. They can be hidden inside you and then it's like they've been switched on all of a sudden. Like a spot on your face, a tumor in your stomach. The kind of thing that drags you down all at once. Like a black hole in your mind."

"I see," she says.

"And that's what you've got. You can feel it a mile off. Something's going to happen. You need to be on the lookout."

What does he mean? She doesn't want to ask. There are splashing sounds from the pool below. A Spanish couple are walking past beneath the balcony, talking loudly and laughing. She leans over the edge and looks down. They are holding hands; they look happy. She gets a lump in her throat when she thinks that must have been exactly what Miranda and Santiago looked like when they were young. She wants to say something about them. That there are people who get it right. A few, the chosen few, sort of.

"The wind is picking up," she says.

"No, it's not," Johnny replies. "The sea's calm."

You can hear it in the distance, the sea, and the sound of the waves is merging with the piano music from the hotel bar. Crickets can be heard from the hill just a bit behind them.

Eventually Johnny goes home. She remains on the balcony with Mercuro. He has put the television on inside, and a woman's voice is talking. They stay like that. Night falls soon afterward and they go to bed.

She wakes in the night and cannot go back to sleep. Her head feels heavy from the alcohol, and her stomach is slightly upset. The hotel is completely silent around them, as if they were deep inside an enormous foam mattress. She knows she's not supposed to start thinking when she wakes up at night. Once

you let the flow of thoughts into your head there's
no stopping it, and hours can go by while you keep
battling away on the unstoppable treadmill of that
unending stream. She can't remember when anything felt meaningful before Miranda and Santiago.
The last time anything felt meaningful before them
might have been at the outset of her marriage to
Martin, or when she was young and studying Spanish in Madrid. It felt like the world was completely
different then. As though it were made of different
matter, spun from another dream. As though *she* was
someone else, the people around her entirely different and even history was not the same. Is this what
getting old is about? it suddenly occurs to her to
wonder. Coming to terms with decay and accepting
the pointlessness of it all? That notion fills her with
a peculiar calm, and she finally falls asleep at dawn.

It is Mercuro who wakes her. Today, he tells her,
he is feeling good. He has slept well and not thought
about Penelope, Soledad, or *Carnality*. She gives
him a tired but encouraging nod. He does look different. As though the sea air has already done him
good, even though they've yet to leave the hotel. He

says he just wants to take things easy today. No museums, churches, or local artisans, the kind of things you might want to see as a tourist.

"No, I don't want to," she says, "not the least bit."

She puts on a bikini and her dressing gown and they go and eat breakfast by the pool. She orders a coffee and a croissant. She thinks the waiter glanced very briefly at her belly when she ordered the croissant. She allows the fat to bulge even more in defiance. You just keep staring, she thinks at him. Then she looks at the Spanish women. Slender, elegant, wearing expensive bikinis and jewelry. They talk in high voices to their husbands, and their husbands respond contentedly, although in monosyllables. You can see from the men's faces that they are happy with their wives, proud of them, satisfied with them as well. They exude a relaxed masculinity, the kind of masculinity men give off who have happy wives, a lot of sex, and nothing to ruin their day. She is feeling embarrassed about herself. She is embarrassed she has not managed to become better than she is. It's impossible to look at those women without thinking of Miranda. Their laughter reverberates around the poolside. She, on the other hand, is invisible to everyone, even to Mercuro, who spends most of the time just staring straight ahead. She sits there in silence and eats her croissant, slightly anxious that Mercuro will suddenly say something about her body, because that is what Spanish men have a propensity for doing when you least expect it.

The hours pass. They have lunch and then dinner. Afterward they go to bed. In the night she is woken by Mercuro screaming in his room. She puts on her dressing gown and goes in to him.

"What's the matter?" she asks, giving him a shake.

"I was dreaming about Lucia," he says.

"Dreaming what?" she asks.

He tells her that in the dream he was walking down the stairs of a darkened house, knowing there was someone standing at the bottom and it was almost certainly her. In the dream he was aware that he was dreaming. Which is why he said: "You can't kill someone in a dream. You might die in the dream but not in real life." Then he heard her voice from the darkness: "Do you know how many people suffer heart attacks in their sleep and die? It often happens because of something that frightened them in a dream."

He says he will never be able to sleep again. She lies down behind him and hugs him from behind. He gets hold of her hand and strokes it.

"It'll all be okay," she whispers and moves in even closer. "It's all going to be fine, perfectly fine."

The next morning they are woken by someone knocking on the door. It's Johnny. He has shaved and put on a white short-sleeved shirt. He appears to have shaved his skull as well and put cream on it, because it is shinier than last time.

"Are you up yet?" he asks. "I thought we could go on a trip."

He sounds as though they've been friends for ages and turning up and knocking on their door was perfectly natural. She doesn't like him now; she can see his shirt is too short and the fat bulges out beneath it. He's wearing tube socks and sandals. You can do that in Sweden, but not in Spain. Dressed like that, you'll be an object of ridicule here. She watches Mercuro look Johnny up and down; his eyes stop at the tube socks. It is then she feels an ache in her groin and remembers the previous night. She turns toward Mercuro and smiles. She wants to say: *You're not impotent at all,* but she can't with Johnny standing there. Instead she says that they've made plans of their own and they don't want to go anywhere, just stay here at the hotel.

"There's nothing to see here," Johnny persists. "We'll go somewhere else instead. I've rented a car."

"What kind of car did you rent?" Mercuro asks.

"A Lexus."

"Wow," Mercuro says. "In that case let's go and find a little cove."

"Exactly what I was thinking," Johnny says. "I was thinking just that. I've packed a picnic and some other stuff. We'll have a great time."

Mercuro turns to her and brushes a strand of her hair off her face.

"What do you think, *mi vida*?"

She is so pleased to be addressed that way, she immediately responds that she'd like to go for a drive and see something of the island.

They pack their bathing things, make their way downstairs, and then drive off in the car. Mercuro and Johnny sit in the front. She is on the rear seat with the picnic basket; she put what was left over from yesterday's supper into it as well: melon, ham, muscat wine, and bread. In Spain they drink and drive, so a glass of wine on the coast ought not to be a problem. So there it is: the basket, sitting rather obtrusively beside her. All packed and ready to go, sort of. The fat on her thighs shakes as they drive over gravel roads. She should have worn long trousers. Thin linen trousers. She gazes out at the countryside. It is scorched and brown. There are cattle on the hills. She looks at Mercuro from behind, thinking of last night. She can see the sheen on Johnny's skull. Johnny accelerates, and Mercuro looks out the window. The cattle are standing still on the scorched hills.

They arrive at a little bay, park the car, and get out; they're sporting large round patches of sweat on their backs despite the air-conditioning in the Lexus. They walk down to the beach, which is full of people. Young people are lying behind large rocks, snogging. They find a spot and unroll the beach mats Johnny bought along. She takes off her clothes and is not pleased to feel Johnny's eyes on her body. I was someone completely different once as well, she would like to say. The bikini is an old one in a brownish shade. She should have bought a new one before she went on a trip with two men. The blue stretch marks on her legs come from valves in the veins leaking, the doctor says. The blood can work its way down but not up. Getting a tan could improve things, the doctor also said, it helps conceal the color. She looks around the beach. Despite all the pretty women there, Mercuro really does seem to have eyes only for her.

"A drop of wine?" Johnny asks, opening the basket.

He gets out the bottle, fills the glasses, and hands them over. She is thirsty, and the wine feels rough on her throat in a good way.

"A bit more, please," she says, and holds out her glass.

Mercuro raises his glass in a toast to her.

"Do you want to do some snorkeling?" Johnny asks.

She shakes her head. Her body is not going to be walking across this beach.

"What about you, Mercury?" he says, waving the goggles.

"Why not?"

Mercuro and Johnny get up and walk toward the water. She watches them glide back and forth, their snorkels sticking out of the water like drinking straws. They hang on to the side of a rock for a while and raise their goggles to talk. They disappear after that, pop up again, talk some more, and then go back under the water. She stays where she is, looking out at the sea, filling herself with light. An African man in an orange sarong comes walking along the beach. He is carrying women's clothes, thin beach dresses, and scarves in one hand and a tray of jewelry, sunglasses, and postcards in the other. He stops in front of her.

"Madame?" he says.

She shakes her head. "No," she responds in English. "Nothing."

"Are you okay?" he asks.

"What do you mean?" she asks in Spanish.

In the same language he replies that she looks sad.

"No," she says.

She isn't sad. Just happy. This is what she looks like when she's happy.

"Just keep calm, madame," he says in English.

"What do you mean?"

"Just keep calm, madame," he says again. "Just keep calm and don't worry."

He walks on and the orange sarong flaps behind him in the breeze. She is waiting for him to turn around, when she will yell, *Just keep calm about what?* But he doesn't. He keeps going, finally vanishing behind a large rock.

It isn't long before she sees them reappear— Mercuro and Johnny—moving toward her out of the water. Mercuro is holding something that hangs down from his hand like the hair of a gorgon. People are staring at him and pointing. He looks happy. When he is only a little way off, he lifts it up and calls out to her: "I caught it with my bare hands."

He swings the octopus back and forth in front of her. She has never seen him smile like that. The Medusa's hair keeps wobbling. Chilly, pink flesh.

"Can you eat it?" she asks when they get to her.

"A delicacy," Johnny says.

"So eat it then," she says lifting her chin at him.

"What?"

"You're the one in the know. Eat it. Have a taste. If it's such a delicacy."

It's the wine bringing out the devil in her, as well as the fact that she ought to be on her own here with Mercuro and not with someone like Johnny. They're a couple now. After the night, the incredible night they just spent together, they are a couple. Johnny looks away from her and at Mercuro. Then back at her again. She gets to her feet, unconcerned about her body, standing in front of him with her arms crossed across her chest and her chin raised.

"Eat it," she says.

"Is that an order?" Johnny asks.

"Yes," she says.

"And what's going to happen if I don't?"

"Nothing. I'll just lose all respect for you though."

She laughs, and Mercuro laughs with her. Johnny's face has turned grim. He takes the octopus from Mercuro. He holds it up in the air. And then slowly lowers it toward his face, opening his mouth and allowing one of its tentacles to drop inside. He closes his mouth around it and before he bites down he turns his head a little to look at her. Then he raises the octopus again and she can see that the arm has been shortened. Johnny is chewing.

"Bravo," she says and claps. "Bravo."

He does it again. Once, twice, until he has chewed off an entire arm. She feels slightly sick.

"You can stop now," she says.

"So now it's my turn to give the orders," Johnny says and chucks the maimed octopus onto the sand.

"How do you mean?"

"You gave me an order. And now it's my turn."

"But that was just for fun."

"This'll be just for fun as well."

She looks at the dead octopus. The suckers are glistening in the sunlight. Mercuro gives her a thumbs-up. Is he drunk as well?

"Okay," she says. "What do you want me to do?"

"Walk naked across the beach."

"Never ever."

"Do it."

"I've got a complex."

"About what?"

"Everything."

There, now she has said it. And now they can lay down their weapons because the power struggle is over. She has grown old and ugly and she suffers from a complex. She's lost whatever points she had as a woman. He's the winner. He's still a man, after all.

"You can have one more glass of wine," Johnny says. "Then you're going to take off your bikini and walk up and down. Slowly, you've got to walk slowly. No jogging."

"I really don't want to."

"Oh come on. You're never going to see any of these people again. What have you got to lose? Put yourself out there. People who take themselves too seriously are so stuck-up."

Stuck-up. What a word. A word typically used by self-important people. She gulps down what is left in the glass, gets to her feet, and takes off her bikini. She even hurls it away from her.

"You don't have to do this," she hears Mercuro say in Spanish.

She starts walking. She passes them slowly, the bodies. One by one. She can see their faces turning toward her out of the corner of her eye. The silence. The offended, shocked silence. Stomachs, hair, limbs. Burnt skin and lips sticky from ice cream. There's not much beach left now. So I'll just have to turn around then. Go back the same way. Here I am, this is my body. The wreck. Not that it matters, because of the kind of rush that comes over you. Once you've kept walking for a bit, you really don't feel as ugly as you thought you would. You may not feel attractive but not that ugly either.

When she gets back to them she lies on her towel without bothering to put her bikini on. Bare-assed, as if it were the most natural thing in the world.

"You never thought I'd do that," she mumbles to Mercuro in Spanish.

"No," Mercuro says. "I didn't."

Is he looking at her thighs? It doesn't matter if he is. She parts her legs a little. Look, for all I care. The wine and the sea are pounding in her ears. Soon afterward she falls asleep.

She is woken by a man's voice she does not recognize. Mercuro is asleep on the towel beside her. The sun has gone behind a cloud, and the beach has begun to empty. A man who must be a police officer is speaking in Spanish to Johnny while pointing at her.

"*No comprendo*," Johnny says with a grin. "*No comprendo, no comprendo. No hablo español.*"

The policeman says he wants to see their passports.

"*Una cerveza por favor,*" Johnny says to the officer, with a grin still plastered across his face.

She gets to her feet, about to sort out the situation in Spanish. Then she realizes she is naked. She wraps herself quickly in the towel and then slips on her beach dress.

"Problem?" she says in Spanish to the policeman.

"Not naked here," he says in English. "Now have to follow me."

Indecent exposure. You're being arrested for indecent exposure. Who'd have thought? Talk about being a prude.

"Hang on, hang on," she says to the officer, "I've done nothing."

"Now you come with me," he says, pointing officiously.

She wakes Mercuro up and, while he starts talking with the policeman, pulls on her panties. In her bag she finds a cap she puts on her head.

Mercuro tells them they have to accompany the officer to the station. They can explain everything calmly once they're there and after that they're bound to be allowed to go back to the hotel. They pack everything up. They follow the policeman to the parking lot. People are staring at them; they can hear laughter and murmuring. She just wants to go back to the hotel and lie on the sofa and look at the tops of the pine trees moving in the breeze. Take a painkiller, go down to the pool, and after a while have a gin and tonic and fall asleep in the cool of the evening, and then wake up and have sex with Mercuro in the hotel bed. And not have to go to some police station with a clown like Johnny at any event. The policeman tells them to follow his car. They drive back out onto the scorched roads. Johnny is humming at the wheel. She is in the rear seat once again with the picnic basket. They follow the police car along the dusty road. The cattle have gone, and the hills look as though they are waiting for rain to fall. You can hear the crickets. She looks at her mobile to see if there is a text from Miranda, but the screen is empty. Her flesh is wobbling against the seat, and she is sweating again. She looks at Mercuro from behind. Everything is spinning. Everything feels odd. She is far from home.

But when they drive out onto the island's main road, Johnny executes a sudden twist of the wheel and, instead of following the police car, they turn onto a small road on the left.

"Let's give that bastard the slip," he yells, and he presses the accelerator to the floor.

"Are you out of your mind?" Mercuro shouts.

Johnny laughs out loud.

"Fucking fascist bastard," he yells. "If you'd just put a bullet in the brains of people like that, you could have avoided that whole Franco farce in this country."

"What the fuck do you know about it?" Mercuro yells. "What do you know about anything, you fat anemic idiot? My grandmother's entire family were executed in their living room by *Republicans*. *Republicans*, do you get that, you bastard? You think this was your war and you can come here and play the hero, but you haven't got a clue. Piss off back to your igloos and shut the fuck up."

For a moment Johnny appears to be at a loss after Mercuro's outburst. The car slows down and he takes one hand off the wheel to run it over his bald head. She gets the sense he is going to say something but then he spits out of the open window and accelerates again. She looks back but can see nothing because of all the dust that has risen in a cloud behind them.

Johnny has evidently managed to shake off the police because they find their way to a small bay with some motorboats hauled up on the shore. Johnny leaps out of the car, grabs one of the boats, and yells at them to join him.

"Quick," he shouts, "Hurry up, this one's got the key in, can you believe it? Come on, hurry up, we can make it."

He pulls her in, and she sits in the middle of the boat. Mercuro appears to have been exhausted by his outburst and allows himself to be steered passively toward the prow. Once they're on board, Johnny runs around and undoes the rope and casts off. It all happens so quickly she has no time to think about any of it, nor does Mercuro. They just sit there, being taken for a ride, and it is only when they have got some way out to sea that it dawns on them they should not have followed Johnny's orders. They keep checking the shoreline but fail to see any policemen. Mercuro tries to get Johnny to turn around but to no avail. They keep going for half an hour, an hour, ninety minutes. She falls asleep for a bit. When she wakes up, Mercuro has her in his arms.

"I think he's mad," he whispers. "I've been watching him for a while now. He's off his rocker."

Half-submerged rocks and skerries begin to appear a little while later. She peers down into the black water. How deep can it be? There are trenches in the Mediterranean two to three thousand meters deep. They suddenly open beneath ships like jaws, like hungry gullets. She twists her rings instinctively. She looks back at Johnny, who is sitting beside the engine.

"Wonderful, isn't it?" he shouts. "The wind, the sea, freedom, Spain! *España!*"

The boat rocks wildly. She grabs the railing and holds on for dear life. The prow is crashing into the waves now. A gull shrieks above their heads, and it feels like a storm is rising.

"Johnny," she says. "Please. Turn back."

"We're almost there."

"Where?"

"Here."

He lifts up a nautical chart which is tied by a small chain to the side of the boat and points to something that might be a small island or a skerry, little dots in a circle on the chart.

"What are we supposed to do there?"

"You'll see."

They get to the spot a little later. It looks as though they have arrived at a large enclosed pool in the middle of the sea, an entirely natural one at that. Steep white cliffs form a circle around a lagoon. Rough white walls that are sheer and stark. It is completely silent inside, as though the sound of the sea were being kept out. It feels like the wind has been cut off by the rock formation, and there are no seabirds shrieking any more. The water beneath them is pitch black. Johnny has turned off the engine and he lets the boat glide until it comes to a stop on its own.

"What a place," Johnny whispers.

The pool or lagoon—she isn't sure what it should be called—must be several hundred meters across. Above them the sky is changing color. It is not dark yet, but shading toward red.

"We should have got here a bit earlier," she says to Johnny with feigned cheerfulness. "We'll have to go back now because it will be night soon. But you're right, what a place…Maybe we could come back tomorrow?"

"We've got time for a swim," Johnny says.

"You want us to go swimming *now*?" she says. "*Here?*"

"It's a kind of marine trench," Johnny says. "On the chart it says it's fifteen hundred meters deep. We'll just have a quick dip. Then we can go back."

She looks down at the still, black surface. She is imagining the depths below. She can feel Mercuro's hand wrapping itself around her own.

"Fancy a swim, Mercuro?" Johnny asks.

"Not on your life," he says. "No way."

"Oh come on, Miss Mercury," Johnny says. "It's one thing if the old girl won't jump in, but you ought to be up to it. Bullfighter! Latin Lover! *Olé!* Come on then."

She's not going to put up with any more of his nonsense, so she pulls the beach dress over her head and dives into the pitch-black water. She does it without thinking because she knows some things have to be done that way. Quickly, recklessly, without reflection, purely on impulse. The ice-cold water closes around her body. She swims up to the surface and treads water while raising her eyes to Johnny and Mercuro in the boat.

"Help me up," she says gasping. "Help me. I had no idea it would be so cold."

Mercuro leans over and reaches a hand out to her, but then Johnny shoves him from behind so he tips over the gunwale. Mercuro is seized with panic the moment he hits the water and starts grabbing for the boat and yelling that Johnny has to help him back in, he's going to die if he doesn't get back in the boat, and there could be anything at all down there, and he's really got to help him get back in. Confronted with Mercuro's panic, she forgets her own fear. She swims over to him, puts a hand on his shoulder, and tells him to calm down. There's nothing underneath them; they're going to get back in the boat and he should go first.

"Help him, Johnny," she says in Swedish, while treading the ice-cold water.

But Johnny shakes his head.

"For fuck's sake, help him, Johnny."

But he just stands there, his arms crossed, and shakes his head. Her mind is racing as it occurs to her that you're supposed to talk to peasants the same way they do, so she yells: "I thought you were more of a man than that!" She should have stopped there, but rage has got the better of her and she goes on: "I really thought you had more balls. Only now I realize I got that wrong, you're all show, a weak and pathetic *chickenshit.*"

"Did you just call me *chickenshit?* Did you just tell me I haven't got the balls? You stupid cow...how are you going to get into the boat now then, eh?'"

She is doing her best to keep Mercuro afloat because he has begun to breathe oddly. She begs Johnny: "Please. Please help him. Help me."

"No way," Johnny says. "Hang on...I saw something down there, right there beneath you. Oh fuck, there's something huge swimming around down there."

A strange gurgling noise is coming from Mercuro's throat. She tells him there isn't anything in the water, and it's just Johnny winding him up. Johnny bends over the engine again and she swims toward the stern and grabs it both to stop him and to heave herself on board. Only something must have been loose because the motor falls off the boat, Johnny grabs at it, but it is heavy and vanishes abruptly into the depths.

"You bitch," Johnny yells and picks up an oar lying in the bottom of the boat. "You fat fucking dummy."

He strikes her hard on the arm with the oar and, as she falls back into the water, he turns and hits Mercuro's hands while he is trying to clamber into the boat. Mercuro screams with the pain, and that scream fills her with a kind of supernatural power. She manages to heave herself back on board. The boat lurches with her weight, and Johnny loses his balance and falls. There's another oar in the bottom and she grabs it, lifts it high, and just as Johnny is trying to get to his feet she aims at his skull and strikes with all her might. Johnny remains on his knees for a second or two, looking her in the eye while a trickle of blood runs across his bald pate and down to his ear and throat. Then he drops lifelessly into the bottom of the boat. She lets go of the oar, grabs hold of Mercuro's hands, and tries to pull him up and in, but fails.

"Come on," she yells, "move it."

Mercuro, however, is completely panic-stricken. He is coughing up the freezing water and she leaps back in to help him stay afloat. She is holding his head up, and he is either groaning or hyperventilating, she hasn't a clue which, but it sounds like he is dying. She swims on her back while keeping his head above water and drags him toward the circling cliffs. She tries not to think about anything coming at them from below, because she realizes she is close to panicking as well. She gets to the cliff wall. There is a small ledge she can reach and she manages to haul Mercuro onto it; he lies there apparently lifeless for a few seconds before opening his eyes. They stay there for a while, then sit up and look over at the boat, which is fifty, maybe a hundred meters away on the black water. Though the lagoon forms one enormous resonator and you can hear even the tiniest motion, the silence is total.

"He's dead," Mercuro says finally.

"He'll just have passed out," she says.

They climb up from the ledge. They are both shaking and they slip and slide and get cuts on their feet. She scrapes her hands and breaks her nails. There is another ledge at the top and when they lift their heads over it, the wind and the sound of the sea hit them. She looks down at the water and feels dizzy. She feels like being sick but gasps for breath, pulls herself into a sitting position, and tries to remain calm. The rock is still warm from the sun. She lies down against it. They remain lying there on the warm rock until the sun has almost entirely set. Then they get up to go and explore. On the other side of the rock face the sea is pounding furiously against the cliff wall. The foam that is being whipped up hits them in the face even though they are standing at least five meters above the surface. They turn around and look down at the black water in the lagoon. From this height they can see Johnny's body lying in the boat.

"Shit," says Mercuro.

"We ought to get over to the boat," she says. "I can swim over and paddle it back here."

"I'm not getting into that boat again."

"We can't stay here."

"I'm not going back out to sea in that boat. I'm not doing that again. Let's wait here. I'm going to wait here in any case."

"I'm thirsty," she whispers.

"Me too."

"Do you think it might rain?"

"Maybe. We'll have to find some way to collect water if it does."

She looks at the horizon. There is only a little slice of orange left now. In a few minutes it will be completely dark.

"We'd best find somewhere to sleep before the light has gone completely," Mercuro says.

They climb down to the ledge overlooking the pool. She lies down facing the rock wall and Mercuro positions himself behind her and hugs her to him. She has the warm rock on one side of her and him on the other. The boat with Johnny's body is floating somewhere out there on the black water. She tries to relax, to feel only the heat from Mercuro and the cliff face. In a few hours it will be light again, and they can work out what to do. The last thing she hears before slipping into sleep is Mercuro's voice asking if she can see the stars.

Lucia

Madrid, August

Dear Bennedith,

This morning I was woken by the wind. I tend
to see that as a harbinger of autumn—but this
was a hot wind, a wind that is said to bring sand
with it all the way from the Sahara and leaves a
thin layer of red dust on the white garden furniture of the convent. As I begin this letter, which
I suspect will be a long one, I am sitting in front
of the open window in my room looking at the
gardener wiping down the chairs and tables
while the wind is ruffling his hair and whipping
up sand from the paths between the fountains.
For some strange reason the knowledge that the
atmosphere is in motion always has a calming
effect on me. This might be because I feel as

though I am a child of nature. Is that something we share, perhaps?

And, yes, this is me, Lucia, writing to you. I realize that my letter will be a surprise. Both because it comes from me and because it isn't every day that you get mail in prison. In light of the harsh words you said to me during your brief visit to the convent, many people would find it hard to imagine I would want to have anything further to do with you. But I understand how outraged you were. Having spoken to the police in Mahón, I now realize that you underwent a troubling and violent experience at sea, together with Mercuro Cano, whom we both know. A Scandinavian, who had the proportions of a giant and all the refinement of a caveman according to the police, is alleged to have tried to kill you on a boat but died instead of a fractured skull. It seems you were stranded on a large rock out to sea for several days. The police told me you had lived on rainwater from hollows in the surface of the rock and shellfish from its steep walls, and after several days the sun and the lack of water had almost driven you mad. The police also told me that they found you and Mercuro Cano unconscious and curled up together like two small children, as though you had become resigned and were waiting for death. The image of two people wrapped around each other on a rocky island affected me. I also felt concerned that you have developed so much fondness for a man like Mercuro Cano. It makes me think that what they say is true and love is blind. If I have understood correctly, you have given yourself to this man body and soul. You have shouldered his burdens and shared his bed. They say that when people fall in love, they fall in love with a scent. That is not entirely true. When someone falls in love, they fall in love with the combination of scents they would produce together with that other person. They are searching for a complete fusion with another element. Stone, which is shaped by time, but also eroded by the motion of the sea. Could that be what is haunting you as well—this primeval human longing for the ocean, for stone and rock?

And now you are being detained while the man you love is probably sleeping with another woman in his arms. You should know that Mercuro Cano's heart belongs solely to his wife,

Soledad Ocampo. Despite his many flings, his heart is hers and hers alone.

So I can understand that what happened with the Scandinavian at sea, the thirst and the sun, combined with Mercuro Cano's disappearance as soon as you arrived back in Madrid and, to top it all off, the questioning you had to undergo on your own, must have thrown you off balance. I presume you simply needed to get rid of your sense of frustration. But to arrive at my convent only a day or so after you had returned from the island, force your way into my room during the siesta, rushing in like an enraged female bear, and then assert that I had stolen your beloved from you, that I had ruined his life from the moment he appeared on *Carnality*... was something of an overreaction, don't you think? You may not know this, because you are not from here, but I am not just anybody. And you are just a tourist, a tourist who finds herself in the women's prison Alcalá Meco II besides, because the police want to make sure you do not leave the country. In Spain, you are, with all due respect, no one, and I could, of course, allow you to rot where you are. Many people have moldered away in there before you, including South American women who smuggled narcotics in order to feed their children, and I really cannot see why you should be privileged to enjoy a different fate. What the police suspect could very well be true as well, and that Scandinavian did not actually stumble, but you, or Mercuro Cano, killed him. From what I could gather from the report, the difficulty they have in tying either of you to the crime is that no weapon has been discovered. There was, however, only one oar in the boat when you were found. What happened to the other oar, as a boat normally has two? In the view of the police in Mahón it could have floated away from the rock formation and out to sea, rendering a continued search pointless. They are reluctant besides to devote major resources to cases that do not involve the local population. If foreigners on holiday choose to kill each other, the police may look the other way, unless the embassies get involved. If you killed the man with the oar, and the oar has floated away, then you have been quite extraordinarily lucky. And that is the kind of luck I put a high value on because it only occurs if our Lord wills it. It has crossed my mind that He may be protecting you. If He is, then He will, of course, be doing so for a reason.

I have taken the liberty of making some further inquiries about you. I hope you will forgive my curiosity, but when I find a person who interests me no effort seems too much. I have discovered that you helped a woman take care of a man suffering from Alzheimer's during your time in Madrid. You went to the couple's flat every morning and assisted the woman in looking after her husband and you did this without demanding any form of payment. I can see that—despite the visit you paid me—you are struggling to be a good and generous person. When I come across that kind of goodness it makes me happy because it shines like a beacon in the long night of our age, when egoism, vanity, and the carnal have been allowed to run wild. The way you have looked after Mercuro Cano testifies to this as well, even if in a more naive way.

So now perhaps you can better understand my interest in you. Is it possible to evoke a

corresponding interest on your part in me?
During your visit you screamed several times:
Who are you, who are you, who are you really?
And you did so in such a way and so emphati-
cally, it made me feel you needed this knowledge
about my past in order to bring about a change
inside yourself. Could that be the case? I know
it could, inasmuch as not all the changes that
occur in people can be self-sown, as it were.
Besides, you have only heard Mercuro Cano's
version, and his loathing for me makes him
blind. If I were to tell you something about
myself perhaps you will understand and, in that
case, this letter might not just be a letter but also
the beginning of a long and rewarding friendship? I mean as long as anything in my life can
be at this point. There may be time enough for
me to enter the fog of dementia before you are
released. And to tell you the truth that would
not be a day too early. I have been longing for
those mists for ages. At ninety-three years of
age I am still completely lucid. I am sitting on a
beach in the sunlight; I remember everything; I
understand everything; I am part of it all. Like a
tired scrap of flesh that has been hoisted as a sail
to catch all the winds of the present and so drive

the ship of human suffering that is my body onward. At a certain point you begin to look out for those merciful fog banks, the mists of confusion. You prefer to see things through the haze and in weak sunlight. To perceive instead of to understand.

I urge you to forget your rancor against me and to read the following pages in peace and quiet. My aim, in addition to telling you the story of *Carnality*, will be to share with you something of myself.

During your brief visit to the convent you nevertheless found time to point out that I am as tiny as a dwarf, and that my maimed hand revolts you. I regret that I made such an appalling impression. My maimed hand is not an object of revulsion to me, however, but a blessing. Without it I would not be the person I am today. I do not intend to say that much about my childhood because I believe it was completely happy, and some people think that anyone who claims they had a happy childhood is invariably lying. The village I come from is hardly celebrated for its beauty, in any case, and there is no reason to go there unless you are a local. Some say it is inhabited by sodomites and illiterates, and while there may be something to that, I take the view that you should not be ashamed of your roots no matter where you come from. Dostoevsky writes somewhere that shame at oneself is the root of all evil in human beings, and I think he is right on that point.

What I remember most are the air, the light, and the countryside. The grass that was perfumed with all the smells of the soil, and the wind that used to caress its leaves when it blew across the interior of Extremadura in the spring. I also remember the forests to the north and the tall eucalyptus trees that were silent during the summers just as in Neruda's poem. When autumn came, the same trees would be completely still as though standing at attention in the face of their own decline. But if the countryside was paradisiacal, my body was a Pandora's box. All bodies are, in fact, Pandora's boxes. What you glimpse inside when the lid is opened are

disease, desire, and sordidness of every kind.
Looking in the mirror one day, I suddenly saw
that I had changed and that though the change
was a blessing, it was also in some way the beginning of a decline...

My father died when I was very young and
my mother was a butcher, like her father and
grandfather before her, so if it did not sound as
odd as it does, you could say I have meat and
flesh in my blood. Though the war was being
waged during my teenage years, it was as if it
never quite reached our village and we were able
to live in peace, as though in a small oasis or a
hidden valley. When I was a child, I was allowed
to play with all the animals apart from the pigs,
because pigs had bitten off the ears and noses of
little children. Pigs' tails were fine, though, and
I would be cutting them up while other children
played in playpens or with kitchen utensils
on the floor. It was the only part of the pig my
mother could spare for my games, apart from the
snout, but she wasn't prepared to give that to a
small child.

My mother loved tools. She would oil, sharpen, and polish them. She had a blacksmith's, or maybe even an alchemist's, eye for metals. One day I saw her chop the head off a hen.

"Did you see that, Lucia?" she asked while inspecting the bloody edge. "The ax is the true queen of all tools. So simple in design and yet so explosive when used."

She taught me to use Skinner, the skinning knife, and the short and broad castrating knife called the Cow's Tongue. The bollock dagger had sandpapered wooden balls above the blade, and then there was the Argentine Brother-in-Law, which was meant for hand-to-hand combat. My mother called the crown jewel of her knife collection the Loving Butcher's Daughter—and, yes, that was me.

Macaria, my mother.

I suppose it is easy to imagine all butchers as grim-looking, hard-hearted bruisers with an ax in one hand, the slaughterer's knife in the other, and dried blood spattered across their broad faces. But my mother was both small in stature and slim and wore trousers she had to cinch at the waist with a belt, while her arms looked like matchsticks you were afraid would snap when she lugged around the heavy carcasses in the slaughter room. She also had hands that were beautifully cared for. The loveliest hands in the village; hands that any pianist might envy. Long fingers, soft palms, and trimmed nails without any black rims. She caught the eye of all the men, and in an attempt to avoid this, wore baggy clothes and would often leave a bloodstain or two untouched on her burlap shirt—anything, as she put it, to discourage them. Her attempts to divert their attention had the opposite effect, however, and some would even come to an abrupt halt, their eyes locked on her, as though they had caught a certain scent, or had suddenly spied an old wreck of a motor from which they could nevertheless hear the self-confident thrum of a sports car's spinning engine. Then she would move away or say something offensive.

"You should be grateful for my attention," a man once said to her. "You'll get old one fine day and no one will so much as glance in your direction."

My mother said to me afterward that that was what it was all about.

"Never let the flesh dictate your terms, Lucia," she said. "In many people the power of the flesh is greater than that of the soul and for many people life is about the carnal rather than the spirit. You need to be on your guard, Lucia, against carnality."

If only she had realized how I would heed her words.

On a lovely day at the beginning of April when the cherry trees were in blossom in Extremadura, and perhaps in all of Spain, an officer strolled into our butcher's shop. He asked for the best Iberico sausages my mother produced, to be grilled by his platoon in their trenches twenty or thirty kilometers north of our village while they were defending their positions against Republicans and anarchists. Although his smile was a bit too broad, his eyes too beady, and his boots too shiny, my mother appeared not to notice. While she was wrapping the sausages in paper, she chatted to him about the war and she did so as if the war were an afternoon tea, at which you might have opinions about the sandwiches or the other guests, but which also allowed you to bring together people who might otherwise never have met. Alfonso Hidalgo quickly adopted the same tone and said that while the war had its disadvantages in his view—that went without saying as war is ultimately war after all—it also offered modest but unquestionable advantages. A war meant devastation, but what was devastation if not also an opportunity to start again? Silence descended on the butcher's shop, and my mother stood there holding the wrapped sausages while looking at Alfonso Hidalgo with a faint gleam in her eyes. When he had left I asked my mother whether she remembered what she had said about never allowing pleasure and vanity to dictate the terms of your life. About the carnal and the spiritual. She looked at me as though she had never heard those words before. They got married as soon as the war was over. At the wedding Alfonso's chest was adorned with several rows of medals awarded for his valor. He moved into our house, took my father's place at the table and in their bed, and so became part of our lives.

Everyone will use certain words more than others, and if you listen to someone long enough

you can work out what those words are and
gain a more profound understanding of the
person in question in the process. I am familiar
with this by now because of the endless hours I
have spent listening to people who come to the
convent for a chance to speak with someone.
The word Alfonso used most was "modernize."
Wherever he turned those chilly, close-set eyes
he would find things he could modernize. The
handling of the animals could be modernized,
the slaughter could be modernized, and the
sale of meat could be modernized as well. In
all likelihood my mother could also be modernized, and I am convinced Alfonso Hidalgo
would have done anything to see her dressed up
and wearing makeup, adorned with earrings and
a pearl necklace, at one of the events that took
place in Madrid and to which former generals
were invited to mingle with the powers that be.
My mother refused, however. She did not want
to travel to the city and absolutely refused to
attend any events with generals who had been
put out to grass, and Alfonso Hidalgo possessed
enough of a survival instinct not to press the
matter. But when it came to making the slaughter more efficient, there was no one to restrain

him. More animals could be kept on a smaller acreage, while allowing them to graze freely was costly and impractical and led to slower growth than if the animals were housed indoors and ate a special kind of fodder. With a big, beaming smile on his face, he remodeled our abattoir and rearranged the routines that guided the slaughter. We no longer slaughtered only our own cows and pigs; animals would be driven to us from the whole of the surrounding area as well. The trucks that arrived once a week stopped behind the abattoir, and the animals were led en masse down the ramp. The engines of those vehicles and the desperate cries of the beasts could be heard right across the square, and all the windows along the street would be closed. Alfonso Hidalgo did not believe you should stop the entire process just because some bone or other got broken or a tail was crushed. The whole point was to funnel the animals forward as efficiently as possible so the soundproof doors could be slammed swiftly shut behind them. Once this was done, the vehicles drove out of the village and quiet descended once more. Alfonso would then start to clean the street and the ramp with a hosepipe while whistling, which served to drown the echoes of the animals' cries. The shop doors onto the street were reopened after that, and the village could start to breathe again as usual.

During the postwar years, Franco's men carried out a number of purges in our village with Alfonso's help. According to him the people involved were refusing to show their true colors and could be intent on harming Spain. Alfonso and his friends would sometimes drive around in a platform truck, picking up people and then taking them out of the village; the people who had been picked up never came home. No one dared call Alfonso to account because he was well known for having fought bravely during the war and for being on good terms with the authorities in Madrid. No one wanted to get into trouble with people like that, and the dead were dead in any case; there was no bringing them back. Occasionally Alfonso would also "take care of" people Franco's men were looking for, and in that case they would be imprisoned in the slaughter room in the basement of the butcher's shop together with the animals while waiting to be collected. I used to try to avoid looking at them. Although Alfonso did not normally involve me or my mother in the handling of these individuals, there was one occasion on which he departed from the routine, and this would have consequences none of us could have envisaged at the time.

That day he had entrusted me with keeping watch. One of them, a woman, had bitten Alfonso Hidalgo on the hand. He had taken them in some food, and the woman had come flying out of the darkness of the pen, according to him, and grabbed hold of his hand and sank her teeth into it. War can make people lose their heads, and apparently the woman in question had children she had been separated from and was no longer able to keep her despair in check. I could hear Alfonso's scream from where I stood in the cold store and was immediately transfixed by the sense that nothing good could come of that scream.

"Lucia," he yelled, "Lucia!"

I ran out into the basement to see him holding his bleeding hand.

"What happened?" I asked.

"The whore bit me," he yelled.

He really was bleeding from a bite on the side of his hand. That didn't stop him from going inside the pen and grabbing the woman by the hair and dragging her across the filthy floor. I could see she had ugly infected wounds on her legs and bruises and dirt all over her face. She screamed from the pain and was spitting so much that saliva was dripping down her chin.

"Alfonso," I called and hurried after him. "Alfonso, wait."

But Alfonso refused to listen and shut the woman inside the cutting room. Then he came back out to find me, virtually paralyzed, next to the pen containing the other prisoners.

"You'll have to watch the scum while I deal with her," he said.

"But they're already locked up," I said.

"*You just keep an eye on the scum*," he said again and shoved over a bale of straw for me to sit on in front of the pen.

I sat on it. Alfonso fetched a pitchfork and handed it to me.

"You have to show them you've got some backbone."

I took the pitchfork from him, but it was so heavy it fell out of my hands and onto the floor.

I sat there trying not to look inside the pen, but it felt like my eyes were being drawn there by an invisible force. Finally I looked into the darkness. There were seven prisoners sitting inside. They did not say anything, but what I noticed straight-away were their eyes. They were all fixed intently on me and they were glowing with a luminous flame. It was then I felt the *hatred*. It came at me through the air like a freezing draft, as if there were only a single person inside, one gigantic soul, throbbing with a great and icy loathing. And as I was being enveloped in that hate-filled and sepulchral silence, the scream sounded. It was a long one, drawn out and panicked. A woman's scream at its most awful, a woman's scream to make the very earth contract in spasms. I jerked to my feet by reflex but then quickly sat back down again and tried to feign calm even though a cold sweat was running down my spine. The scream went on, and the prisoners in the pen began to move anxiously around in the straw, talking to one another in their fear. One of them looked like he was about to have a panic attack and was groaning and gasping for breath. I ran over to the door to the cutting room and leaned my ear against it, but it had gone quiet. When I turned around I could see that all the prisoners in the pen had got to their feet and were leaning against the bars in a tight group, their eyes on me. I turned back to the door and pounded on it hard.

"Alfonso," I yelled. "Alfonso, what's going on? Open up."

The door opened then, and Alfonso and the woman came out. Her face was now black and blue all over and streaked with tears. A blood-stained piece of cloth was knotted around her hand. Alfonso opened the pen and flung her inside.

"Come, Lucia," he said, and he walked over to the door.

But I was unable to move from the spot and kept looking at the woman and the other captives. She said, "He took a finger."

It looked like she was opening the cloth to let them see because they all screamed and one of them seemed to turn around and vomit into the darkness. I had to run to catch up with Alfonso.

"What did you do," I yelled, "what did you do, you can't just chop someone's finger off!"

He did not reply.

"What did you do, you bastard?" I said and aimed a blow at one of his kidneys.

He turned toward me then and I was looking up at his broad blood-spattered face. He grabbed me tightly around the throat with one hand and squeezed.

"My duty," he said. "I did my duty, as a man, a soldier, and a citizen of this country."

"Your hand smells of blood," I managed to get out.

He let me go and then aimed a blow at my head that landed with such force I was hurled into the cement wall. Once I was on the floor he put his foot between my shoulder blades and pressed me down against the asphalt.

"Talk back to me again, and it'll be your finger next time."

He took his foot away and started to walk down the street. But then he turned and raised his index finger toward me: "Not a word to Macaria about this!"

A few days later Franco's men arrived to pick up the prisoners. Alfonso Hidalgo was lauded once again for his efforts. In the end the police

felt so confident of him, they said that under his
leadership the villagers could take matters into
their own hands and handle any troublemakers
as they saw fit, because it was both a long and a
costly trip to drive all the way from Madrid and
with Alfonso in charge matters would be handled just as if they were actually on the scene.
Some weeks later he got a financial reward for
his zeal and courage. He was also invited to
send a box of charcuterie to Doña Carmen,
Franco's wife, who thanked him personally in a
letter written on pink paper that, when opened,
gave off the scent of an exclusive lady's perfume.

Over time Alfonso's hatred me of me would
become more intense. He said he could not
understand what my mother could possibly
mean when she said I had the makings of a good
butcher, because I lacked all the qualities a good
butcher ought to have, as he saw it. I lacked
courage. I was squeamish and compassionate, to
a ridiculous degree.

"That's because she's a girl," my mother
said.

"That's no excuse," Alfonso replied. "I have come across women as tough as granite who had hearts of steel. There's you for instance, Macaria. No one ever coddled you, and you grew up to be a thick-skinned and formidable female. Come over here and sit in my lap so I can have a squeeze."

According to Alfonso, the human race could be divided into shellfish and finfish. Good people were shellfish who protected their innards with a hard surface. In keeping with the shellfish principle, a person with any value to them had to become thick-skinned. This was all about the pearl inside, or a sense of self-worth, if you prefer. It followed that only people who were completely worthless could be kind to their very core.

"Lucia," he said, "is the perfect finfish. As soft on the outside as on the inside and just as unprotected from the natural challenges and constructive reverses that life entails."

But his lectures failed to help. It might have been the memory of the woman and her chopped-off finger as well as all the other things that went on in the abattoir that made me start to cry inconsolably every time a slaughter was due. My mother and Alfonso did their utmost to get me to control my feelings, mainly by forcing me to help with all the practical arrangements during the hours I was not in school. I obeyed them, but the tears flowed while I did what I could to be useful. Alfonso gave me a hiding on more than one occasion out of pure rage. My mother could also get really upset over what she called my "squeamishness" and smack me with her plastic glove-covered hands, which sometimes left a bright red bloodstain or a scrap of meat on my cheek. From time to time they also tried to harden me, in line with the motto *What doesn't kill you makes you stronger,* by forcing me to carry out the cruelest of tasks. These included the castration of young boars and the slaughter of the piglets. My mother and Alfonso must have thought that turning my hands into granite was simply a matter of how many metal implements I proved able to stick into the soft parts of pigs, or how many animal body parts I could cut off and, at Alfonso's orders, throw to the sows, which devoured them greedily. Several years later, when I arrived at the convent and talked about these experiences, the *madre superiora* said to me: "That explains why you are so short, Lucia. Some people cannot deal with all the challenges that confront them and may then stop growing, out of sheer terror."

My mother and Alfonso had no plans to produce any children of their own. Motherhood had been torture, my mother said, and I think she said that to please Alfonso. We had been happy for a few years while my father was alive. The three of us against the world—there had been something inviolable about us. Alfonso had no time for children in any case. He thought we were like animals who did their business where and whenever they fancied and always seemed to do their utmost to cause trouble.

Then one day Alfonso Hidalgo died. Those malicious voices that insist I had something to do with his death are, of course, barking up the wrong tree. I hated him, it is true, but how could I—a fifteen-year-old girl—have killed a fifty-year-old man who had come through all the horrors of war, and not just with his life intact but with rows of glittering medals on his muscular chest as well?

Alfonso Hidalgo was bitten to death by a sow. I apologize for putting it like that because one should always honor the memory of the dead and not make fun of them without good reason, nor pigs either if you ask me. But I have come to realize that it simply cannot be put any other way. Alfonso Hidalgo died because a sow bit him to death, and that was not the least bit ridiculous because if, like me, you had been standing there watching the sow that did the biting, you would understand there was nothing even vaguely humorous about the situation. Some people claimed, it should be said, that I was neglectful because I allowed the sow, once her piglets had been taken from her, to remain in the same enclosure as Alfonso. But ever since I was little, I have learned to handle animals in my own very different way, and those particular safety procedures had not become engrained in me. We never had anything to do with piglets while my father was alive because he thought that was the height of cruelty. So the sow was still in the pen and beside herself with fury. She charged Alfonso the way only a creature that knows the battle has already been lost can mount an attack. Alfonso was entirely

unprepared because, despite the precautions,
he insisted on clinging to the mistaken idea that
rage had been bred out of domestic pigs. When
he took the piglets from the sow, he did so in his
usual way and stabbed them to death one after
the other while humming cheerily to himself.
The sow moved away and took up a position
at the other end of the pen, pressing herself
against its wall the way some animals do when
feeling grief. I was aware she was there but must
have turned to look at something else, because
I completely failed to notice she was about to
charge. When she hurled herself at Alfonso, she
had gathered so much momentum that he lost
his balance and fell over. In a matter of seconds
she was grinding away at his face and throat
with her teeth. I have seen pig's jaws at work
ever since I could just about walk and they can
make short work of flesh very quickly, let me tell
you. Although I was frozen to the spot at first, I
was not much help when I did regain my senses
because I had no idea what to do. I rushed to get
my knives because I knew the sow would have to
be killed come what may, and if Alfonso Hidalgo
survived, he would subject her to all the tor-
ments of hell before she died. I had seen him do

this with other animals, and in all likelihood he would force me to watch, out of some perverse desire to harden me further. I took the Loving Butcher's Daughter out of the knife bag, flung myself over the animal, and thrust the blade with all my might into her flesh just below her throat. The sow froze, took a few tottering steps, and then fell over. Alfonso Hidalgo lay beneath her, and I could barely make out any part of his face, which was a mass of blood and torn skin. The ambulance arrived twenty minutes later, but it was too late. Alfonso died somewhere on the motorway to Badajoz. Although my mother was devastated, all that need be said in my view is that a sigh of relief was heaved throughout the abattoir. And throughout the universe and the heavens too, for that matter.

Bennedith, I would never forgive myself if I am boring you. Could you drop me a line to let me know if you are interested in meeting me? In that case I could visit you in prison. If not, we might perhaps continue our correspondence? Writing is so delightful. A weight is lifted off your heart, and you are able to see yourself from outside. If you want to remain in touch with me, I promise I will get to the point before long and tell you about Mercuro Cano. I will also speak to the convent's lawyer to see about speeding up your case.

Yours sincerely,
Lucia

Madrid, August

Dear Bennedith,

Thank you for your reply. It made me so
happy! Happy you actually replied, first and
foremost, and happy you are getting used to
being in prison—insofar as it is possible to get
used to a prison, I mean. It was distressing,
however, to hear that the warden is making
advances. I assume that learning to handle
that type of uninvited appreciation is one of
the many ordeals women face in real life? Let
me know if you need help because then I could
visit the prison and meet him in person. I
might be able to talk some sense into him.

——— ———

I have problems of my own as well, of course; we all have our crosses to bear, as they say. I am very old, and something inside me is burning out and fading away, to the point of disappearing entirely. I sit in my rooms in front of my windows and drink my vermouth. Now and then Miss Pink and Mister Blue from *Carnality* turn up to discuss a forthcoming episode with me, and then I am enveloped in the joys of youth. They are so easygoing; they smell so nice; they are so lovely and full of life. I feel so well when they are here. Do you have any children? Someone you would do anything for no matter what, someone who is your greatest source of pride while keeping your heart clenched in an iron fist.

Carnality is my child.

I told you about Alfonso Hidalgo; after his death, my mother made it clear she no longer had any interest in being a butcher. She used the inheritance to set up a small restaurant kitchen and furnish a space with tables and chairs in the premises the shop had previously occupied.

Downstairs—in the former abattoir—we would create something resembling a museum, in memory of my father, Alfonso Hidalgo, and all the animals that had lived there.

The scent of blood and machinery disappeared. I thought that the time had come to be properly happy at last. Our tormentor had gone; the filth had been cleaned out. The air in the country around us seemed a little crisper, the sunlight that bit brighter and the water in the streams even clearer. My mother looked happy running her restaurant and, as for me, I was happy as well now I had time to be outside and to go for walks in the fields.

But history is always spinning its threads in the present, and people have to answer for the actions they have committed. If they are no longer with us, then the survivors must do so. We are muleteers, as the saying goes, and in time our paths will cross.

I suppose it is a natural part of childhood that events in the heart of the home, under the warm evening lights and in the company of one of your parents, are imbued with a sense of reassuring normality. It is not until much later, years or decades later, when the events become detached from that setting, that they can suddenly seem strange, horrifying even. I mention this because the fact that we had a man imprisoned in our basement—however strange that may sound—never felt particularly odd. There are doors that shut, hasps that catch, after which there is no going back. The truth is that while my mother may have imprisoned Sergio Alameda, Sergio Alameda imprisoned us too in a sense. Everything we did from the moment he was locked up had to be done with Sergio Alameda in mind. Unlike other families we could not go away on holiday for a couple of weeks. We could only be away for two days at most, and over time, even being away for that short a period would make my mother feel uneasy. She didn't like to think of Sergio Alameda being alone in the basement without anyone to come down and see to him, without freshly prepared food or any of the sounds that made their way downstairs when my mother left the door to the restaurant open. I suppose she was also afraid she might come home and discover that Sergio Alameda had gone. It would be impossible to know in that case whether he had escaped—with the police arriving in a matter of hours and our lives ruined—or if Sergio Alameda was still somewhere in the house just waiting for the right moment to kill us both.

It all began one chilly evening toward the end of winter a few months after my stepfather's death. Rain was clattering against the windowpanes, and the square in our village was empty. It was then a car stopped outside the restaurant and a man came inside. He was elegant—elegant in the way people from the city are. The man who was entering our restaurant exuded the wider world; he was someone. My mother, who was watching him through the windowpane that looked out onto the square from the kitchen, decided he was an actor. Both his suit and the black broad-brimmed hat suggested as much. In one of her women's magazines she had read about a film that was currently being made in Madrid and the stars, who had been assembled from all over Spain, were making the city glitter. She thought she recalled reading in the same magazine that one of those actors had a mistress in Portugal. Perhaps that was who the man was. He was getting away from all the glamour and romance of the capital and driving through the desolate

wastes of Extremadura on his way to Porto or
Coimbra for the next bout of sensual pleasure.
During the trip he had become hungry and
turned off toward the first village he could find,
which happened to be ours. The other restaurants on the square had already closed, which is
why the actor had ended up at our place. That
was what my mother was thinking as she watched
him from the window, which naturally meant she
was unable to make out the intent etched across
the stranger's face or detect the zeal in his eyes, or
the mute excitement in his tall gangly figure.

"Good evening," my mother said as he
entered.

"Good evening," he replied.

My mother wiped her hands on the towel she
had hanging from her waist and said he could sit
at whichever table he liked. She also said he was
the only customer, so he should just come inside
and not stand in the half-open doorway, letting
in the freezing wind. The man nodded at my
mother and sat down.

"What can I get you?" she asked him once
he had looked at the menu.

"The dish you consider your best," he said.

"Very good," my mother replied.

She went into the kitchen and prepared her best dish (it is easy to create something extraordinary when you have meat of the highest quality). While the stranger ate, she kept an eye on him through the kitchen door and mentioned to me that something fishy might be going on. She decided that he did not eat like an actor, but more like a food critic whose job is to perceive the whole symphony of tastes in a meal. And it was true that the man chewed slowly and with the utmost concentration and even closed his eyes every now and then. Neither of us could have guessed that he was simply attempting to keep calm in preparation for what he was about to do and was probably not paying any attention to those flavors at all.

"I've heard there is a daughter in the family as well," he said when my mother went in to collect his plate.

"And where did you hear that?"

"Earlier this afternoon from the people in the village."

"I see."

"Is it possible to see her?" the man said. "I heard she's extraordinarily short in stature. They say she is almost a dwarf."

"A dwarf she may be," my mother said, "but she's not a performing monkey."

"I do apologize," the man said.

My mother must have accepted the apology because she came into the kitchen and told me to take over the service. She said I was to be extra attentive toward him because whoever he really was, he wasn't just anybody. It wasn't every day our village was visited by that kind of person, and it was vital she and I made the most of this potential boon. If we were to get a good review in one of the major food magazines, we might receive busloads of pensioners on a regular basis, and then our fortune would be made.

I went back and forth between the kitchen and the dining room.

"So you are the daughter of the family?" the man asked after a while.

"Yes," I said.

"And how old are you?"

"Sixteen."

"That would make you short for your age."

"I stopped growing before I was supposed to."

He nodded but failed to ask me anything more about that.

"Would you mind sitting with me for a bit?" he asked.

He pulled out the chair beside him. I hesitated at first but then sat down. We sat together for a short while before the unthinkable happened. I had been searching for something to say because he was not saying anything, and the silence was becoming increasingly oppressive. I could hear my mother in the kitchen, stacking the dishes and humming to herself. And then all of a sudden the man grabbed my hand, pressed it flat onto the table, pulled out a knife and in the space of an instant severed my thumb from the rest of my hand. It happened so fast, and the cut was entirely clean. My thumb lay there on the dark tabletop looking as though it had never been part of me. White, lifeless, and utterly alien. A pool of blood was spreading around it. I looked up at the man's face and thought I could see horror there, a horror I was incapable of feeling myself. I looked at the bloody knife in his hand and his quivering lower lip. I looked down at my hand again, and the only thing to occur to me was that he knew nothing about butchery because even though he had managed to achieve a clean cut, he had used entirely the wrong knife for the purpose. It felt as

though my ears were blocked, and I could only
see things, not hear them. The blood continued
pumping out, and I was struck by how red my
blood was, not at all like the dark brown men-
strual blood that had been making an appearance every month for the last year or two. It took
another few seconds before I managed to gather
my wits enough to let out a scream. But my lungs
finally filled with air, and I screamed out the pain
and the horror I was feeling; my mother came
rushing out of the kitchen in response. I held
out my hand toward her. She remained standing
where she was for a moment or two. Then she
performed a very fast movement with her hand as
if something had come flying toward her through
the air and she was warding it off instinctively,
and then she turned and flew into the kitchen,
grabbed a clean towel, and rushed back into the
dining room to press the towel around my hand
to stop the bleeding.

"What the hell have you done?" she yelled at
the man. "Who *are* you?"

"I am Sergio Alameda," the man announced
calmly.

The steadiness of that voice must have been
achieved with great effort because you couldn't

help noticing that not only was his lower lip trembling but so was the hand holding the knife. He appeared to be doing his best to cope with the situation all the same, and he exuded the kind of resolute peace of mind you imagine hit-men display as he began to wipe the knife blade clean with a napkin.

"And I really am sorry I have maimed your daughter," he said. "In my defense, I would add I did it so quickly, she shouldn't have suffered any psychological damage."

"Psychological damage!" my mother shouted. "*Psychological damage*, you've got a nerve!"

"However crazy it may sound, Mrs. Hidalgo, I simply had to do it." My mother stared at him. The stranger cleared his throat and went on: "This is my revenge against Alfonso Hidalgo, who kept my comrades and me prisoner during the war and who maimed my beloved sister Paloma in exactly the same way I have just maimed your daughter."

"Alfonso maimed your sister?" my mother yelled.

"He maimed my sister, and I have just maimed his daughter. So now we are even, you might say."

He was just about to move toward the door when my mother came out of her paralysis. She took a couple of steps across the floor while pulling out a kitchen knife from her apron. I was still clutching the cloth around my bleeding hand and was incapable of understanding anything of what was going on. However strange it may sound, I was not in any great pain. But I was aware I had lost a part of my body and that my mother, who had always appeared to be a fairly peaceful person, was holding a large knife against the belly of my assailant.

"Get back inside," she hissed.

Once again the stranger showed how little of a hardened criminal he was, because he had already put the knife back in the sheath that hung from his belt. He had also automatically raised his hands above his head at my mother's shrill command. He moved slowly back inside.

"Take his knife, Lucia," my mother said.

I moved over to him and with my unencumbered left hand pulled the knife off his belt and threw it into a corner.

"You just stand still and keep your arm raised," she told me. "And I'll deal with this bastard. Everything's going to be all right, Lucia. It's all going to be all right."

She wiped a sweaty strand of hair off her forehead with the back of her hand.

"We're going down those stairs over there," she said.

The man turned around and continued in the direction she indicated. I could see the light vibrating along the edge of the blade in time with my mother's trembling. She steered him slowly in front of her down the spiral staircase to the former abattoir in the basement and then into one of the pens. Once she had shoved him inside, she locked the door. We stood there like that. My mother and I on one side of the barred door and Sergio Alameda on the other. His stylishly combed hair was disheveled, and sweat rings were blooming across his white shirt.

"Who the hell did you say you were?" my mother asked, once she had pulled the bar across the door.

"Sergio Alameda," the stranger repeated, still in that same dignified voice. "I was held captive by your husband during the war. One day he chopped a finger off my sister Paloma's hand, as I just told you."

He appeared to be walking a tightrope between rigid self-control and unbridled panic. My mother kept staring at him in silence.

"Have you completely lost your mind?" she finally said.

"I am assuming you knew nothing about it? Your husband must have been very good at concealing his bestial nature."

"And just how did your warped little chicken brain see this all working out?" my mother asked.

"An eye for an eye, a tooth for a tooth," the stranger said. "I think that covers most of it."

"You're an idiot," my mother said. "You realize you'll be sent to prison, don't you?"

"I assumed so," Sergio Alameda said with a nod. "The thing is, though, I don't really see I've got anything to lose."

"As long as you remain alive and healthy, you've always got something to lose," my mother said.

Sergio Alameda shook his head. "Paloma died a month ago. The last thing she said to me on her deathbed was: 'Take revenge on the man who tortured me, make sure he has to pay dearly for what he did.' I'm ready to accept my punishment, Mrs. Hidalgo, because a promise to someone dying is not to be taken lightly. Besides, I've already found out what the punishment will be. One year in jail for bodily harm. That will be worth it."

His fingers closed around the bars and he nodded slowly, as if to convince himself of what he had just said. My mother was catching her breath.

"You need to listen carefully to me now. Alfonso Hidalgo is dead. And he was not the father of the child. Some people even think that the girl you just maimed *caused* his death. Although she denies it, there's no doubt she always hated him from the very depths of her soul. With all her heart, the way people hate in our family."

Even though the lighting down there was negligible, I could see Sergio Alameda turn pale inside his pen. He raised his hands toward his head in a gesture of desperation. "That can't be true," he whispered.

"You are a lousy criminal," my mother said.

The man groaned.

"The least anyone could expect is for you to find out who you were going to maim before you actually did it. You should have done your research! Haven't you ever seen a film?"

"I would like to return home," Alameda said.

"You'll be staying here tonight," my mother replied.

"Sorry," he yelled, "so sorry, sorry, sorry, Mrs. Hidalgo, please, I'm sorry. I realize I have made a terrible mistake and I really want to—"

My mother uttered another scream and kicked hard at the door to the pen.

"I'm going to stuff you in the meat grinder!" she yelled. "I'm going to grind you slowly to death, you bastard, and throw the mince to the pigs and your head to the dogs."

I had never seen her like this before, and I wonder if it was a side of her she had been concealing or that was unknown to her as well. Whatever the case, she showed no hesitation about anything she did that evening.

"Let's talk about this," Sergio begged. "We should talk about this, Mrs. Hidalgo. Calmly, like civilized people. Ring for an ambulance, maybe something can still be done."

"Sew it back on, you mean?" my mother said. "I will deal with the cut. And if you say 'civilized people' again I will fetch my former husband's rifle and shoot you on the spot."

She moved toward the stairs.

"Come, Lucia."

"Please, forgive me and let me out," Sergio Alameda yelled. "Call the police, but don't force me to stay here. I've already been locked up in this place."

But we had already gone up the stairs. Then my mother tripped the switch and the basement must have gone completely dark. Sergio Alameda seemed to be panicking down there in the pen, because he kicked at the walls like an animal while pleading and begging like a condemned man.

"That soundproofing will come in handy now," my mother said as the door closed, and his cries immediately vanished.

We went back to our apartment and treated my hand. We went to bed several hours later and were only woken up the next morning by the police knocking on our door.

The policemen who turned up that morning were the same officers who had known Alfonso

Hidalgo and attended his funeral. They respected my mother greatly and deferred to her,
apologizing for disturbing us while insisting that
as Hidalgo's widow, my mother was the most
reliable source they had in the entire village.

My mother made them coffee and listened.
The policemen told her about the disappearance
in confidence and provided details they empha-
sized were not public knowledge. A picture soon
emerged. Sergio Alameda was fifty-three and
drove a white Volkswagen. It had been parked on
the square, not far from my mother's restaurant,
around eight o'clock the previous evening. The
last time he had been seen was a few hours earlier
when he had had a coffee at a bar just outside the
village. He had told one of the waiters he was on
his way to Portugal. He had also asked detailed
questions about various people in the village, including Alfonso Hidalgo. No one had given him
any information of value as no one knew who he
was. Something must have happened to the man,
though, because the way his car had been parked
indicated that the driver only intended to be away
from it for a little while.

"So we were wondering if you had seen him,
Macaria," one of the policeman said. "You did

keep the restaurant open yesterday. Did he eat there? His wife has become quite hysterical and is desperate to find out what has happened to him."

Silence filled the room.

"If only that had been the case," my mother said, "but yesterday was one of those hopeless evenings when not a single customer turned up the entire time. Lucia and I just sat there waiting for someone to come along, but it stayed as empty as only the square can be on a winter's evening in our village. In the end we closed up and went home."

I made sure to keep my hand hidden under the table. The police asked what time that had been.

"Eleven," my mother replied with a shrug.

The officers thanked her and got to their feet. My mother said that since they were already in the village, it would be nice if they went over to the churchyard and visited Alfonso Hidalgo's grave. She stood at the front door with her arms crossed to shield herself from the cold wind. The policemen thanked her and said while they might not have time to go to the churchyard right now because it was vital to find the man in question, next time they came to see us they definitely would. My mother nodded and said they were welcome to come back to the restaurant for lunch later on, but they replied there wouldn't be time for that either.

"Next time, Mrs. Hidalgo, we'll have time for everything including remembering the old days."

When they had left, I said, "I can't believe how good you are at lying."

"Lying is easy, Lucia," she replied shortly. "You just have to make sure there is a grain of truth in everything you say."

"You're not turning evil, Mum, are you?" I asked.

"Evil?" she said.

Then she reached her hand across the table and grasped mine.

"You do realize, don't you, that it's those who are really kindhearted who become the bitterest people of all over time? The ones who fail to exact retribution and then feel betrayed."

Despite my mother's words that morning I am convinced she would have released Sergio Alameda the following day—or the one after that at least, if it had not been for what happened next.

My mother would have let Sergio Alameda go, in other words, if I had not received the revelation that would change my life. Writing about it is difficult, because the only thing you can say for certain about revelations is they cannot be explained. Not to someone, at least, who hasn't experienced something similar themselves, which I doubt you have.

The revelation made my mother go crazy, and all her concentrated rage was focused on a single point: Sergio Alameda down in the basement. Sergio Alameda became the target for years of repressed rage and frustration. Frustration and grief at everything time had taken from my mother, because just when you think you have built something, it is snatched away with all the cruelty inherent in the way life works and you have to start all over again. That had been the case with my father, and the same went for Alfonso Hidalgo. I had been the one constant thing, the only thing that was left, and when I received my revelation, my mother believed I had been snatched away as well.

As I write this my right hand is resting on one side of the piece of paper, and so I keep seeing

the stump where the thumb should be. Today
I am grateful for this stump. It has saved me
from so many battles. From the moment I
received my revelation, it felt as though what
had previously been my hand had become
another that was completely different in kind.
I was gazing at it the next morning and at the
bulky knot that covered it, and I could feel the
holiness.

It was that same morning, after the policemen
had left. I was walking along the paths beside
the pastures. The late winter sun was shining,
and the yellow flowers of the broom bushes
around me were glowing. In the distance I
could see animals moving tranquilly. A few
eagles were circling on thermals in the air
above, along with what might have been the
odd vulture. My maimed hand was covered in
a large white bandage, and I had been given
so many painkilling tablets I could feel no
pain at all but just this calm sensation of heat
running through the lower part of my arm and
a lovely feeling like cotton wool in my head. I

was humming. I could hear the church bells in the village some way off and I was considering walking toward the churchyard and my father's grave, but then it occurred to me that Alfonso Hidalgo was buried there as well, so I started walking in the opposite direction, toward the meadows and the little stream that flowed across them. Everything was so vibrant and so beautiful and so much a portent of what was to come. I sat on a rock and watched the clear water in the stream flowing past. I closed my eyes and turned my face toward the sun, listening to the ripples. So I was entirely unprepared when I actually heard the words. There they were, though, and spoken so clearly I leaped to my feet, convinced I was being spoken to from a distance and that some kind of acoustic phenomenon had carried the words to me. *You shall lead them through the apocalypse,* the voice said. I thought someone was pulling my leg. I sat back down on the rock and listened intently in the hope the voice would repeat what it had just said, but all I could hear was the water, and far off, the church bells and the motorway toward Madrid.

"What did you say?" I called. "Say it again, and who are you?"

But there was only silence, of course, because when God says something, He only says it once.

So that was my revelation. One sentence, a few words said just to me. Or was it? I rushed home to tell my mother and share the joy I felt with her. But when I entered the kitchen, sweaty from the walk across the fields and a happy smile plastered across my face, it felt as if the steam were already coming out of her ears.

"Say that again," she said icily from where she was standing in the kitchen with a towel hanging from her waist.

"God has spoken to me," I said.

"And what did He say?"

"That I am to lead someone through the apocalypse."

"What are you raving about, child?" my mother yelled. "Who's that supposed to be? And what apocalypse? Have you gone completely crazy?"

After a while, when I failed to respond, she grew resigned and said in a rasping voice: "I see it now. It's all been spoiled, even you."

The same evening, while sitting on a stool in front of the bars of Sergio Alameda's stall, my mother declared in an appallingly matter-of-fact way that the torment of yesterday had made something go wrong in my brain, so I now believed I had a vocation. I was convinced God had spoken to me and believed that I was capable of saving the human race. Sergio Alameda looked horrified, but my mother went calmly on. Without being aware of it, I had gone insane in an attempt to make sense of my maimed hand. I was most probably lost forever because the smile she had seen on my face when I told her about the revelation was the kind you only see on incurable fanatics. There was no coming back from that, and the healthy part of me was gone for good.

"Couldn't it be the painkillers having some kind of hallucinatory effect on her?" Alameda asked.

"You didn't just maim her hand," my mother
said, "you maimed her soul as well."

This, she went on to say, was not something she could forgive Sergio Alameda either.
No mother could forgive someone who had
murdered her children, because that would go
against nature. Revenge, my mother said, was
the only logical thing in this situation.

Sergio Alameda listened attentively, and
it should be said in his favor that he seemed
utterly and quite genuinely crushed. Unfortu-
nately he also wept, which was stupid because my mother never liked men who cried.
She thought that crying was one of the few
privileges reserved for womanhood and that
when men wept it felt as wrong as when snow
falls in the summer or when animals that are
supposed to sleep through the winter awaken
early from their hibernation. My mother
would have preferred Sergio Alameda to
clench his teeth, keep a lid on his feelings, and
ask how he could make things right, how he
could atone for his crime and compensate my
mother. But he didn't do any of that; instead
he just sat there in the darkness with tears running down his chin.

"You'll have to stay here," my mother finally said and got to her feet.

"For how long?"

"Until I know what to do with you."

It is not my intention to excuse what my mother did, but as time passed the situation became part of daily life while Sergio Alameda became both part of us and our secret, and that was a secret we could tell no one for the simple reason no one would understand. If the truth came out, his crime would end up overshadowed by ours. We were the real victims, not him, and it was important, my mother said, to see justice meted out *as it should be*.

Sergio Alameda was our prisoner and would stay where he was until my mother could decide what she was going to do with him. Until then he had a roof over his head and food, as well as a pot my mother emptied several times a day. Sergio Alameda wanted for nothing, as my mother used to say. And as time passed she began to devote an almost exaggerated care to preparing

Sergio Alameda's food—so much care that eventually she would place the finer cut of meat on his plate rather than on mine or her own, and she would even wipe the edge of Alameda's plate with a paper napkin if some of the sauce happened to splatter there. The expression on her face when that happened was a mixture of incomprehension and determination; it was also the one she wore when she was trying to solve a crossword and could not come up with the solution. Sergio Alameda preferred coffee with hot milk in the mornings; it was important to take the coffee downstairs to him immediately so he did not have to drink it cold, because if there was anything Sergio loathed it was coffee that had cooled. Just like my father while he was still alive, and Alfonso Hidalgo as well, he expected a baguette with an omelet as well as beer in the morning. He ate lunch and supper when we did. He was always given a cup of tea before bedtime, and if he felt cold in the winter and needed extra pillows or blankets, those were supplied as well. The business of pillows and blankets was important because my mother worried about Sergio Alameda becoming seriously ill. If that happened she would have to decide whether to take him to a hospital, let a doctor in on the secret, or kill him. I am not trying to defend her or in any way justify her actions, but I know that that last alternative had a kind of paralytic effect on her. She had the tools, the skills, and the strength required to take someone's life, it is true, and would have been able to make Sergio Alameda vanish from the face of the earth as though he were no more than a damp spot, an exhalation of water vapor in the process of evaporating. My mother had been butchering meat for many decades and knew all about the stages and changes meat went through. How to carve joints, how to grind meat and package it, and even occasionally make it vanish. Handling a body would be no more difficult for her than dealing with dead flesh in all its guises. There would be no drama involved. Sergio Alameda could die without presenting her with any practical problems, and he would not have to suffer either. I had heard her going over the details of his possible disposal. She would put sleeping pills in his water, and once he was asleep she would go in and put the cattle gun to his head. Sergio Alameda would fall asleep without a qualm and never wake up. I have no doubt at all

that she would have handled Sergio Alameda's
death in exactly the same way she and my father
treated their animals while he was alive. Always
seriously, respectfully, painlessly, and efficiently:
thought and deed in complete accord, working
so perfectly together that words were no longer
needed.

While I am not saying Sergio Alameda had no
right to complain, there are prisoners in Asian
jails, for instance, or people kidnapped in
South America, whose conditions were much
worse than his. During this period whenever
my mother bought herself a book, she would
always buy two and give him a copy. The books
she bought were often about the civil war and
provided witness reports from both the Republi-
can and the fascist sides. Sergio Alameda would
pointedly leave some of the books outside the
bars of his pen. Literature was not, however, the
only distraction we offered him. Occasionally, if
there was football on the radio, she would take
the set downstairs and then they would sit there
listening, my mother outside the barred door
and Alameda behind it. They would both have a

beer and every now and then my mother would say something about the match. It has to be said that as time passed Sergio Alameda became very fat. This was because my mother forced all that food on him but never let him move about. It only took a few months of captivity for him to lose that aura of the fashionable film star that had shone around him when he first entered the restaurant, and he was slowly beginning to decay down there in the dark. The police rang to say he had most likely run away from his family and was probably living in secret with a mistress somewhere else, maybe in one of those hot countries like Guatemala, the Dominican Republic, or El Salvador.

One day my mother said that if I was determined to continue pretending to be holy, it would be better if I faced up to the consequences and became a nun in some convent or other in Madrid. I didn't want to go, but she said she couldn't put up with a child who put on airs, and it wasn't healthy for a young person to live with a single woman and her prisoner. I could either stay on and become a normal person like her, finding a husband, moving into a home of my own, having kids, and doing a lot less talking. Or I could pack my bags and get on the bus at the stop on the main road to seek my fortune in Madrid.

I have spoken with the police in Mahón again. They have still not found a weapon of any kind and if they fail to do so in the next few days, you will probably be released. The convent's lawyer has done his utmost to speed things up and also spoken to the warden about you. You are currently under my protection, and I hope that will help give you a feeling of calm. The thing is, you see, that the more I write the more I want to speak with you. I have heard writers say that when they feel paralyzed by writer's block they imagine a single recipient for their words. A particular individual who will read them. For some reason I do not understand, you appear to be the person who can make the words pour out of me in such a delightful way.

In the land you come from—was it Sweden or Norway?—do you live in the country or in a town? Although I have lived in the city for a great deal of my life I have always longed to go back to the countryside. I cannot reconcile myself to the death that asphalt spreads or to all the areas filled with neither buildings nor greenery. I remember the way I saw them the first time I came to the city on the bus. Tall buildings made of concrete that were unfinished, a kind of graveyard of the lack of human love, and a shock to eyes that had only seen hills, fields, and streams. I watched people eating while they were walking, and their eyes kept wandering as though they were being pursued. It reminded me of the way the rats lived in our village. But the city was also huge, powerful, passionate, and all-embracing. I could sense its power the closer the bus got, as though something dark

and formless was coming toward me—or rather
I was heading toward *it*—and no matter what
kind of darkness was involved, it was bound to
be much easier to enter than to exit.

I would really appreciate a few lines from you at
this point! Can you write to me and let me know
how things are for you in prison, and ideally
what Mercuro Cano actually told you about me?
If you were also willing to tell me what happened on the island I would, of course, be all
ears. I will forward everything to our lawyer and
keep you informed.

Yours sincerely
Lucia

Madrid, August

Dear Bennedith,

Thank you for your letter. As soon as I had read
it I was filled with a great sense of unease and
immediately made my way to the prison to see
the warden. He could not see me until some
time after my arrival, so I was given a tour in the
interim by one of the staff. I kept an eye out for
you but to no avail. I did get a chance, however,
to speak to some of the women who work in the
hall that looks like a Chinese clothes factory.
They were on their break and were sitting inside
what resembled a gigantic, enclosed cage in the
inner courtyard of the prison. When I saw them
there, I asked if I could speak with them. The
prison officer looked as though he had no idea
how to respond, but when I repeated my request

he shrugged and said why not. He fetched me a
chair and a cup of coffee, introduced me to the
women in the cagelike construction, and then
stood a little way off to have a smoke while I
took a seat and spoke with them. I asked how
they had ended up inside and they told me
about their husbands and their children, the
crimes they had committed, and how old they
would be when they got out. They were debating with a touching matter-of-factness what
would be too late by then to experience, and
what might still be left for them. Most of them
had smuggled drugs. They also confirmed
what you had written—that the warden asks
you to perform oral sex on him in exchange for
certain privileges. I told them then that while I
clearly had no experience in that area, if I were
a man I would be wary of stuffing my genitals
in the mouth of someone who hated me. They
laughed, all of them, in concert. The sun was
shining, and I thought that the countryside
around your prison looked quite lovely at that
moment, despite the drought-stricken soil and
the high fence that surrounds you. But then I
turned around only to discover that the warden had appeared. I gathered from his grim

expression that he had probably been standing there listening to our conversation. I was escorted by him to his office in any event, and I put my maimed hand on the table when we got there. He crossed his legs in front of him like the hinged ramp on a car ferry to protect his body, as though he thought I might perform some devilish trick on him if I was allowed direct contact with his flesh. I told him what I had heard in the courtyard.

"A prison is not a resort," he replied, "and the people inside are here because they deserve to be."

I said I could arrange regular visits to the prison, given that the inmates had no contact with the church and no representative of ours had been to visit them.

"No thanks," he said. "The last thing I need is some bitter old maid running a campaign against me from in here."

"Old I may be," I said, "but I have not yet allowed bitterness to sour my disposition."

"It's really weird the way you talk," he said. "You sound like an old book."

"And as to age," I said, "in the eyes of the Lord I am still but a little lamb."

"A little lamb!" the warden exclaimed with a laugh. "You kill me. You—a little lamb!"

Then he stopped laughing and leaned toward me.

"All due respect, nun. I heard what you said out there and let me tell you one thing. Anyone even thinking of biting me down there would get her skull crushed with just the palm of my hand."

He held up his palm as if to illustrate the force of what he had said. I thought it looked dirty, dirty and slightly greasy, like the floors in the corridors connecting the various parts of the prison that I had just traversed. I also thought his hand gave off a musty smell. But I kept in my seat and we stayed looking at each other like that while I was wondering how long he could keep his hand in the air. The only thing you could hear was a fly against the window. It beggars belief that a fly could find its way in there. Through all the iron doors and the hermetically sealed, unbreakable glass.

"They're smugglers, the lot of them," he said finally as he lowered his hand. "They thought they could improve their lives and make themselves financially secure by transporting cocaine as well as provide a better future for their kids."

"There is supposed to be a saying in Naples," I said. "That if you steal, you are a criminal, but if you do not steal you are an even greater criminal because then you cannot feed your children."

"Stupid idiots," he said, shaking his head as though he had not heard what I had said. "Stupid idiots."

I laid out briefly what I had come to say. That if he touched a hair on your head I would be unable to resist the impulse to harm him. Though I might not be able to resist in any case given what I had heard in the courtyard.

"Harm me—how?"

"Don't worry, I'll think of something."

He looked at me as if what I had said had filled him with an urge to laugh once more, but something in my face must have told him I meant business, because he failed to laugh and his smile faded. He got up finally and said he had to bring our meeting to an end, although I had no need to be concerned about you because there were more appetizing pieces of meat on his table and he was not so desperate he needed to stoop that low. That's just sour grapes, I told him, and then repeated my pledge to look into

the possibility of arranging further visits to the
prison after you had been released.

I hope that this will help you see that my concern for you is genuine and that, as promised,
I will do all I can to ensure you are released
quickly and that your conditions are as good
as possible until then. Having read your letter,
I am more curious about you than ever. I now
realize that your relationship with Mercuro,
when you found yourselves in such a predicament on that island, was deeper than I had understood when I first wrote to you. To share a
resolution, as you did—a resolution to improve
yourselves and do good—is bound to create
powerful ties. One moment you feel intoxicated
by the nobility of your intentions and the next
disheartened that it is proving so difficult.
Believe me, that balancing act is a familiar
one, and I have been forced to make compro-
mises on numerous occasions to cut out a path
through the dense thickets, the crassness, of
the real world.

My life was restricted to the convent in the period that followed. When I arrived and first saw the sisters—so stiff, dignified, and out of reach—I felt simply ridiculous. My immediate impulse was to grab my bag, rush back out into the city, and take the next bus home to the village and never, no matter what happened, leave it again. I was seated on a chair in the rooms I now occupy and which were then occupied by Sor Maxine. She was sitting in her chair regarding me with compassion, and I realized from the expression in her eyes that she had sat there many times before facing confused young girls while having no idea what to do with them.

"So you want to become a nun?" she said.

I nodded in terror. She asked why I had chosen their order in particular and not another. Why not the Franciscans or the Carmelites? I shook my head and could not get a single word out. I couldn't tell her the truth, after all, that this was the convent closest to the bus stop where I got off, so I lied and said the Lord had told me to come here.

"Oh," Sor Maxine said with a touch of irony in her voice. "If He is the one who told you, then, of course, you did the right thing."

I was just about to get to my feet and leave both the room and the convent when I heard some chickens clucking as clearly as I could hear Sor Maxine's voice. The sound could not possibly be coming from the city outside, which meant the animals had to be inside the convent walls. I got up and went over to the window that overlooked the courtyard.

"Where's that clucking coming from?" I asked.

"Clucking?" said Sor Maxine. "Why are you asking that?"

"I can hear it quite clearly," I said. "Where's it coming from?"

She sighed. "It's the hens."

"The hens? I can't see any."

"They're in the kitchen. Immediately below us."

"Don't tell me you're keeping hens in the *kitchen*?" I said.

"Where else can we keep them? I wish we didn't have any hens at all. But since we keep being given them, they've got to be kept some-where, don't they? When there are just too many of them we take them down to the butcher's by the roundabout. Although none of my sisters are keen to make fools of themselves leading that gaggle of feathered flesh."

"Can you show them to me?" I asked.

"You want to see *the chickens*?"

"I do."

Sor Maxine shook her head but got up and moved toward the door.

"If you insist," she said. "Follow me."

While we made our way down to the kitchen, she told me that the convent received a great many gifts every week, and that almost all of them were in the form of food—frequently preserves and ready-made dishes, for which the sisters were grateful, but then there were the gifts from the very poorest people, those who could not afford to buy either preserves or pastries and would turn up, instead, with live animals from their farms. They came into the city from the countryside, sometimes on carts drawn by donkeys. From time to time the convent would be presented with piglets, chickens, and turkeys. The only thing the sisters could do was to accept the animals, which they shut into a storage area in the kitchen, because they had no idea what else to do with them.

"I don't understand," I said.

"That was the only place we could come up with. It's just the moment we open the door, something will come flying out at us and we have no idea how to deal with it."

We had entered the kitchen where some nuns were slicing eggplants and peppers to make a *pisto manchego*. I moved slowly up to the pantry door Sor Maxine pointed at and opened it. Sure enough, out flapped two hens and a turkey. I leaned forward and peered inside. The pantry was stained with droppings and bits of old food. An embarrassed Sor Maxine asked what I was doing and said the pantry was going to be cleaned and someone would have to take the animals to the butcher's the very next day, she would make sure of it. The other sisters nodded in agreement. It was while I was holding the pantry door open that I realized this was the Lord's way of helping me enter the convent. And the one thing I wanted at that moment was to have something practical to do because ever since I had stepped inside the building my brain had been spinning, and when the hands are working the brain is resting, they say. I told Sor Maxine I had been working with animals all my life, and that I had always set great store by never depriving an animal of its dignity, not even at the moment of death. I said that on some profound inner level the way a person treats animals is how they treat themselves. I said some other things I can no longer remember, because talking had suddenly become a breeze. The chastened sisters in front of me listened without interrupting.

Finally Sor Maxine said, "What can I say? You are so clearly right. What do you need?" I said I needed cleaning equipment, rolls of plastic, and my bag. It took a while to get hold of the plastic, but once I had everything at hand I covered the floor and the chairs with it and then got my knives out of the bag. Why had I brought them with me? I'm not sure, perhaps because they were things that felt like a part of me and I could not leave them behind. The sisters looked appalled when I unrolled the cloth sheath. I showed them all the knives and told them what they were called and what they were used for. Fascinated, one of the sisters raised the bollock dagger to inspect it, while Sor Maxine spent a long time gazing at the glittering blade of the Argentine Brother-in-Law. I also talked about handling animals, about empathy and suffering.

I did not mince my words and I acted without
hesitation. A few hours later, and the kitchen—
including the pantry—was sparkling clean, and
the hens and the turkey had been slaughtered,
plucked, and cleaned out, each on a dish of their
own on the table.

When you become part of a convent community,
you have to feel that community can contribute something to you as a person, while the
community also has to feel you can contribute
something to it. I had been given an opportunity
to give them the full picture right from the start,
and the sisters liked what they saw. They gave
me a room that overlooked the inner courtyard.
They said I could stay until they, and I, had
figured out whether this was the right path for
me. I lay on my cot that very night, thinking
about my mother and Sergio Alameda in the
basement. I was also thinking about my maimed
hand, which the nuns had stared at while I was
working but had asked no questions about. And
about my revelation, the meadow and the little
stream in the morning light. Meanwhile the
night breeze kept rustling expectantly through

the canopies of the trees outside as though it were whispering to me that this was my path, and that everything would turn out fine now.

The years passed. My life became a different one, and I became a different person. Apart from the conversations I had every Sunday with my mother and Sergio Alameda, I had very little contact with the world outside in the years that followed. My mother finally opened the pen, and Sergio Alameda was released. But despite his imprisonment, there must have been something about my mother he valued highly, because he never went back to Madrid. I think they became happy together as time passed. In any case they are buried in the same grave in the cemetery in our village, in a grave that lies in the new section, at a fitting distance from both my father and Alfonso Hidalgo.

Bennedith, I do so hope I am not boring you with my stories. As I said, I could never forgive myself if I added to the gloom of your time in prison. If you have grown tired of the memoirs of an old woman, do take a break, but please do not skip anything. You may think I am rambling, but bear in mind that everything I write could actually be of the utmost importance. For you, but also for me. I really believe that my immortality is dependent on you. You may think I'm being vain, but being vain is doing things for your own gain. I, on the other hand, am doing them for the *world*. Because yes, Bennedith, I really do think that the world benefits by my soul being allowed to linger here. And even perhaps by my becoming more firmly attached.

After a few years I confided the secret of my revelation to the *madre superiora*. She did not make fun of me, as I had expected, but showed reverence instead for what I had experienced and even spoke with the priest who had been appointed to supervise us about my being allowed to hear women in the confessional. Women are, of course, not allowed to hear confessions, never, but in the light of his experience it was the priest's view that women would often remain silent when they had to confide certain things to men and it would be an advantage, in those situations, if they were able to speak with a woman. He said that as long as the penitents who wanted to confess agreed, they could come to me. It was then the path that lay ahead of me began to take definite shape.

I listened to all kinds of stories over many years and it felt as though I too could experience some of what the people in question had undergone, as though I were able to make up for my own inadequate experience of life through theirs. I did not have much to say to begin with, but as time passed I began to give them more specific advice. I tried to get them to become stronger, to turn away from the kind of thing that did them harm. Thanks to the cultural education I had received from the *madre superiora* in the convent, I could also counsel them to listen to a particular kind of music or read a certain book or a poem while being able to picture exactly how the music or the book would affect them internally, in the same way a chemist concocts the correct mixture of different substances to produce a particular solution. I was able to help a lot of people in this way. Though there were also days when my sense of powerlessness was so great and my dejection so paralyzing that I felt I was unable to do anything for humanity at all, and that there was just too much suffering and too much resistance for any kind of improvement to take place.

I confided in the *madre superiora*, who responded laconically, "Everyone suffers, Lucia."

So how were you supposed to help in that case? I would have to find out for myself.

When I left the domain of the confessional behind in order to intervene in a practical manner, things turned out so well it could only be seen as a sign that the Lord not only approved but had actually been waiting for someone to act as I was doing. Let me make a leap forward in time at this point. A woman whose husband had been unfaithful came to see me at some point in the early 1960s. She was being eaten alive by jealousy. I have seen many women being endlessly consumed on the low flame of that awful fire, but those flames were blazing in this woman like a burning brand. As she was sitting there in the confessional, the expression on her face would have terrified even a mother confessor as battle-hardened as myself. That was how much insomnia and all those embittered thoughts had disfigured her; the furrows had made her skin crack like a landscape racked by drought. She was hissing insults at her husband, and it felt like little torrents of saliva were coming through the lattice.

"Calm yourself," I said, but she didn't hear me.

I understood from our very first conversation that the unfaithfulness of her husband would be the spiritual death of this woman. I could see myself spending ages doing my utmost to persuade her to accept her lot while keeping her dignity intact, and I could also picture her learning to control herself while the suffering in her eyes was extinguished and replaced by a kind of fog, as she was slowly but surely transformed into a vegetable, drained of all vitality and completely numbed. I have seen this happen so many times and always consoled myself that a fog is better than a forest fire. I heaved a deep sigh under my breath. Abusive language continued to pour out of the woman, like lava erupting from a volcano.

"He's in our home with the other woman now," she whispered. "While I'm here being tortured, he's having it away with her in our flat. With the whore, and as for him, the fornicator, I'm going..."

And so on. I got up and stepped out of the booth. It took a while for the woman to realize I was no longer sitting on the other side, and I could hear her tortured lament continue for several minutes. But then she suddenly fell silent.

"Sor Lucia?" she said. "Are you there?"

She must have leaned toward the lattice and tapped it lightly, as though I might be huddled on the floor or collapsed from sudden illness.

"Sor Lucia?" she said again. "Where are you? Are you okay?"

"I'm standing outside," I said then. "Please step outside as well."

After a few seconds of silence the door to the confessional opened and out she came. Her embittered expression had been replaced by one of sheer astonishment.

"What's going on?" she asked.

"You said your husband and his mistress are at your home now," I said.

"Yes," she said hesitantly.

"So let's go there."

"Sorry?"

"So let's go there. Where do you live?"

Clearly distrustful, she came out with an address, and thirty minutes later we were getting out of a taxi in front of her building.

I can remember how I felt as we were standing there. A ticklish sensation in my stomach, the kind of thing you can experience when there is still some youth left in your blood and many years of living ahead of you. That was the first time I acted on my own initiative. It was the starting block for the phase of my life that would now begin. I can remember that curious white facade towering above me. A yellow sheet was fluttering on a line outside a window, and water was dripping onto the street as it does after people water the potted plants on their balconies. It was hot and the air was still. I hummed quietly to myself while thinking. The scorned wife beside me got a pocket mirror out of her handbag and then put it back, only to get it out and put it back once more. The dance of meaningless gestures an anxious person will perform. The dark and imposing front door was open, and in a booth a few meters inside was the concierge. As we entered he looked at us with a mixture of surprise and disapproval. He obviously knew what the woman's husband was up to several floors above us, because the husband would have gone past him with his mistress some time before. He came out of his booth and made an obligatory little bow to me before starting to talk to my companion. But I grabbed her under her arm and pulled her gently toward the lift.

"Wait," the concierge said.

"Yes?" I said and turned toward him.

There is something in the common man that makes him fall silent when a nun looks at him in a certain way, as though his objections were a challenge not just to the nun but to the whole of Heaven. He shook his head, made a dismissive gesture, and returned to his booth. We took the lift and were soon standing in front of the door to the couple's apartment.

"What are you going to do?" the woman whispered.

"I don't actually know," I confessed.

"You don't know?"

"No, but don't worry. The Lord will show me once I'm inside."

She shook her head in doubt but obeyed my instruction to insert the key into the lock. The door opened. It was immediately obvious that the woman's suspicions were well founded. A pair of high-heeled ladies' shoes had been slung on the floor just by the door and clothes were scattered along the hall, which continued farther inside the apartment. A little gasp escaped the woman. For my part I sighed. Though I have never liked the unfaithful, I have always made an effort to help them as well. Adultery is one of the dirty little scandals of human life, and were it not for an instinctive disinclination toward all forms of moral preaching, I would have liked to expand on my ideas concerning that subject. I have, however, refrained. We could hear distant laughter and the clink of glasses. And then I saw it. In the space of an instant it was clear to me what needed to be done. I gestured to the woman to come inside and close the door silently behind her. Then I whispered to her that she should stay where she was while I stepped quickly down the hall in shoes that never make a sound and picked up the clothes. When I had all of them in my arms I placed them on the floor in front of the woman.

"Fold," I said.

And fold we did. We folded the underwear quickly and elegantly (if you will permit me a minor detail, the lace panties bore marks that were a lurid yellow in color), then the jeans shorts and blouse, the man's jacket and trousers. I even smoothed out the stockings and then folded them over and under four times in so exemplary a manner I am convinced even Lourdes who cleans my rooms would have been impressed. When we had finished there were two very neat piles arranged beside each other on the floor. The man's and the woman's shoes were placed in front of their respective piles. Loud groaning noises could now be heard from one of the rooms in the apartment and I opened the front door, pulled the woman out into the stairwell, and then closed it behind us.

"So that's that," I said. "It went better than I expected."

The look the woman gave me was a mixture of sadness and hope. We took the lift down to the concierge who bowed once again when he saw me coming. I asked him if he could keep our visit secret or if I would be forced to buy his silence. He gave me an appalled look and said his lips were sealed, and that he hadn't seen us arrive or leave. I thanked him. Then I said goodbye to the woman, hailed a taxi in the street, and went home.

She returned the next day, but this time her face was very different. I would almost go so far as to say she was glowing. She came into my room and I couldn't help exclaiming, "Today you look like you're *alive!*"

She told me that once I had left she had eaten a good lunch at a restaurant and even had a glass of white wine in the shade. For the first time in ages she had been able to think about something other than her husband's infidelity. She had watched the people around her, *felt* the air against her skin, and really *tasted* her food.

"Very good," I said.

She had returned home a few hours later. The concierge greeted her with a new degree of respect, or so she thought. In the apartment upstairs her husband had been beside himself with worry. He had asked her all kinds of questions— if she had been in the flat that afternoon, if she knew whether someone else had, if she knew anything at all.

"About what?" she asked.

"Do you know anything, anything at all, about what happened here this afternoon?"

She had shaken her head in silence and replied she did not know what he was talking about, but that he could ask the concierge if something had happened because he kept an eye on everyone who came and went.

"I think I'm going mad," he said, holding his head in his hands.

After that incident he stopped seeing the other woman. This confirmed my theory that infidelity depends on a secret emotional charge and if you can drain that charge of excitement, both adulterers will then see themselves in the full light of their sordid behavior and their mendacity. The woman came back to see me several more times and continued to thank me.

"Such a simple little thing," she would say time after time.

I felt pleased as well. I had helped someone, and entirely without bloodshed into the bargain.

That leads us, rather conveniently, more deeply into the nature of my activities. It isn't always possible, you see, to help people if you insist on never shedding blood. This depends, in turn, on how thoroughly you want to immerse yourself in the process, how far you are prepared to go to actually provide relief, and, of course, how brave you are. I have never been someone interested in half measures, so I was prepared to risk everything to follow the voice I thought I could hear inside me.

One of the people I helped was Francisca León. That was a mission I carried out to perfection, if I say so myself. This was in 1992. I drove out to an old people's home, the House of the Butterflies, as it was called, some twenty to thirty kilometers outside Madrid. I decided to drive there myself that day, and I no longer felt nervous; that is how self-evident my vocation had come to seem to me by then. My pulse was as slow as when I had my coffee in the morning in front of the open window of my dining room while looking out across the tops of the trees in the inner courtyard of the convent. I even remained in the car for a while after turning off the engine to relish the grandeur of the setting I had arrived at. The leafy canopies of horse chestnuts and plane trees towered over my head, and that improbable greenery provided shade for the few, though top-of-the-range, cars parked there. A large country house could be seen a hundred or so meters farther away, nestled among the kind of flowering plants that are commonplace in Valencia or Alicante, but that require great effort and extraordinary amounts of water to maintain here in Madrid. I opened the door, grabbed my bag, and got out of the car. The heat of the wind came at me like a blow, even though it was almost evening. I walked into the garden that surrounded the building. Garden isn't the right word—it was more like a park. A large park with streams, bridges, rose hedges, manicured lawns, and a wealth of exotic trees that had little plaques on them. The grounds of the House of the Butterflies might once have been a botanical garden or a park that belonged to an eccentric nobleman who had collected plants from other continents. I sat on a bench in the shade in keeping with the instructions I had received in the letter. There was a little pond close to the bench with a shiny, orange carp swimming back and forth through its murky water. Even though my task was imminent, I felt able to delight in this place. I tell you this so that you may understand the importance of calm. A cool head is the most fundamental ingredient of any and all success. A cool head and, perhaps, a chip of ice in your heart as well.

I must have dozed off sitting beside the carp because I came awake at the sound of a clock striking six inside the old people's home. Some elderly women and men were being pushed in wicker wheelchairs across the pale-colored paving toward a shaded arbor. For a while the staff went back and forth carrying trays on which I glimpsed stemmed glassware and tall bottles in different colors. Cheerful voices could soon be heard from the arbor talking and laughing. I thought then, and I think it now, that nothing can turn a person into an Epicurean like the presence of death. It is part of human nature to want to ensure that the passage to the other world occurs as painlessly as possible and—where possible—as gracefully too. And yes, if you have not already realized, Bennedith, from time to time I had made it my mission to help people make the crossing to the other

side. I considered it to be part of that mission
to explain to them the various means available
to achieve that goal. The substance I used most
frequently provided a light-hearted, bubbly
feeling, like the sensation of being slightly
tipsy in spring, and I referred to it as "Mozart."
Anyone can experience a good death to Mozart.
It does not require previous knowledge or a
particular ability to put yourself in a state where
you are receptive to the joys of life. Mozart
seeped inside, took possession of the person,
and refused to relax its hold on the brain until it
had grown cold. Though there were people too
who would not be satisfied with Mozart. There
were those who thought that if you were going
to die you might as well take a risk or two—if
you were going to die, you might as well go the
whole hog. The individuals who chose to die to
the substances I called "Bach" and "Schubert"
may have been thrill-seekers, but they could still
be handled. If I were to summarize some of the
most meaningful and profound experiences of
my vocational life, they would always be linked
to those two substances. And then there was a
third category; all I had left to offer them was
"Rachmaninov." These people were what you

might call territories without maps. They could change their mind at the last minute or take the plunge long before I was ready myself. They were unpredictable, and unpredictable people are also dangerous people in a sense—to me, in particular, because I always felt obliged to operate according to a very detailed plan that had been set out in advance. Besides, you cannot afford to feel the least doubt, not in my field. If you are predisposed to brooding, you will quickly end up dead as well, by someone else's hand, someone who will not hesitate to pull the trigger. But I have never had doubts, because I have always believed that you have to be the master of your fate and the captain of your soul, as in the poem by William Ernest Henley, and that of all the people He may choose to help, God prefers to choose those who can help themselves.

I knew I would have to wait a while longer for Francisca León, as the specified time had not yet arrived. I got the letter out of my bag and read it once again. There was nothing unusual about it per se. The sender was a ninety-year-old lady who wrote that while she was "content with her life and with all that had been," she felt she had now reached the end of the road and therefore wanted my help, as she put it, "to leave the stage while she could still do so with her head held high." She did not mention how she had obtained my address, who had informed her about my operation, or whether she was aware of my fee. I could tell, though, from the handwriting, the paper, and the general tone of the letter, that the fee would not be a problem. Once I had done some research into the House of the Butterflies, I knew that it was hardly a home for those in need. The cost of a stay of a few months was astronomical, which meant that there were two possibilities—either Francisca León was wealthy or she belonged to the category of people that devote all their resources to financing the last period of their lives, but who then live on longer than expected and, once their accounts have run dry and their property has been sold, would rather die before their time than move to a more modest home with vinyl flooring, poor food, and the stagnant though penetrating smell of cleaning fluid and urine in the corridors.

But when at exactly six-thirty a single woman was wheeled out through the open terrace doors, I knew my client belonged to the category of rich people whose assets have been virtually unlimited throughout their lives. I could read that from her face, which exuded a sense of security, and in those detached but searching eyes, which appeared to be peering into all the dimensions of the hereafter at one and the same time. This type of person is different from those who become rich as adults and allow money to bewitch them to the very depths of their souls. People that deeply bewitched give off a faint scent of corruption, the scent of those who have been guided by the principles of capitalism all their lives.

The woman was wheeled toward a secluded corner of the park, close to a little waterfall that found its way out from a rock wall and tumbled into a small stone pond. Soon I could no longer see her because the arbor she had gone inside was completely cut off from the rest of the park by a tall dense hedge. There could be no doubt though that she was the person who had sent the letter. As soon as the female staff member had vanished back inside the house, I got up from the bench and went over.

"Francisca León?" I asked.

The body in the wheelchair froze.

"Oh," she said. "It's you. Lucia. At last."

"I got your letter," I said.

"You could have come earlier. I've been sitting here every day waiting."

I couldn't help smiling. The park around us was so lush with greenery; large peony heads were bobbing in the breeze, and the leaves of the poplars were rubbing against each other with a rustling sound.

"You have to admit that this is a lovely place to be in," I said. "A privilege. Not everyone is so fortunate. There are people who die alone in the cold and the dirt."

"That may be so. But it changes nothing. Not for me."

"I assume that you know that I take my time when preparing my missions," I said. "If we decide to work together, my priority will be to devise a plan. And then you too will have to make preparations of your own."

"Preparations?" Francisca León asked with a furrowed brow. "Me?"

"I usually start by going through their lives with my clients. There may be farewells that must still be said, letters that have to be written, and things that need to be sorted out. Posterity is real and it will remember them."

"I've already written the letter I need to write," she said with a dismissive gesture. "It is in my suitcase, along with everything else. I would like to get everything decided now. And then you can come back some day very soon and... carry it out."

Her sentence remained hanging.

"I will pay, of course," she added and gave me a piercing look. "You can have the money right away. As long as you say yes. Please. Just say yes. I am begging you."

That piercing look vanished, and now there was desperation in her beseeching eyes.

"Let's not rush into it," I said. "This is a major decision. How long have you been considering this?"

"For as long as I can remember. And I think we can skip this entire conversation, if you don't mind. The question is not actually if but how. Whether you are going to help me or not. If you're not, then you leave me no other choice but to take matters into my own hands."

———

I always feel a chill run down my spine when confronted with that kind of determination. I know what a relentlessly sloppy, violent, and ridiculous form it can assume once it has been put into effect. Suicides are a destructive breed but an impractical and naive one first and foremost, who consistently and just as gravely underestimate the contradictory mechanisms of dying. I have seen the corpses of people who cut their own throats halfway between the bed and the door, their hands reaching out as though the last thing they ever did in their lives was to call for help in mute despair. And I have seen the hands full of splinters of a suicide who hanged himself and then grabbed at a ceiling beam once he had kicked away the table. That is God's punishment: to change your mind at the last moment, and for that to be the last image of the dead person posterity will preserve: of desperate and ridiculous regret.

"It does seem as though I cannot dissuade you from taking this path," I said.

"Well then," Francisca said. "It's up to you to say when and how."

I opened my bag and got out my calendar.

"How many people have you actually killed with those pianist hands of yours?" Francisca León said.

"Seventy-six," I responded.

"So that would make me the seventy-seventh," she mumbled. "Seventy-seven is a good number."

"I'm happy you see it that way." I got to my feet. "Have a lovely afternoon, I'll be in touch."

"Hold on," Francisca called out. "Please, Lucia. Wait. We haven't decided anything yet."

"I can come back on the Friday of next week," I said. "If you've completed all your preparations, we can put it into effect at that point."

"I've already done all my preparations, I told you that. Couldn't you come any earlier? Sunday? Please on Sunday!"

"I'm going away this weekend," I said.

"Going away? But nuns don't go away for the weekend, surely?"

I laughed out loud. "I said next Friday. Next Friday is when I will be here. Goodbye, Francisca León."

I offered her my hand, and she shook it rather hesitantly.

"Is it true what they say that you believe you are God's emissary?" she asked.

"No," I replied.

"Is it true what they say," she asked then, "that you have a team of nuns and monks supporting you who believe that that is what you are?"

But I did not reply to that question and started walking toward the parking lot.

"Goodbye, Sor Lucia!" she called after me. "And thank you."

I might have gone ten, at most fifteen paces, before I stopped, turned around, and started to retrace my steps. I was looking at Francisca León's back and her thin shoulder-length hair that was moving in the warm breeze. She appeared to be staring straight into the evening sun, but as I got closer I could see from one side that her eyes were closed and there was a little smile on her lips. I took up a position behind her and put my hands on her jaw and cheek. She flinched at first, but when I put my hand on her shoulder she relaxed. I ran my hand quickly over her hair, down her throat and across her jawbone. When I could sense she was not only not resisting but had relaxed and surrendered completely to my touch, I performed that small almost imperceptible wrench. Her hands dropped beside the seat of the wheelchair and her head dropped back against my stomach. I remained like that for several minutes. The breeze was still rustling in the trees, and the sun had now become an orange sphere on the horizon. I carefully laid her head against the table in front of her. I also folded her hands and put them in her lap. The last thing I did to Francisca León was to draw back her hair so that the faint smile that was still playing around her lips was the first thing the female attendant, who would soon be returning to wheel her inside for the evening, would see. I also read a short prayer and made the sign of the cross over her. Then I took her bag, opened it, and found what I was looking for. The payment notes were placed neatly in a full envelope. The letter to posterity was also inside the bag, addressed in handwriting that was just as neat; the envelope even had a stamp on it. I left the park by a little winding path at the back of the arbor. Twenty minutes later I was pulling onto the motorway heading for Madrid.

I have just spoken with our lawyer, who informed me that you will very probably be released in a matter of days. I was so cheered by this news I couldn't help ringing the Alcalá Meco prison to book a call with you. When you rang me a little later you sounded happy. That was good to hear, because I had only heard you speaking when in a state of rage before. Maybe your good mood can be explained in part by the fact that you have been invited to Salou to see the woman with the invalid husband as soon as you are released. Of course I'm pleased for you because, unless I misunderstood, something took place that led you to believe the friendship was over. And now you will be going there. All's well that ends well. I am so pleased, as I said. Do you think you will have time for a visit to me first? I would be so grateful.

———

I realize I must hurry up and tell you about *Carnality* so you have an opportunity to reflect on certain matters relating to Mercuro Cano before we meet.

The years in the convent went by. I was one sister among all the others. I had my work on the side, a mission that was valued highly by some and ignored by others. Did I have enemies? Of course. But I have always believed enemies are a good thing. Loyal in their hatred and constant in the wickedness of their intent, your enemies will always be there, waiting. It is thanks to them you have the energy to get back up when you have been shot down, and it is thanks to them you become hardened. The very thought of them drives both fatigue and any sense of ease from the body and puts you back on the right course. I owe my enemies so much—without them I could never have achieved any of my successes.

Maternal feeling, though, Bennedith,
oh those maternal feelings. The greatest ac-
complishment of my life is Ada and *Carnality*
along with her. When Ada entered my room in
the convent, I felt reduced to a tiny wounded
animal, a queen in beggar's clothes. That was all
those repressed maternal feelings inside me immediately welling up to the surface and demanding their place in my life. How could something
like that just happen? I was over eighty years
old and ought to have become reconciled to my
fate as a woman without issue. But my heart was
wrung instead by an invisible hand—the same
hard and relentless hand that wrings the heart
of a mother from the moment her child is born
until her death.

She turned up with her father, who was a
simple man. It was apparent that being obliged
to sit opposite an old nun made him nervous.

Sometimes I feel an impulse to scare people when they tense up like that. To put my maimed hand on the table and drum with the fingers I have left and watch the people I am facing turn pale and stammer, their eyes flickering from my hand to my eyes. But I sat there in silence this time, my hand perfectly concealed beneath the table, and waited patiently. The father sat there for a while and looked away from me to the windows, the spines of the books, the plants, and the candelabra. Once he had taken a breather and scratched his beard and scalp, it came out.

"We're here because we've got a problem," he said.

"Has it to do with this girl?" I asked.

"Yes," he said. "The thing is she..."

The sentence remained unfinished.

"Tell me," I said.

"She has had her sexual debut," the man said quickly, as if he were afraid the words would evaporate if he failed to spit them out.

"I see," I said. "And why have you come to see me?"

"The thing is," he said, "now Ada believes she is carrying a holy child."

"How do you mean?"

"She thinks she is carrying a holy child. As if she was the Virgin Mary. You see?"

I looked from the man to the girl. Her eyes were locked on the floor as though the conversation had nothing to do with her.

"I'm ashamed of course," the man said.

"Why?" I asked.

"Why!" he exclaimed. "Because she is my daughter and she's certainly not right in the head."

I got out my notepad and pen and cleared my throat. Then I turned toward the girl.

"What is your name?" I asked her.

"Ada," she replied.

"A lovely name," I said.

"That's not what I think," she said.

"What would you prefer to be called instead?" I asked.

"Miss Pink," she said. "I've always wanted to be called Miss Pink."

She turned her head and looked at her father defiantly. He appeared to be about to break out in a torrent of reproaches, so I made sure to head him off.

"Why do you think you are carrying a holy child?"

"Because the act was an annunciation," she replied.

I have to admit that the girl had risen in my estimation. Her forthright speech, her eloquent vocabulary, and the clarity with which she uttered those words. But what made the deepest impression on me was the sense of conviction she gave off when speaking of the annunciation. To be able to transform an unfortunate sexual situation into a blessing calls for a special kind of temperament.

"There you have it," the father said, gesturing at me, "Now you can understand. And we're just an ordinary family, you know. I really want to make that clear. We've never had any fanatics in our family. We're perfectly ordinary people. Just ordinary people, Sor Lucia."

I couldn't help raising my eyebrows. "If you really were so ordinary," I said, "there would hardly be any point in emphasizing the matter."

The man fell silent, and I could turn to the girl once more.

"Have you started menstruating?" I asked.

I could see the father reacting out of the corner of my eye.

"What kind of question is that?" he asked.

"Just answer it," I said to the girl.

"What kind of question is that?" the father yelled. "What is all this, and who do you think you are? You're supposed to help us and instead—what do we get? Fanatics plotting together."

I realized I could not ignore him and so I swiveled to face him:

"In order to understand whether she is carrying a holy child or not, the first thing I have to establish is whether she is menstruating. You must know enough of your Bible history to be able to see how the two things are connected?"

He stayed in his seat, his eyes locked on me, and was finally silent.

"So have you begun menstruating?" I asked the girl once more.

"No," she said.

"In that case you're not pregnant. Not even Mary could become pregnant without menstruating first."

The girl nodded.

"It's just I feel holy anyway," she said. "As though there was something special about *me*, me in particular."

The father nodded and pointed at her.

"Exactly," he said. "That's exactly what I mean. So now you've got the notion of pregnancy out of her mind, maybe you could be so kind as to rid her of the idea she's special in some way."

"In what way is there something special about you?" I asked the girl.

"I've been told there are two kinds of women," she said, "and that would be the Madonna and the whore. You are either one or the other. I feel really strongly I must be the Madonna."

Ada rose even more in my estimation at that. I realized she had got completely lost in the male narrative and that her mind, which had to be both sensitive and sharp, had been absorbing fragments of it here and there and compiling them into a logical account of herself. The holy Madonna cannot simply have sex in its most basic form. The act must, of course, lead to something magnificent.

"You heard it out of her own mouth!" the father exclaimed. "That's it! Now say something miraculous so she'll be cured."

I shook my head in concern. An idea had begun to take shape, and even if it was a crazy idea, I couldn't let it go until I had explored all the possible angles.

"I can't tell whether she has been chosen or not just like that. I need time to look into it."

"What do you mean?" the man asked.

"All I am saying," I said with a slow shrug of my shoulders, "is that some things take time."

"How much time?" the man asked. "How long would that take?"

"A few weeks," I said. "Maybe a month."

"And how would you go about it?"

"Ah," I said. "We have our methods. You can safely leave her here with me if you want to. She will be given a room, and we will also give her lessons in everything from the history of the Bible to French."

The man looked rather alarmed at that, but the girl's face lit up. I assume the family lived in some cramped and unhealthy hovel on the out-skirts of Madrid and the girl did not even have a room of her own.

"If you can stay a bit longer I can show you around the convent," I said and stood up. "It's still too hot to go outside at this time of day."

I then showed Ada and her father around all the open rooms of the convent. I escorted them to

the leafy inner courtyard where they were served
an array of small dishes from the kitchen, as the
cook was trying out the menus for the coming
week. I may have appeared relaxed, I am confident in fact that I did, but my brain was actually
working feverishly. I had to find out whether
what I wanted could actually be done, whether
the girl possessed the necessary qualities, and I
also needed to understand whether a period of
apprenticeship at my side would be possible. I
had seen a seed inside her, but I did not know
if it could grow into a tree. It is very difficult to
come up with a reliable sense of what exists inside
another person in a short space of time, what
abilities she might possess, how much elasticity
her mind would permit her, and what guises she
could adopt. But I did the only thing possible
in the situation, which was to put my trust in
the spur of the moment, even though I felt like a
stranger to myself in doing so. It was as if all that
accumulated maternal feeling had clumped together to form a huge snowball, and that snowball
was rolling behind me down a steep slope. In the
end, while doing my best to sound indifferent, I
proposed that Ada should stay in the convent for
a while, starting immediately.

"But what would she do in return?" the man asked. "I can't afford to pay."

Oh, the tedious conscientiousness of the little man. What is the point of always trying to do the right thing in a world that exploits you and that you hate? But I felt obliged to persuade that same man and had to rack my brain for any possible kitchen or janitorial duties. I named a few jobs at random and hoped the kitchen staff would not mind too much having an unsolicited assistant. To my surprise the man nodded, and everything was resolved with astonishing simplicity, as will happen when the Lord approves.

The fact that I failed to take Ada's mother into account turned out to be an error, a minor error, but one that would prove consequential when she turned up a few days later. I have done a lot of thinking about the fact that a woman like her could bear a child as formidable as Ada. It must be one of the chance equations that creation generates. She was furious, and she was swearing and dripping with sweat, because she had walked all the way to the convent from the bus stop in the heat and had not brought a change of clothes with her, but chose to enter the inner courtyard in all her unvarnished and perspiring flesh.

"You planning on taking my child from me?" she said when she came into my room.

She had skipped all the phrases of greeting and just stood there with her hands on those substantial hips.

"Not in the slightest," I said.

"Oh yes you are, that's exactly what you're planning on doing," she said with hatred in her voice. "Because that's what nuns do. You take the children away from us *real* women. You did it during the dictatorship, and you're trying to do it now. You've all got this wound inside you because you never got to be mothers, and this is your pathetic revenge for what you can't heal by yourself."

My heart started racing at those words, but I replied as calmly as you can when facing an enraged animal that she no doubt had a point. There probably was a wound like that inside me, but everyone has a myriad of wounds inside them, and what is important is that you have something else inside you besides those wounds. Little islands where you can find peace and rest and that you can stand on as you jump across the endless quagmire of disappointments life has to offer.

"What a load of drivel," she hissed.

Then she yelled I shouldn't try and get the better of her with a load of biblical rubbish. I replied that nothing of what I had said to that point was biblical, and she yelled back at me that the very fact we were in a convent and I was a nun was biblical enough to last her a lifetime.

"A whole godforsaken fucking lifetime!" she yelled.

She paused to catch her breath for a moment and said she was the one who had given birth to the girl and you couldn't know anything about real maternal feelings and real pain unless you had squeezed a kid out of your own womb.

I had to wipe the sweat from my brow with a handkerchief. We—my sisters and I—sometimes forget what being part of the world beyond the convent is like. We tend to forget that the people out there are actually capable of looking one another in the eye while spitting out indiscriminate insults and we forget that there are people whose daily goal is not to show humility and understanding for one's fellow men but to crush them

with all the finesse of a dog devouring a bowl
of its food. I put the handkerchief on the table,
cleared my throat, and tried to put on a smile
as well. I said it was true I couldn't know what
it was like to have a child of my own. That was
true. It was perfectly true as well that I had not
squeezed anything out of my womb, and even
though I was grateful for that in some respects, it
was possible I lacked insight into certain aspects
of female life for that very reason. I wiped my
brow again with the handkerchief. She nodded
at me, and the look in her eyes said, *Told you
so.* So I said there were other things I did know
about, things that had been significant for me.
She moved over to me at that point, leaned
across the table, and put her index finger under
my chin. She raised my face toward her and
said: "Just because you use a lot of posh words
you think you can trick simple folk like me out of
the thing they love most. Only you're not going
to trick me, you dried-up lying old nun!"

Dried-up lying old nun? I stared into her
eyes, and if not for the fact I could see Ada's eyes
in there as well, I would have countered with a
devastating retort. Instead I felt my heart clench
and a tenderness well up like lava. I wanted to

hug her, press her against me, ask her to be my friend, stay for lunch and a glass of cold white wine in the garden and listen to the water with me—but before I had time to say anything, she had grabbed the flesh under my chin and pinched it. It was terribly painful and decidedly not conducive to my finding something for us to talk about or issuing an invitation. I presume she interpreted my silence as indifference to what she had said, because she turned and walked over to a chair in the middle of the room and sat there doggedly, her arms crossed, as though she never intended to leave. She stayed there for a good while, looking around with an expression of distaste across her face.

"Carpets, candles, canopied beds," she mumbled and waved her hand. "Potted plants, curtains, fruit bowls, floral displays. Life in this convent really is holy. Some paupers you are."

Then she stopped talking and locked eyes with me. She drummed her fingers for a bit against the edge of the chair. Meanwhile I was trying to appear as unconcerned as I could. I looked out the window, down at my nails, and then I picked up my pen and drew a little scribble on a piece of paper. The skin under my chin still hurt. I was wondering where Ada had got to and thinking it would be unfortunate if she were to come in now and find out about her mother's resentment toward me. But she did not turn up. Instead the mother got to her feet, grabbed her bag, and said, "Just so you know, nun, the little miracle is defective."

"What do you mean?" I asked.

"Ada. She's *defective*."

I shrugged and said I still did not understand. With a peculiar sort of calm all but beaming from her eyes, she said, "Her heart is made of stone."

"Her heart? What do you mean?"

"It's made of stone, Sor Lucia. Just wait, you'll see for yourself."

I remember the gardener was humming outside my window while watering one of the bushes and a member of the staff was walking across the gravel path and then there was the sound of the door to the street closing. That moment would remain with me like a photo in an album you get out many years later.

"What do you really mean?" I repeated.

"You're going to regret ever letting her inside the walls of this convent."

And with that she turned and with a contemptuous expression still plastered across her face she left the room.

I quickly shook her words off, it should be said. You have to believe the evidence of your own eyes. In Ada, I had seen the possibility of something magnificent. She thrived in the convent, she was studious, now and then verging on brilliant, and most importantly she loved spending time with me. She wanted to come into my room whenever she had a free moment. I had Jaime, our factotum, carry up a desk for her that was placed at the other end of my study. We would sit there and work in front of the open window. I answered letters and began writing little instruction manuals on the art of living, the art of growing old, the art of dying—manuals that actually became very popular and which the sisters in the convent, the priests, and the monks began to hand out to the general public. We talked, Ada and I, and I told her about my childhood in Extremadura and about what my mother had told me: that for many people life was about carnality, about the flesh rather than the soul. I also told her, just as my mother told me, that she should watch out.

"Watch out for what?" Ada asked.

"Most things," I replied.

I also told Ada about my revelation, about the woman with the folded clothes, about Francisca León and all the other people I had helped. Ada listened attentively and when I had finished one episode she would often ask me to tell it again, as if it was a fairy tale. Time passed. Weeks, months, years came and went. Ada did not want to return to her parents, she completed her studies with us instead. A few years ago she also started playing computer games. This latter interest failed to please me as much. I have always wondered why people do things like that when they could be reading a book or listening to music. Ada, for her part, always insisted that the games helped develop her intelligence and that every individual must try to form a connection to the age they live in. I allowed myself to be convinced. But her passion for the games forced me to behave furtively as far as the other nuns were concerned, because I knew they would never consent to that kind of worldliness existing within our walls. And while I had no great problem, personally, with the games, I didn't think it fitting for Ada to devote so much time to something that did not *lead* anywhere, so to speak. But if you labored this point with Ada, you ended up in long and complicated arguments involving theories about what actually did lead anywhere and what it meant for something to lead somewhere. The probing, existential nature of the young. She would sit with those huge headphones on in front of the computer and play games and watch video clips. She could sit like that for hours, while I worked, drank my vermouth, and took my naps.

Weeks and months passed in this way. Ada, who had been filled with a kind of holiness that made me think of the holiness that had filled me when I was young, had suddenly become an introverted girl in her late teens who seemed to have barely any memory of the Madonna she once believed herself to embody. I tried to take this gracefully. But when I received a visit from a sister from another convent one afternoon, it dawned on me that Ada had no idea how to behave properly in the presence of a stranger. She sat silently in one corner, sipping her coffee and nibbling the

almond cookies, but appeared not to know how
to contribute to the conversation or how to make
herself heard in any way at all. She did not seem
bothered about this either. Sor Ana pretended not
to notice, of course, but I could see her stealing
glances at Ada, as if she were wondering how
this girl could have ended up in our convent. I
racked my brains for an explanation once she
had left. Hoping that Ada would become a kind
of successor to me, might I not have clipped her
wings instead? To have become a part of the
outside world while living in the convent would
have been impossible for her. The more I thought
about it, the more I realized that I had to give
Ada room to grow, so to speak. I was determined
nonetheless to ensure that she grew in the right
direction. I wanted the sun to shine on her so she
could grow the right way. Toward me, I mean.
I have, of course, come to regret this with hindsight. Everyone needs to be allowed to grow in
the direction of their choosing. If you intervene,
you risk producing... distortions.

As someone who writes, you will no doubt understand why it was reading in particular that I put

my faith in. To determine what someone reads is to shape them. Ada had only read selected portions of the convent literature, and impressive though that may be, it cannot teach you much about the world. And so I spent an entire morning and half an afternoon walking up and down the corridors of the convent pondering the matter, while listening to the clatter from the kitchens and the church bells of Madrid and the distant traffic. Giving a seventeen-year-old a collection of books you know that young person will actually read and think about while also making those texts part of her and a foundation on which to build her future self can only be described as an opportunity both magnificent and breathtaking. To be allowed to sow seed in fertile ground and in furrows that have not yet become rigid. To be able to mold someone, to be God when he created Adam. As Pico della Mirandola puts it—"I have placed you at the center of the world so that you can mold yourself." This is how I created Ada. I selected the pearls, the crown jewels of literature—she deserved as much because only the best was good enough for my apprentice. I started with the epic of Gilgamesh, continued with the Old Testament, the Greeks, the New Testament, the German and Icelandic epic narratives of the early Middle Ages, and then Dante, Ariosto, Cervantes, and Shakespeare. I did wonder for a while whether I should include the Romantics, but then decided to skip that part of literature entirely. Because I despise suicides I thought it was entirely unnecessary to include *Young Werther* in the collection or any of the other hemophiliac works of the eighteenth century. So I skipped straight to Nietzsche and the Russians, and then thought that the nineteenth century could wait until the next round.

Content with my compilation, I was seated in my study contemplating the riches I would be bestowing on Ada. I would ask Jaime to drive to the appropriate bookshop to acquire all the works and make a great parcel of them. I was imagining Ada's joy as she opened the parcel, presumably with a huge smile on my face, when there was a knock on my door. It was Jaime, who had come upstairs with my afternoon drink.

"How convenient," I said and took the glass from him. "I have a shopping list ready for you, as it happens."

I handed him the piece of paper and took a swig of my vermouth. I closed my eyes and relished the wave of intoxication that rose to my head.

"Oh," Jaime said, "books."

"Yes, for Ada."

I was expecting him to leave the room at that point.

But Jaime stayed where he was.

"Yes?" I said.

He looked from the list over to me with an anxious expression.

"Can't you read my handwriting?" I asked.

"Yes, I can."

"So what's the problem?"

"If you'll permit me, Sor Lucia, to raise a point?"

"You wish to make an objection?"

"Yes, if I may."

"Of course. Where is the problem?"

"They're all white men."

"Sorry?"

"On your list. They're all white men."

I took back the list and glanced through the names. Jaime was right. They were all white men. I gave the sheet of paper back to him and said, "And you're not a white man, I suppose?"

"No, I am."

"God is a white man," I said. "And if you have a problem with that maybe you should find work elsewhere. Somewhere there aren't any white men like yourself."

I leaned back in my chair. It was vexing to be corrected. And I really did not understand, to be perfectly honest.

"Jaime," I said. "What do you really mean? Do you think I have poor taste?"

"No," he said. "It's just maybe you could include some other writers as well. Male or female, from some other part of the world. If your aim is to mold Ada's mind and spark her interest, then maybe you should use the *present* as your starting point."

The present. It was the way he said it.

"The present can wait," I said, "but I promise to bear it in mind when I compile the nineteenth-century list."

He remained standing there as though there was something more he wanted to say.

"The thing about privilege," he began, "is that you can't see it, if you're—"

"Leave now, Jaime," I said.

Jaime left but my feeling of joy had been clouded. I considered what he had said, which was easier once he was no longer physically present. After a while I decided to add some works by Sor Juana de la Cruz and Teresa de Ávila. When he returned he would have to drive all the way back and buy them as well. The idea of him having to go back out in the heat and the traffic cheered me up, and I was able to enjoy my vermouth to the full once more.

I should have prepared myself for a degree of disappointment when giving Ada her books, because when it comes to gifts you always run the risk of things not going as you expected and of you being happier than the recipient. And that was what happened on this occasion as well, because she opened her present, lifted out the books one by one, and regarded their spines with a jaded look.

"Thank you," she said finally, without any noticeable expression.

"Not at all, Ada," I replied. "I'd love to compare notes while you're reading them if you wanted."

What I hoped, of course, and what I was expecting, was that Ada would continue to come to my room and sit at her desk while I sat at mine, and that we would have long and interesting conversations about the contents of those books. But that is not how it turned out at all. In all honesty I barely saw anything of her once she had been given the books. Jaime carried them over to her room, and then she closed her door and it felt as though she had vanished into thin air. I had to spend my afternoons alone. And the convent became so quiet while she was reading, or that was what I felt at least, though it was obviously no quieter than usual, not that it has ever been really particularly quiet for that matter. But I presume I felt it was quieter than usual because I knew that Ada was in one of the rooms reading all those pages that had inspired me so strongly, and I was wondering how those words would fit in her universe so to speak, whether they would put down roots inside her and what would start to grow and what would be discarded. I found myself wondering what her face looked like while she was reading and wondering about her eyes moving along the lines of text and how she was sitting.

How long did the metamorphosis take? How long did Ada need to change from larva to butterfly, to make those golden leaves part of her blood? It took an eternity in my view. An eternity of silence before the day came when she knocked on the door to my room. Happy to see her, I asked if she had finished her reading.

"Yes," she replied.

"And?" I asked.

"And what?" she responded.

She was so lacking in expression I was forced to ask myself how anyone could read such masterpieces and still look so vacant when they had finished. As if they had not changed her at all, as if they had entered her and then left again, like a highly nutritious foodstuff the body cannot actually absorb.

"What did you think?" I asked. "About the books, the masterpieces?"

"They were good."

"Anything you want to talk about?"

"In time maybe," she said.

That's it, of course, I thought, and I nodded. She had been given so much to think about, it was naive and embarrassing of me to imagine she would come to my room to tell me at length about what she had read. Besides, reading is a private matter. Everything has to be left to mature, like the coal that will turn into diamond over time.

"There's something I've been wondering about," she said.

"Yes?"

"I was wondering if you could help me get a program started."

"A program?" I said. My first thought was that she wanted to start some kind of literary program.

"Yes, a show on the Internet."

"What do you mean a show on the Internet?"

"A show I'd be helping people on."

"Helping people, in what way?"

"Like you, Lucia. Like you've done all your life. Just a bit more modern."

Like you, she said. I had been waiting for this moment for so long. When Ada would tell me she wanted to follow in my footsteps, along the way I had paved, and maybe even *take over from me when I was gone.* I had been waiting so fervently for something of this kind and for so long that I had actually begun to give up hope. It struck me that this was a far greater gift than if Ada had entered my room to reel off a series of self-important ideas about the books she had just read.

"How can I assist you?" I asked.

"I need a place to work from, and someone who can do programming and the financial stuff, someone who can help me to create a cryptocurrency and a secure website."

"Cryptocurrency?" I asked.

"Yes," she said. "We'll have to find an Internet bank that will allow us to open an account and we'll need to come up with a way for people to prove they have a right to access the site."

I failed to understand anything of what she had said.

"Everything has to be encrypted, you see," she continued, "because it's not going to be, I'm not sure how to put it ... it's going to be a bit obscure."

That last bit sounded worrying. I asked her to elaborate.

"Nothing really," she said. "Only if you're going to help someone, you have to do it to the max."

That was true. Though you should always try to do it wearing silk gloves, if you have to take them off, so be it. Silk gloves are worthless if you're trying to row across a flooding river or muck out a stall. All the same I felt that I needed to understand a bit more about the nature of what she envisaged.

"Have you got something particular in mind?"

She looked me right in the eye and leaned across the desk so her head was only a few inches from mine.

"Lucia," she said, "don't you get it? You've given me wings. Do you want me to use them to fly or do you want me to drag them over the ground? Like an eagle, or like a lame duck with a chain around its neck? Is that what you had in mind with all this?"

Oh, the way she was talking. Finally, a voice inside me rejoiced.

"So how do we go about it?" I said to keep the conversation on a practical level and not become emotional.

"We'll start with the IT person," she said. "He's going to be called Mister Blue."

"You appear to have thought of everything," I said.

"If you know why, you know how as well," she said.

"You just quoted Nietzsche," I said.

Ada had started heading for the door but turned and smiled at me before she closed it behind her.

Creating Carnality is among the most stimulating and exhilarating things I have ever done. I still cherished the illusion that Ada was a kindhearted person I had helped mold and that she belonged in some way among the elect. In her I saw all the ideas, all the energy, all the joy of youth, qualities I could sustain with my knowledge and my wisdom and my financial position. We sketched out ideas and looked at various programs, including one in which a Mother Angelica from Ohio meets her audience.

"Can you see the audience's faces?" Ada asked. "They're begging to be *watered*. She isn't really saying anything much because they'll hear what they want to hear in any case. You could have done that so much better."

There was the affirmation that I still possessed a place in the world. That I wasn't consigned to the wings. What is old age if not primarily the fear of no longer being relevant and of becoming an extra in a play in which you once played the lead role? To realize that your ideas are obsolete and do not apply to the present day and that people are just waiting for you to disappear so they can fill your place with someone else? *Carnality* saved me from that kind of tedium and pointlessness. I would sometimes wake up in the night and think about the program. I imagined there would be an introductory piece of music and that the image on the screen would be slightly dreamlike, blurred, and shimmering.

But Ada said, "No, not like that at all. Not like that, Lucia. There's not going to be any shimmering intro."

"So what's the program going to be called?" I asked. I'd been considering *A Network of Miracles* or perhaps *The Hour of Miracles*.

"It's going to be called *Carnality*," Ada replied.

I said I thought that made it sound like pulp fiction.

"That doesn't matter," Ada said. "That's what it's going to be called. *Carnality*, Lucia. Your mother told you that, didn't she, that life was about the flesh, the carnal. People can turn to us with their problems of the flesh, and we will help them find their souls."

It was impossible not to be drawn in. Ada's hopefulness, her joy and excitement. She managed to find her Mister Blue, who is actually a Dominican hacker by the name of Yulman de la Cruz. They would sit together in the garden planning the whole thing and then come up to discuss things with me. They were exemplary in their attention to detail, as if they had already created hundreds of Internet shows. It felt as though they were able to pluck these ideas out of nowhere. I know very little about the practical aspects Mister Blue dealt with, as he was clever enough not to attempt the doomed enterprise of explaining the technical side of things, but as soon as they got going he insisted I should watch all the episodes. During that first year I found nothing to object to. Ada and Yulman accepted all kinds of people with every sort of

problem. They all got to sit down with them
and talk about themselves and what they wanted
help with in a calm and composed fashion,
while Ada and Yulman listened intently and sincerely. When they felt they couldn't do anything
for them, they explained this without a fuss, and
the guest was able to leave the location without
any further drama. They simply got up and
left, that was all. I watched the episodes from
my sofa on the large screen that Yulman had
installed in my room. That was always the high
point of the day for me. Ada did such a good
job in front of the camera and I felt so proud of
her. Yulman told me their followers loved her. I
had no idea though about who these followers
were exactly, because there were some things
only Yulman oversaw. I did realize all the same
that they could hardly be nobodies, because
the sums credited to the show's account every
month were considerable. I told them early on
that I did not want any of the profits, but then
Ada and Yulman said that because I was the
one who had made the seed money available, I
should have my share of the money just like any
other venture capitalist. I obstinately refused. I
said that having spent my entire life as a nun, I

wasn't going to die a venture capitalist. Besides, I spend hardly any money. My pleasures are largely free. Sitting in front of an open window and writing is free, and so is lifting your eyes to watch the treetops and the sky behind. Lying awake at dawn and listening to the blackbird in the tree outside is free. Listening to the wind is free, and so is walking through Madrid's old neighborhoods in the evening when the sun has set but the asphalt and the stones of the buildings are still hot. My rooms are mine until I die, and the convent pays for my food. I don't need clothes or beauty products, and the rare times I go on trips it is because some institution has chosen to invite me, and then everything is as free as it is lavish. I actually have an incredibly good life and I am convinced that the linchpin of my good fortune is my lack of interest in money.

The change occurred after a year or two. It was nothing I could put my finger on to begin with, but it felt as though the atmosphere on *Carnality* had changed, as if a kind of *contempt* had crept in. Ada might suddenly start to make fun of the guest, and occasionally the guest would get up and try to get out of there only to find the door was locked. While the guest was banging on the door, close to panic, onscreen you could see Ada and Yulman smiling with satisfaction. I cannot say that I approved of that. I ended up squirming on the sofa. I told Ada and Yulman I could not imagine how this could be helping anyone, but then they said that sometimes a person needed to "be dragged though the mire to be properly helped." A certain kind of person needed to be "spooked" so they could find the strength within themselves to appreciate what they had. Fair enough, I conceded. There was a logic to that. Yulman also said it wasn't just the guest who had to be considered, there were the followers as well. The number of followers had risen dramatically after they began the periodic humiliations.

"There is a hunger for humiliation," Ada said.

"Think of all the public executions and gladiatorial games of the past," Yulman said. "All of that existed to meet a *need*."

I understood what they meant, but I still felt there was something about their reasoning that jarred.

"The only thing I want," I said, "is for us to be on the side of the good."

"The good?" Yulman asked.

"What I mean is, they shouldn't have to be *destroyed* in order to be forgiven."

"Although—," Yulman began.

"—it would be too easy if forgiveness were completely free," Ada finished the thought.

"The voice in my revelation said I should help, you see," I said. "And I honestly don't feel right now..."

"Lucia," Ada said. "You are guiding them through the *carnal*. The corruption that lurks in every pore, the stench that lies under the millimeter-thin surface of the skin. You are helping them get past all of that. You are leading them toward their souls, and when they find them you let them go. They can fend for themselves after that. What is that if not *help*?"

"You are the light in the labyrinth of the flesh!" Yulman said.

We laughed, even though I felt slightly chilled inside. I repeated that the important thing as far as I was concerned was that we were on the side of the good. Ada replied that I was the one in charge. Besides, I controlled all the formal

rights to the program. I owned the website, the
server, the account, and God knows whatever
else they had registered in my name. As soon as
the program had been set up, Yulman had given
me an envelope containing all the contracts, the
encryptions, the passwords, and the other information. As a result I was free to control everything; but even though mine was always the final
word, I gave way to Ada and Yulman. They were
the young ones, and not just any young people
besides. They were attractive, powerful, informed, and calm. Unlike my generation, whose
education was more general, theirs was narrow
but deep. They did not know much, but what
they did know they had mastered completely.
They were the new, and they were going to phase
out the old and the obsolete. Me in other words.
I felt no bitterness—I was, after all, the mother of
the show. The thing we shared—*Carnality*—was
an exquisite hybrid of the very best of us. I told
them this in an attempt to express my appreciation. Yulman's eyes narrowed at that point and he
said, looking at Ada, "So why isn't Lucia on the
program, in the flesh I mean?"

Ada nodded and said that was what she had
imagined from the outset, only then the idea had

got lost. I raised my hand and said no thanks, I was happy with things the way they were. I was only too pleased to remain at one remove. I had no desire to be Mother Angelica and make myself an object of ridicule. All I wanted was to hold my hand over them, nothing more.

"You should be sitting in the background," Yulman said, "like a kind of...judge."

"No, no, no," I said.

"You and your maimed hand!" Ada exclaimed. "Lucia in the background with her maimed hand and her glass of vermouth. That's brilliant, Yulman."

I wasn't quite as thrilled. I am familiar enough with my reflection to know what kind of impression I would make onscreen.

"People might be scared," I said.

"People *want* to be scared," Ada replied. "Please, please, *please*, Lucia!"

I have never been able to resist Ada or Yulman on their own, so how was I supposed to resist them in concert?

"I suppose so," I said. "My one condition is it mustn't be sordid. If it becomes sordid, we'll have to shut the whole thing down and do something else."

Ada and Yulman nodded.

"Don't worry," Ada said. "Sordid is so very not *you*!"

After that I began to appear on *Carnality* at carefully selected moments. Ada wanted my appearances to be out of the ordinary: "an extra prophetic resource" for special cases. A sort of oracle that, whenever it spoke, always uttered words of the utmost importance that everyone was obliged to heed. I was encouraged to speak in riddles. Ada and Yulman would then interpret these riddles. I felt like someone who had been dressed up by a crowd of kids, and though you know the clothes do not suit, you do not want to disappoint the children. Let them have a bit of fun, I would think every now and then, I'm going to die soon anyway. In the end I acquiesced to everything, while thinking to myself that Ada and Yulman might very well be capable of seeing things I was blind to.

Now and then I would think about Ada's mother that time she came to see me and told me that her daughter had a heart of stone. I recalled her words: "The little miracle is defective." I wanted to get in touch with her mother, invite her to the convent and talk with her, try to understand what she meant when she said that. But somewhere inside me I felt ashamed, knowing as I did that I had, in fact, deprived her of her daughter. During the years Ada had been living at the convent, she had gone home for the odd weekend, but it had become completely impossible for her mother to gain the hold over her daughter every good mother ought to have. Had she been a better mother, on the other hand, Ada would probably not have chosen to stay with me.

I make no bones about the fact I had begun to have doubts about Ada by the time Mercuro Cano approached us. Soledad Ocampo actually turned up first. Ah, Soledad Ocampo! Have you ever caught an eel in a well? The eel is a cold and powerful creature, a leftover from those aquatic beasts of prehistory. You have to sit on the edge of the well and stare down at the black water until the eel comes to the surface. And that can take time, because eels appear to possess a sixth sense about when and where a danger may be lurking. Some people have "eel souls" like that. It is as if you had to decode them, decipher them, grab hold of their inner lives when they least suspect and yank them up to the surface to examine them in the light of day. When I heard Soledad Ocampo speak, I could sense that was the sort of soul she had, and for all Ada's precocity, she did not possess the kind of knowledge that is required to tackle a person of that kind. You need to have had more experience of life, to have made your way through many different people if you are to see them properly. But, sitting there in my chair, I was able to see. And what I saw was the question that lurked deep inside Soledad Ocampo: Why do I have to die when the man who betrayed me gets to live? Perhaps she had been visualizing Mercuro Cano, his flesh still possessed of its body heat, rolling around with another woman in sheets that she had bought, washed, and ironed while her own body had grown cold a couple of meters beneath the earth and was being perforated by worms. I'm not saying she was aware of this; it is by no means certain she was. But the idea was quite clearly there, inside her. And what was obvious to me was that Soledad Ocampo would never get over the harm her husband had done her. The bitterness and rage had accumulated inside to form a dark sludge she was no longer capable of eliminating. I could see that sludge in her eyes as she was sitting there. I could see the eel one moment and the sludge the next, and I froze. I, Lucia, the butcher's daughter and the accomplice—froze. Ada and Yulman, on the other hand, were absolutely thrilled by the figure she presented: her dark skin, her black eyes, her gravity. Those long nails painted a dark shade and that soft voice. The followers loved her and Penelope too, which obviously did not bode well for Mercuro.

Soledad Ocampo began by telling us she was ill and would die unless she was given a new heart. That was a matter we could very probably help her with. It would not have been the first time I had helped arrange something similar. Whenever this situation crops up, I ring Mr. Huei. I always emphasize that I do not want an innocent person to die.

"People die all the time," he will then reply, "and a lot of perfectly good hearts get incinerated or buried. We will, of course ensure that among all those hearts there won't be one from an *innocent* person."

It is sometimes difficult to grasp exactly what Mr. Huei means by "innocent," however. I usually emphasize that organs may only be taken from people who are going to die in any event and who have given their consent. He always nods and smiles. He is always agreeableness itself, and I have come to understand that there are nuances to that amiability I am unable to interpret; there are smiles of honey and smiles of edged steel, and I cannot tell the difference in his case because every now and then the blade of the knife appears to have been smeared with honey.

No matter. Before the episode that featured Mercuro Cano, I told Ada and Yulman I did not want some hardworking father in India to be obliged to provide Soledad Ocampo with a heart. They promised. They would not involve Mr. Huei unless they could come up with a specific donor for Soledad Ocampo who Mr. Huei could then get in touch with.

"How's that going to work?" I asked. "Who could that be?"

They shrugged mysteriously. Whether it was Ada's ability to manipulate, Yulman's

camera angles and the questions they put
during the conversation with Mercuro, or God
Himself that made it turn out the way it did,
I do not know. At any event everyone hated
Mercuro Cano even before we began. As soon
as Soledad Ocampo had left, the Comments
field went completely haywire, with people
working themselves into a frenzy. Although I
asked Yulman to calm the irate mood, there's
no denying Mercuro Cano was extraordinarily
dislikable throughout his appearance on the
show. Everyone hates a liar when the lies are
being uncovered, and everyone hates a violator
when the violation is exposed. Everyone hates
the sexual urge when it is badly packaged or
revealed in all its sordid crudeness. He was
polite and obsequious into the bargain, and
that combination provoked the full force of our
predatory instincts right from the start. The
truth is that from the moment his taxi pulled
up outside everyone was anticipating seeing
Mercuro Cano torn to shreds. *Carnality* had
been transformed for the day into a popular
spectacle, mob rule, a gladiatorial circus.

———

The program was recorded on a Thursday. Jaime drove me there. When I arrived Yulman opened the door and helped me down the stairs and into the studio I had put at the show's disposal. And there he was, Mercuro Cano, sitting in the beam of light.

I listened to him, and the moment he started making those pretentious comparisons of his inner life with the *Titanic*, I knew he was going to be offered up. So yes, I did know that. I sat there in my chair and knew beyond all doubt that unless Mercuro Cano got to his feet, hurled himself at the door, and made his escape, Ada and Yulman would make sure he was sacrificed. I could see the gleam in her eyes. I could sense the eagerness in Yulman's fingers on the keyboard. The whole thing was like a train running downhill—at any moment it would start to accelerate, and then it would be too late. So I put my maimed hand on the table and began to drum it against the tabletop. That usually scares the shit out of people, if you'll pardon the expression. Mercuro Cano may have fallen silent as well, but he stayed where he was. I drummed a little bit harder, but he remained in his seat. You've only yourself to blame, I thought eventually. I tried to help you, but you refused. Serves him right. He doesn't believe in anything anyway. No God, no principles, no goodness. The human soul in all its wretched nakedness.

The episode was almost over, and I had dozed off in my seat when I heard Ada say, "I've decided to try and cure you using the six methods of the philosopher Friedrich Nietzsche for improving self-control."

"What do you mean?" Mercuro asked.

"Friedrich Nietzsche's six methods for the taming of powerful urges, such as attraction and aggression," Ada responded.

"What do they involve?"

Yulman offered a piece of paper to Ada. She took it and then read aloud. "Allow me to summarize: Method number one: *Avoid all opportunities at which the urge or desire could be satisfied.* Method number two: *Introduce a rule for the urge to the effect that it can only be satisfied at impossible intervals.* Method number three: *Devote yourself without reservation to the urge such that an aversion is created toward it, and use this aversion to control it.* Method number four: *Associate a highly embarrassing idea with the satisfaction of the urge such that the satisfaction is ultimately contaminated by the embarrassment.* Method number five: *Subject yourself to exhausting labor and by this means channel your physical energies into other paths.* Method number six: *Replace the powerful urge with another powerful urge.*"

There was silence. Ada looked at Mercuro Cano.

"After our conversations with your wife Soledad and your mistress Penelope, in our judgment methods one, two, three, and five have either already been tried or have no chance of success for other reasons. The remaining methods are therefore method number four and method number six."

Mercuro Cano shook his head. "I don't remember which ones they were."

"Method number four: *Associate a highly embarrassing idea with the satisfaction of the urge such that the satisfaction is ultimately con-taminated by the embarrassment.* And method number six: *Replace the powerful urge with another powerful urge.*"

A skeptical Mercuro Cano shook his head once again. It is possible he had begun to realize where this was headed. I had, in any case, and I was squirming with distaste.

"How much time is there left?" Mercuro asked.

"Enough," Yulman said.

"What kind of highly embarrassing idea?" Cano asked.

"Take your clothes off," Ada said.

In this world there are people you can negotiate with, that you can disagree and argue with, and then there are people who can say things with so much force and conviction and with an underlying and unspoken threat of potential destruction that any attempt at dialogue or protest is pointless. Ada belonged to the latter group, as I had now realized. There's no denying, however, that all at once the show had recaptured its intensity. The kind of charge you can sense when something is *for real*. Mercuro failed to obey her nonetheless and did not take off his clothes, but got up from his chair and moved to the center of the cement floor, where he remained standing with his arms crossed while shaking his head.

"I'm not going to do that," he said. "It may be true as you say that if you force me to submit to this kind of humiliation—the urge might vanish, for a while at least. I know you can drain someone of their potency so, yes, your German philosopher is right. But you might want to consider the possibility that there's a point to allowing me to retain my desire. If only for my wife, who actually happens to derive some benefit from it now and then."

"Good point I admit," Ada responded. "Sit down."

Mercuro went back to his chair.

"Maybe method number four would not be effective enough in your case," Ada said. "So that leaves method number six."

"Christ Almighty," Cano said. "You're killing me here."

"Aptly put," Ada said. "Method number six stipulates that you should replace the urge you want to control with another one. In which case the second must be stronger. And what instinct is more powerful than the sexual one?" She looked at Yulman with a smile while pointing at him.

"The survival instinct," Yulman replied.

"Exactly," Ada said. "The survival instinct."

"What do you mean?" Mercuro said.

"Your problem will soon be solved because you'll be spending so much time surviving nothing else will matter."

Thus began what you referred to during your visit as *the persecution of Mercuro Cano*—a harmless game that was staged by two innocent young people and that may have frightened "the plaything" more than intended. Can we not consider the subject closed now?

I have become aware that the gentle mists of confusion are settling in my brain more and more frequently. While I have been writing these pages, I have had the feeling every now and then that I am sitting in front of an open window, a different window from the ones in the convent, listening to the rain falling. The soft clatter against the pane, and the breeze that

is slowly making the wet leaves rustle... As if I
were in Extremadura, in the spring... as though
nothing had happened yet...

Forgive me. I hope that you feel as I do that
these letters have brought us closer together.
I also hope that we can meet as soon as you
leave the Alcalá. Let us sit in the courtyard of
the convent and talk about everything that has
happened, not to mention everything that may
do so. I would also like to introduce you to Ada
and Yulman. I am already expecting you.

Yours sincerely,
Lucia

Is it true what they say that you reach a point in certain sequences of events when everything suddenly runs amok as though a mechanism had been tripped by an invisible hand? And if it is, how do you know which point it is, where it lies, and what can be done to counteract it afterward? Could you have been shedding your skin, and once the old skin, now worn thin and dried out, is beside you on the floor, you realize that in order to live your old life you would have to crawl back inside it? And that, you know right away, is impossible; the die is cast and you have become someone else.

This is what she is thinking the morning she is supposed to be released. She is standing in front of the mirror in the toilet in the prison's reception area, and this is the first time in a very long while she has actually seen herself in a mirror. So this is me, she thinks. Bennedith. There are new shadows on her face. Her eyes seem to sit deeper inside her head than when she arrived, and the healthy tone the sea air had lent her skin has faded completely. She notices that her fingers must have swollen, despite the prison food, because she can no longer pull her rings off.

She goes back out and is given her case and other belongings in a bag. The warden turns up to say goodbye. He is dressed in a worn leather jacket and corduroy trousers that sag just enough to tell you they have not been washed. He winks at her and says quietly that though she may be free he wasn't born yesterday and he's got the picture.

"What picture?" she asks.

"You don't get fractures in the center of your skull when you hit your forehead on the gunwale," he says. "You should be grateful to your patron."

She gives him a vacant look. "Is that it?"

He tells her one of the prison's cars is waiting and she should look after herself out there.

She leaves the brown-brick building behind and is driven across the cracked countryside toward the center of Madrid. Summer lies heavy on the soil like an enemy who never tires, and the scorching morning sun has found a way inside the car. Even though the driver says not a word, she can sense him looking at her in the rearview mirror every now and then. He is slowly rotating something in his mouth while looking at her, maybe a sunflower seed or a piece of chewing gum. She knows he thinks she is a criminal because whenever she looks up and meets his eyes he immediately looks away. She gets out her phone and rings Mercuro, who fails to answer. Then she rings Miranda, who sounds genuinely happy to hear from her.

"To think they could misjudge you like that," she chirps, "you and your heart of gold."

"You did too, Miranda," she says.

"And I haven't been able to stop thinking about it. I'm so sorry. Anyone could lose patience with an invalid, and your intentions were so good. I feel so sad about everything you've been through."

"There's no need."

"So when are you coming out to see us in Salou?" Miranda asks. "The sea air has done us all so much good, and Santiago is in a positive mood almost the whole time."

When she gets to the flat on calle Goya, she walks in and out of the rooms. First through the whole flat to the bedroom, where she turns around and makes her way back, working through the living room and the hall and into Mercuro's room. She runs her fingers over the pillow on his bed. It occurs to her she should write or call home, tell someone the truth. She has been involved in an incident, locked up in a Spanish prison, and the police had to rule out murder before they could release her. You'd never have thought that about me, would you? she would say. But it is the truth, and she has come to feel that the truth is her business and hers alone. She doesn't need any outsiders getting involved. Out of respect for the outsiders but out of respect for herself as well.

She goes down to the street again. The breeze is both hot and strong and she thinks it feels different from before—as if it were bringing with it sounds from another place or another time—though maybe that is because she has spent so long inside a hermetically sealed building. She relishes the feeling of the warm wind against her legs. She is remembering the kind of thing Mercuro used to say on the rocky island. He was completely lucid to begin with and would come out with things like "We're not getting out of this alive" and "I wonder if anyone has been asking about Johnny," or "Maybe he lives on his own at home as well" and "You need peace of mind to be able to go on living, only how are we going to find peace of mind after this?" He would also climb up and down the steep cliff over and over again to look across at the boat before it was driven out to sea, as though he could not grasp that Johnny was actually lying inside it. She felt strangely indifferent herself. She told him to take it easy and not to get all stressed. The body needed more energy when you got stressed, and the best thing you could do was just to lie still until you were found. By the way, she had added, he had hardly been enjoying peace of mind before this had happened, so from that point of view nothing had actually changed.

"Look on the bright side," she said. "Your persecutors are very unlikely to look for you here."

After that he lay perfectly still beside her for several hours. He woke up in the middle of the night and asked her which writer it was who said that if you stare into the abyss for too long, the abyss will look back into you? She said she didn't know. The next day it was as though the thirst was affecting his brain. "How could all of this happen?" he yelled, sitting at the top of the cliff. "We were supposed to do better, weren't we? How did we end up here?" His eyes blazed with desperation, and his skin was red

from sunburn. She yelled at him that he was paranoid and should calm down.

That night he woke her up to tell her Johnny was
sitting up in the boat out there. "He's not dead," he
said. "He's alive. He's out there, and he's fine." She
peered out across the lagoon but failed to see anything. All she could see was Mercuro's smile in the
dark, and she thought he must have gone mad for
real this time.

She hails a cab to go to the convent. She needs
answers to some of her questions. She knows the
nun has those answers and may actually provide
them if they are eye to eye instead of leaving her be-
wildered in the labyrinths of an old woman's past.
Why was Mercuro not taken to the same hospital she
was when they were found? Where did he go after
that? She reports to the watchman at the entrance
and is shown into the courtyard. She sits on the same
bench as she did last time. A novice comes out to ask
her if she wants anything to drink and once again
she is given a glass of ice cold sparkling water that
rasps pleasantly as it goes down. She dozes off on the

bench and is woken by a woman's voice talking to the watchman at the main door.

"I've come to see Sor Lucia," she hears the woman say.

"Your name?"

"Soledad Ocampo."

Sitting in the sun, she turns to ice.

"Have you got an appointment?" the watchman says.

"No, I don't."

"What's it about?"

"It's about my husband, Mercuro Cano. He disappeared some time ago and I'd like to ask Sor Lucia if she knows where he is."

She sits up straight on the bench, wide awake. She does not want to turn her head, but when she hears the woman being invited to wait in the courtyard she thinks there will be time enough. She will be able to look at Soledad Ocampo undisturbed. Soledad sits on a bench that is positioned facing the one she is sitting on but at an angle, just by the fountain. When she sees her, she is filled with a sense of being confronted by someone legendary, someone from a story, someone she has only seen on film or encountered in her dreams. Soledad's face is concealed by large black sunglasses that have detailing on the sides in a silver color. Her hair is jet-black and glossy, and has been gathered so it hangs in a loosely coiled ponytail. Soledad gets out a lacy black *abanico* that she starts to fan herself with. When she sees this, she recalls with a pang of jealousy what Mercuro said about Soledad radiating a kind of "mature glamour." That is true; there could be no more apt phrase to describe the woman in front of her. She looks as though she dedicates meticulous care to her appearance. And with marvelous results, you'd have to say. While she is looking at the other woman's body, she remembers what he said about her breasts and all the joy they brought him. She is overcome with a paralyzing feeling of jealousy and decides to try to get a conversation started quickly in order to keep it at bay.

"It's so hot; it feels like you're going to die." Her voice sounds unnaturally constrained but Soledad Ocampo responds in a friendly way.

"*Es horrible*," she agrees. It's ghastly.

Her voice is darker than you'd expect when you see her. Apart from moving the fan, she is sitting perfectly still, and it is impossible to make out whether her eyes are open or closed behind her sunglasses.

"A few weeks ago I underwent a major operation," Soledad continues, "and while I was coming around the air-conditioning in the hospital broke down. When I opened my eyes I thought I had died and ended up in Purgatory."

"Really?" she says. "What sort of operation was it?" Her voice sounds muffled and just getting the words out feels difficult.

"I was fortunate enough to be given a new heart," Soledad says, smiling broadly at her. "And even though I have to take dozens of pills now to stop it being rejected, I feel totally different in myself. I've got a new heart and a completely new life along with it."

"A new heart?" she says.

"Look," Soledad says.

She opens the topmost couple of buttons of her blouse and pulls the fabric aside. A long scar starts from the dip in her collarbone and runs straight down.

"It's just so strange," Soledad Ocampo continues with a little laugh as she closes her blouse, "that everything can feel so *different*."

"In what way?" she asks.

Soledad Ocampo shrugs and that jet-black ponytail coils like a snake across one shoulder.

"My husband, just to give you an example," she says, leaning against the back of the bench. "We were finally getting a divorce. I thought I hated him. I just didn't have any hope left by then. My aversion had become... how to put it? *Instinctive.* As if the very sight of him was worse than the sight of anyone else. It was as if he felt like a threat, and my entire being went on the defensive as soon as he came close. He was always saying he wanted to make up for everything he had done wrong, all the adultery and so on. And even though I felt like I wanted to forgive him, I really did, I couldn't get over my aversion. But with this new heart..."

"Yes?" she says. "What about the new heart?"

"Everything feels so different with this new heart," Soledad says. "The hatred is gone. I've got no ill will left. Now all I want to know is where he is and when he's coming home. When he does come home, we're going to fix the life we have together. And that's what I need to ask Lucia. If she knows when he is coming home and where he actually is ..."

She stops listening because it feels as though a tiny, fragile twig has just snapped inside her. She can feel that quite distinctly: just as though a small branch or a little bone really had broken inside her, followed by the echo of the barely audible sound that is produced when something tenuous but vital snaps. Completely motionless, at first all she can do is stare at the other woman. Soledad fails to notice because she has taken out a powder compact from her handbag and is touching up her makeup. With a little smile on her lips Soledad also powders the top of the scar beneath the collar of her blouse. For her part, she turns her eyes toward the ground as she feels her face turning red and her eyes beginning to smart. Soledad is humming a tune under her breath that she recognizes, because Mercuro used to hum the same thing while he was making breakfast in the flat on calle Goya.

"You have to be able to forgive," Soledad says, putting her compact back in the bag.

"How do you mean?"

"You have to be able to forgive. When someone really repents."

"And is that what your husband did?"

"Yes, that's what my husband did. He would have done anything for me. He adored me. And I was so cold to him."

She is considering making a break for the closest toilet until she can regain her composure, when she sees Soledad cross one leg over the other, lean forward, and regard her with a worried expression.

"Are you feeling all right?"

"No," she says. "I think it's the heat."

Soledad nods in sympathy. Soon afterward the novice returns and says that Lucia cannot receive visitors today.

"But I have to see her," Soledad says indignantly.

"I'm sorry, that isn't possible," the novice replies. "Sor Lucia cannot be reached."

"*Can't be reached.* What can you mean?"

"It is a recent development. She'll just sit there for hour after hour as if she were not present. Why not come back another day?"

"When?"

"Why not come back in a week's time, and we'll see how she is then."

They stay where there are, seated opposite one another on the benches. The novice vanishes inside the building. They are alone in the courtyard. While she is doing her best to slow the beating of her heart, which feels like it is running riot in her chest, Soledad Ocampo is looking around in bewilderment. She closes her eyes and takes long deep breaths. When she feels calm settling through her body she gets to her feet, moves across to Soledad, and takes her hand.

"Come on," she says. "I know which room is hers."

Soledad gets up and joins her. They pass through the colonnade and then up the narrow winding staircase. The door to Lucia's room is ajar, and they simply step inside. The first thing they see on entering is the back of a small, hunched creature sitting in a wheelchair in front of the window. She is completely still, and her hands are folded in her lap. Once they are standing beside her, they can see that her eyes are closed.

"Lucia," says Soledad. "Lucia?"

The woman opens her eyes and turns her face toward them. Those eyes are as bright green as they were the last time she was there, but it is clear from their absent expression the nun no longer recognizes her.

They remain like that for a while, the three of them. She has no idea what to do. But Soledad says she needs to go home now as she has to take her medicines and she will come back another day.

"Maybe we'll see each other again," Soledad says before she leaves.

"You never know," she replies.

Soledad walks toward the door and just before she leaves she turns and waves merrily at her. She is standing in a patch of sunlight, and the bracelet on her wrist glitters like a little waterfall of sunbeams. Once the sound of Soledad's steps has faded, she moves over to Lucia again. She notices something has fallen on the floor as if Lucia had something in her lap that had slipped out of her fingers. She bends down and picks it up. It is a large envelope and her name is written across it. FOR BENNEDITH. She looks around, worried she will suddenly be caught. Then she crosses to a chair at the other end of the room, opens the envelope and reads the card that lies on top. She can see that the words have been written with great effort because the handwriting is meandering and uneven as if it had been written very slowly and with a shaky hand.

Dear Bennedith,

My prayers have been heard at last, and this can only be the end. I ought to say something lofty, but when it comes down to it lofty is not in my nature. The only thing I can come up with is a sentence I heard on one of Ada and Yulman's television shows when someone said there isn't anything sadder than an outdoor cat that thinks it's an indoor cat. You are not an indoor cat, Bennedith. You are meant for something greater. The door has been opened; all you have to do is step out.

I feel absolutely sure at last that you are the one I was waiting for, which is why the Lord is allowing me to leave at this point. My beloved Ada is a formidable creature, but a formidable creature that lacks compassion and whose hardness I have only made worse. You, on the

other hand, possess the empathy Ada lacks.
Your concern for the man with Alzheimer's
and for Mercuro is ample testimony to that. But
you also have the capacity to take action when
the situation requires. The encounter with the
Scandinavian in that boat is the proof. Your time
in prison has shown you another side of Spain—
you are no longer a naive tourist, and you have
created a shell for yourself. You have heard my
story and hopefully understand my actions and
what drove me. You can tell my story to other
people in the future and help me embody the
legend that gave birth to *Carnality*. You can
help Ada and Yulman. You are old enough to
be their mother but young enough to have many
years of good deeds ahead of you.

I have never been inclined toward nostalgia
so I will skip the farewell and simply ask you
to take charge of the rest of the contents of this
envelope. Inside you will find all the passwords,
addresses, codes, account numbers, and autho-
rizations you will need. That is it. May the Lord
keep His hand over you, Ada, and Yulman.

Yours sincerely
Lucia

It takes five hours by rail from Madrid to Salou. She takes the express to Barcelona, and then another train from Estación de Sants south toward Tarragona, before finally reaching the resort. The journey is fast and trouble-free and she receives encouraging text messages from Miranda the entire time. *The right decision! Staying in Madrid during the summer would be stupid!* and *Everyone is dying to see you and Santiago is talking about you.* A taxi Miranda ordered in her name is waiting at the local station. Once she has checked in at the hotel she walks around the lobby and then out to the pool, but there is no sign of Miranda, Santiago, or their daughters. In the end she goes up to her room, changes her clothes, and lies on the balcony in a sun chair, wearing a bikini. She has a view of the beach and the sea. This is what the Spanish coast is like in the evening—relaxed, with a breeze off the sea, and the noise from bars and restaurants that are about to open. No scorching sun, just a gentle warmth in the air and the smell of the sea. She feels a warm tide of exhaustion rising inside her and dozes off. She wakes up later to the sound of a familiar voice beneath her balcony. It is Miranda, giving instructions in her customary manner to a troop of people about how to treat Santiago.

"There has to be a cushion on his chair," she says. "The swimming ring has to be fully inflated, and you must ensure the valve has been properly closed. He should have his shirt on until we reach the water so his shoulders do not get burnt. And, yes, that really can happen at this time of day, it did last year. Gema, can you take the bag, and Camila, the towels? Watch your step. He needs to have his shoes on when you carry him over the sand!"

She leans over the balcony railing and gazes at the industrious little crew.

"Miranda," she calls.

"Oh, there you are!" she calls back. "Come down. We're going swimming, come on down."

Miranda keeps gesturing while continuing to walk toward the beach with that long linen shirt fluttering around her thighs. The daughters, sons-in-law, and then the bodybuilders carrying Santiago between them walk behind her. She points out to sea and says something that is inaudible from the balcony. Then Miranda heads toward a parasol with blue trimming that has been put up at the edge of the beach. She gets her towel, beach dress, and bathing shoes out of the cupboard in her room and hurries after them.

It is a wonderful evening. An extraordinary evening, an evening capable of embracing everything, even the bewildering events of the day and Santiago's illness. There he is, sitting among them, the natural center of the company, with a demented gleam in his eyes and a smile on his face as he looks at each of them, one by one. Every so often he raises his water bottle and says "*Cheers,*" whereupon everyone clinks their water bottles against his and toasts him back. "*Santiago! Cheers, Daddy! Cheers, darling!*"

It is Miranda who comes up with the idea of having champagne. They have all just gone into the water. The bodybuilders have made their way back to the beach now that they have lifted Santiago out of his chair and placed him in the large white swimming ring. He is floating around with an even broader smile on his face.

"Champagne," Miranda shouts. "We shouldn't be drinking toasts in water but in champagne. Now we're out here, we should be raising our glasses to this moment when all the family have gathered together, all the family and Bennedith, and the evening is so lovely, so warm and Santiago is so...

She looks at him and appears unable to complete her sentence.

"Come on, Mum," Gema says, "let's get the champagne."

"Cava would be just as good," Camila calls and hurries to catch up with her sister.

"Is that okay?" Miranda calls to her. "We'll only be gone a little while. Paco and the others are over there on the beach, just yell if you need help."

"Not to worry," she says. "I'll look after Santiago."

Gema and Camila each give their father a kiss on the cheek and then dash with Miranda toward the beach and up to the hotel. She watches them race merrily away in the evening light—the daughters in bikinis and Miranda in her beach tunic. Paco and his mates wave to her from the beach and she waves back.

When they are alone she places her hands on Santiago's swimming ring and pushes him slowly forward through the water. The sun has all but set behind the mountains and the beach is empty of people. Only the two of them are out here. They lie on the surface, floating side by side, for some time.

"Can you see the sky?" she asks.

"Yes," he says. "I can see the sky."

After a while she starts to push him farther out. He floats along in his swimming ring and she keeps swimming behind him.

"Is this the right speed?" she asks.

Then he turns his head and looks at her.

"I have to say something."

He is speaking perfectly clearly, as though for a moment he were not sick at all.

"Yes?" She says, holding on to the ring. "What is it?"

"What I'd really like is if we could do it now."

"What?" she says.

The question is superfluous, though, because she knows. It feels like she has always known, and the last twenty-four hours have simply helped to crystallize a course of action her only choice is to surrender to. She looks up at the sky. A high haze is veiling the last of the sunlight and lending the water around them a luminous green color.

"What, Santiago?" she asks again. "What do you want us to do?"

It has already been set in motion, though, because she has already started to help him as his clumsy fingers fumble to remove the plug from the valve of the swimming ring. The air starts to hiss out. All she can hear now are her own heartbeats and the air slowly leaving the ring. Finally she pulls it over his head and lets it drift away.

"Stretch out," she says. "Look up at the sky and just let yourself float."

The stiffness of his movements has vanished, and there is something almost pleasurable about the way he is able to stretch his thin, wasted body in front of her. She is supporting him gently under his back and the nape of his neck.

"I've never done this," she says. "I don't know if I can."

He smiles. "I wouldn't have asked you if I didn't think you could," he says. "Help me."

He shuts his eyes, and she takes her hands away. She lets him drift away. Very soon he has floated ten, twenty meters away from her and is still floating perfectly calmly while looking at the sky. The swimming ring has drifted off in the opposite direction and is on its way into land.

"You've got to help me!" he yells. "It won't work like this; you've got to help me."

Later when she is telling Ada and Yulman about what happened she will try to describe the feeling she experienced at that moment: the first real act of her entire life. And then she will wish she could say all she felt was the elation that comes with mercy and the power to act, but she knows she felt something else as well in that moment. Something she neither will nor can explain. But that muddy, churning surge of envy pure love creates in the lonely person has completely subsided as she starts to swim toward him.

"Santiago!" she calls. "Santiago!"

LINA WOLFF was born in Lund, Sweden, and lived for several years in Spain and Italy, where she worked as a translator. She arrived on the literary stage in 2009 with the publication of *Många människor dör som du*, a collection of novellas set in Spain and in the south of Sweden. In 2012 her debut novel, *Bret Easton Ellis and the Other Dogs*, won the prestigious *Vi Magazine*'s Literature Award. In 2016 her novel *The Polyglot Lovers* won Sweden's highest literary award, the August Prize for Fiction, and has been translated into seventeen languages. *Carnality* was awarded the prestigious Aftonbladet Literature Prize in 2019.

FRANK PERRY's translations of Sweden's leading writers have won prizes from the Swedish Academy and the Writer's Guild of Sweden. His translation of Lina Wolff's *Bret Easton Ellis and the Other Dogs* was the 2017 winner of the Oxford-Weidenfeld Prize and was awarded the triennial Bernard Shaw Prize for best literary translation from Swedish.